Nicole
TROPE

Blame

ALLEN&UNWIN

First published in 2016

Allen & Unwin
83 Alexander Street
Crows Nest NSW 2065
Australia
Phone: (61 2) 8425 0100
Email: info@allenandunwin.com
Web: www.allenandunwin.com

Cataloguing-in-Publication details are available
from the National Library of Australia
www.trove.nla.gov.au

ISBN 978 1 76029 315 4

Internal design by Lisa White
Set in 13.5/18 pt Minion LT by Midland Typesetters, Australia

10 9 8 7 6 5 4 3 2 1

For D. M. I. J.

Chapter One

'Excuse me,' says Anna to the policewoman standing behind the counter. She says it quietly, barely whispers it, preferring not to be heard at all. The policewoman doesn't respond. She is in the middle of a conversation with someone else. A man wearing a long grey coat, despite the heat, is trying to explain what his lost dog looks like. He keeps saying the word 'dog' and sticking out his tongue and pretending to pant, in case the policewoman has forgotten it's a dog he is talking about. Even though he's standing a few feet away from Anna, she can smell the heavy unwashed odour coming from him. With his shaggy beard and long hair, he is starkly out of place in this suburban police station.

Anna looks around her at the peeling fake leather chairs, grey laminate counter and cream-coloured walls, and tries to imagine someone actually designing the room. It's not even ugly. It's just nothing. If she closes her eyes, she immediately forgets what it looks like.

The man at the counter waves his arms and his smell assaults Anna again.

The policewoman doesn't seem to notice the odour—or she's very good at ignoring it. Anna furtively dips her head towards her chest and smells the perfume she sprayed on as she was getting dressed. The floral scent mingles with the man's smell, making her feel slightly sick and reminding her that she only had coffee for breakfast this morning. And that she only had wine for dinner last night. She doesn't usually drink wine, or any alcohol at all, but she was trying to see how much the rich, berry-coloured drink could alter the way she felt. 'There must be a reason so many people do it,' she had thought. She had not expected to have acid in her throat this morning and now doubts that she will ever be able to drink wine again.

She was trying to see if, with enough alcohol, she could feel like her old self, or a different self—anyone but who she was right now. One glass of wine had slowed her heart rate a little and smoothed the rough edges of her thoughts, but before allowing herself to enjoy the sensation, she had poured another glass and then another. This morning, she had chewed on an antacid tablet and dismissed the idea of rediscovering even the smallest atom of her old self as ridiculous. Her old self hadn't existed for so long, she couldn't even be sure what feelings and thoughts she was trying to recapture.

Looking in the mirror as she applied her make-up, she acknowledged that she was an entirely different person than she had been two weeks ago. Her face looked strange, filled with shadows and angles that she had never seen before. She had had to reapply her make-up because it looked wrong, as though she were a teenager making her first attempt at decoration. It didn't look much better the second time but by then she was running late, and so had shrugged her shoulders at her reflection and given up on finding her old face.

There is a mirror on the wall behind the policewoman and Anna glances at it, wondering if there are other police officers behind it, watching her. She straightens her shoulders a little. In its reflection, she looks, as Caro would say, like she belongs in some country house. 'Oh my dear,' her friend liked to say, affecting a British accent, 'don't you look fabulous.'

Anna smiles down at her shoes as she thinks about Caro's terrible accent that always came out sounding more New Zealand than British and never failed to make her laugh. Caro loved accents despite being hopeless at them. Only four weeks ago, she had insisted on pretending to be Italian when they tried out a new coffee shop. Caro's ruse had fallen apart because the owner was actually Italian and had attempted to have a conversation with her. Anna had eventually excused herself to go to the bathroom because she could see her choked-back giggles were irritating the woman. Caro had simply pretended that she was speaking Italian until she finally gave up and went away.

'She probably thinks you're insane,' Anna had said on returning to their table.

'That's Mrs Insane to you,' Caro had said, stealing the last piece of mud cake.

Anna had left for school pick-up feeling lighter than she had all day. She had breathed in the late-spring air and felt, if not content, at least better than she had. For what seemed longer than an hour, she had just been a woman having fun in a coffee shop.

Anna looks at the mirror again and quickly stops smiling. She smooths down the front of her wraparound dress, which she bought last year. The fabric is soft and has a delicate rosebud print. She remembers how excited she was to find it on sale, marked down three times to a price that she could finally afford.

'Buy it,' Caro had said as she watched Anna twirl in front of the boutique's large gold-framed mirror.

'But it's still expensive. When will I ever wear it?'

'We'll have a night out together,' said Caro. 'We'll go drinking without the husbands and pick up gorgeous young men.'

The dress had hung in her closet ever since, waiting to be worn. Anna had only pulled it out this morning when she had run out of other options. She had held it to her cheek for a moment, remembering. 'I found somewhere to wear it,' she would like to tell Caro.

Because it's a wraparound dress, she can wear it even though she has lost weight in the last two weeks. 'Eat something,' says Keith every time someone else brings over a meal. There are at least five different kinds of lasagne squashed in the freezer, all in dishes she knows their owners will require back.

'Why can't they just use something disposable?' she said to Keith as she watched him note exactly who the latest one was from.

'I suppose they think these look better. I'm heating this one up now; please eat some of it with me.'

'What's the point?' she had replied, making him shake his head. She left him in the kitchen and curled up on the couch in the living room, switching on the news but muting the sound.

She hadn't asked that question to be difficult. She really would like to know if there is any point in her continuing to exist, continuing to feed and dress herself, or even get out of bed in the mornings. She doesn't think she has ever looked this thin and this old. At a certain point, she seems to have crossed a boundary between waif-like and haggard. 'So what,' she thinks, staring at the reflection of her collarbones in the police station mirror. 'So what.'

'You need to eat, Anna, because there's going to be a day when you're ready to move on, to move forward,' said Keith, who had joined her in the living room. He'd handed her a plate of lasagne and given her a fork. 'You want to be physically strong enough to get on with your life. We both need to be strong enough to get on with living.'

'What if I don't want to get on with living?' she had asked and put the plate on the coffee table, next to the sandwich he had made her for lunch.

'I don't know,' he had replied, and then she had watched him shove three large forkfuls of the lasagne into his mouth, barely even chewing one mouthful before opening his mouth for the next one.

'You'll choke,' she said and he had shrugged.

'You can do something with your life, Anna; really do something,' he said, as though she were now free to embark on some great adventure. 'You could go back to school and study for your master's degree in art, or you could study teaching . . . anything!'

Anna had been unable to suppress a bubble of laughter. Sometimes the things Keith said were so stupid that she thought about hitting him.

'We could try for another child,' he said quietly after she had finished laughing at him.

Then she *had* hit him. It had happened so quickly that she had barely felt herself move as she leapt to her feet, whirled around and slapped him across the face. The stinging sensation on her palm made her aware of how numb she had been feeling and she had looked at her hand, almost enjoying the tingling.

She had never done anything like that before and had a vision of herself powered by rage.

'What the fuck is wrong with you?' he had yelled. He had dropped his plate of lasagne on the floor and the congealed mess of yellow and brown made Anna feel sick.

'Arsehole,' she had replied and then had gone to the kitchen and found an unopened bottle of red wine. 'Well what have we here?' she'd heard Caro say so clearly that she had turned around—expecting her to be there.

Now she swallows twice, reliving the cheap acidic taste that she had managed to ignore in order to finish half the bottle and collapse into bed, only to be woken four hours later by a raging thirst. 'You're such a lightweight,' Caro used to say whenever she managed to convince Anna to join her in a drink.

Anna takes a step back, so she is further away from the man who has lost his dog, pats her hair and straightens the dress's belt. She knows, without another check in the mirror, that to the outside world she looks well put together, regardless of how she looks to herself. She could be on her way to lunch at a beachside café or she could be planning a day of shopping. She could be anywhere but instead she is right here, waiting for the policewoman to notice her.

'I'll come with you,' Keith had said when he came into the bedroom before he left for work and found her sitting on the floor, surrounded by dresses and pants that, not knowing what to wear for this interview, she had rejected, but she told him not to. She is sure that they will not allow anyone else to be present in the interview, and she is also sure that she does not want Keith sitting next to her today, or, possibly, ever again. Anna had known that he wouldn't mention her slapping him. It has never been his way. Keith had always been able to compartmentalise their arguments and dismiss them as single moments in time. He'd just pretend it had never happened. Perhaps he'd been afraid to push her for an explanation in case it pushed her too far or opened a discussion he didn't want to have. Either way he said nothing and she did the same.

'You should have hit me back,' she wanted to say but knew that Keith would have been profoundly shocked by that.

'He is . . . dis . . . dis . . . ,' says the man, trying to indicate, Anna thinks, that the dog has spots of colour. 'Is . . . is,' he continues and then looks around, and not finding what he's looking for, growls at the policewoman.

'Like a leopard,' she says. Anna has no idea how the policewoman has understood what the man was trying to say.

'Dat,' he says, pointing a finger at her. 'Like dat.' His accent sounds European but Anna doesn't know from which part. Keith, as he tells her all the time, always knows. He makes a habit of talking to strangers with accents, just so he can enjoy their incredulous expressions when he picks, say, the state they're from if he's talking to an American, or the county they're from if he's speaking to an Englishman.

'Pity it's not the sort of thing you can make money from,' she always thinks as she smiles and congratulates him on his accuracy. 'Keith is easily impressed with himself,' she told Caro once when they were exchanging confidences about their husbands. 'Most of them are,' Caro had said.

Anna smiles again as she remembers how Caro's laughter had set her off and the two of them had giggled like much younger women. There was a freedom in uncontrollable laughter, a feeling of being right in the moment, and Anna had not experienced such moments with anyone but Caro since she was a child.

The policewoman sighs and writes, in a small notebook, the dog's description. 'Okay; we have everything we need. We'll call you if we find him.'

The man nods and smiles and his shoulders slump forward a little, as though he is relieved that the police are on the case. He shuffles out of the station and the policewoman turns her attention to Anna. Her hair is tightly slicked back into a short ponytail. She is wearing a vest covered in pockets and has a gun holstered at her side.

'Do you really find lost dogs?' Anna asks.

'No, not really,' she replies, giving Anna a small smile, 'but he comes in every week to report it. I used to try and explain that it's not something the police do but he doesn't seem to understand, or want to understand, so it's easier just to take down the details and tell him we'll do our best.'

'Doesn't he wonder why you never find him?'

'We don't think the dog actually exists, but it makes him happier to report it missing.'

'But surely you need to help him understand that?' Anna asks, finding herself aggrieved on behalf of the old man.

The policewoman seems to realise that she has unwittingly found herself in a conversation and stops smiling. 'Can I help you?' she says.

'Oh yes. I'm ... um ... I'm here to meet with Detective Anderson,' Anna replies and feels herself flush at the words. This is not a situation she has ever imagined she would find herself in.

The policewoman consults a computer on the counter.

'You are?' she asks.

'Anna McAllen.'

'Yes, Anna McAllen,' says the policewoman, agreeing with Anna that she is, indeed, who she says she is.

'No one else would want to be me,' thinks Anna.

'Come this way, please.' The policewoman's tone is low and her voice formal. The change is alarmingly sudden, making Anna wonder what she's heard. She glances at the mirror again, wondering how many people are judging her.

She is no longer a nice woman seeking help. She is here to be interviewed, to help police with their enquiries. No one has said these words to her but she is thinking them. Whenever she's heard the phrase on the news, she's known instantly that while it sounds like a friendly exchange of information, it is anything but.

I'm here because they suspect me of something. I'm here because I am a suspect. I know that, she knows that. Everyone knows that.

'It's just routine,' Detective Anderson had told her when he called yesterday. 'It's just so we can get all the facts down.'

'But you already have the facts,' she said. 'You were there.'

'I wasn't there when it happened, I was only at the hospital. Trust me, it's no big deal. We just have to do it in a formal situation so we can get your statement on camera. It can wait if you're not . . . ready.'

'Why does it need to be on camera?'

'Anna, I don't want you to get upset about this. It's more to do with how the case against the driver is going to proceed. We just need a clear statement from you. But, as I said, it can wait if you're not ready.'

'No,' she had said. 'I'll do it. I'll come in and do it.'

It was, for a moment, a relief to think that she could leave the house, that she *should* leave the house. Bereaved people were supposed to stay home, out of sight and away from people who were trying to get on with their lives. Last night, she had looked at the walls of the hallway leading to their bedroom and wondered if they were moving closer together. She's found herself standing in the garden at all hours, sucking in deep breaths of air to carry back inside with her.

Anna follows the policewoman through a door into the back of the station, which is really just a collection of small rooms. The air-conditioning seems to be failing in the face of the heat and she feels her lip bead with sweat. She reaches up to touch her cheek and finds it wet. Again, she has been crying without having realised. Anna had always assumed that crying involves the whole body, starting with heaving shoulders and guttural sounds, but now she knows better. She can be standing in the kitchen, thinking about whether she would like a cup of tea, and absent-mindedly touch her face and find it wet. She is always embarrassed when this happens and is glad Keith hasn't caught her.

Even when she thinks she is coping, she is not. Anna wipes her face quickly.

She reaches into her bag and touches her phone but instantly withdraws her hand. She cannot call Caro now. She cannot call Caro ever again but, oh, how she wants to. More than anything, she wants to call Caro on her phone and say, 'You won't believe this but . . .'

Detective Anderson is sitting in an office with the door open. He is reading something on a computer screen when the policewoman knocks on the door. 'Detective Anderson, Anna McAllen is here for her interview,' she says.

'Ah, Anna,' he says, standing up. 'Good of you to come.'

Anna nods at him, maintaining the charade that she is doing him a favour. 'Thanks, Missy,' he says to the police-woman, and she nods and leaves. He leans back a little and braces his hands against his back, and Anna is struck, as she was when she met him two weeks ago, at how tall and broad he is. He towers over her, and when Keith stood next to him, her husband looked like a boy in comparison.

'Follow me; we'll pick up Cynthia along the way. Are you okay?'

Anna wipes her cheeks again and nods. 'Just fine.'

Detective Anderson grimaces a little, in recognition of the outright lie.

She follows him down a corridor, waiting while he knocks quickly on a closed door and then moves off without saying anything. Behind her, she hears the door open and knows that Cynthia, whoever she is, is walking behind her now.

Once all three of them are seated in a small room with a table, three chairs and little else, Anna feels a shift in Detective Anderson's demeanour. He sets up a camera, and then sits down and looks at it.

'It is eleven am and this is the West Hallston police station. Attending are Detective Sergeant Walter Anderson and Detective Sergeant Cynthia Moreno.

'To begin with, Mrs McAllen, I want to make sure that you understand we are going to ask you some questions but you do not have to say or do anything that you don't want to. Do you understand that?'

'Yes,' says Anna softly.

'I also want to let you know that we will be recording this interview. Are you happy to let us record it?'

Anna looks at the camera, 'What happens if I say no,' she asks.

'Then we can use a tape recorder or we can type up our questions and your answers as we go,' says the detective.

'No, no it's fine, you can record it.'

'Okay, and one more thing, Mrs McAllen. I just want to let you know that you don't have to say anything but if, for some reason, this ends up in court then there may be a problem if you bring up something that you have not mentioned in this interview. And anything you do say may be used as evidence in this case. Do you understand that?'

Anna nods.

'Can you answer that verbally please Mrs McAllen.'

'Yes, I understand that, and please call me Anna.'

'And lastly,' continues Detective Anderson, as though he hasn't heard her, 'you have the right to let a friend or relative know where you are and you have the right to talk to a lawyer.'

'A lawyer?'

'Yes—would you like to speak to a lawyer?'

'Do I need to speak to a lawyer . . . I mean, I don't know; I'm sorry, I'm sorry, I'm just . . .' Anna feels a light sweat of humiliation break out all over her body as she scrabbles in her bag for her last remaining tissue.

'Control yourself,' she thinks.

'That's okay, Anna,' says Detective Anderson and is then silent, giving her time to finish blowing her nose.

Anna has never been one to cry in front of other people. She feels humiliated any time she does it. She has always thought of herself as being made of stronger stuff but is aware that tears are the expected reaction to what has happened, especially in front of the police, especially in front of family; otherwise, how will anyone know that she is grieving?

'It's okay,' he says again, and Anna takes a deep breath and looks straight at him. In addition to his height, he has thick black hair and green eyes. There is a light stubble on his chin, and Anna clutches her tissue tightly to prevent her hand from reaching out to touch him. 'What kind of a person are you to be noticing his looks?' she thinks.

'I just need to ask you these questions and I need to let you know again that this is being recorded,' he says. His tone has softened and Anna sees the man she met two weeks ago but, having had a glimpse of his professional demeanour, she reminds herself that she is in a police station and that anything she says, as he has just explained, may be used against her.

'Words can be weapons,' her mother always told her.

'Our local weapons expert,' was how Peter and Anna used to refer to her when they were teenagers, because no one was more devastatingly accurate than their mother.

'Yes, yes, I can see that,' says Anna, gesturing to the camera. 'I'm sorry, I'm sorry, but can I get another tissue?' She is feeling flustered and wishes that Keith were sitting next to her.

'Here you go, Anna,' says Detective Anderson, sliding a box of tissues across the table. 'Just relax. I know this is a really difficult time. We can leave it for another week.'

'She'll still be . . . be gone in a week, Detective. I just want to get this over with.' Anna tries to say the word 'dead' every day but simply can't. She remembers that only a couple of weeks ago, she would, as most people do, say she was 'dead tired,' or that she'd 'rather be dead than wear a bikini again' or that 'the stores were dead today'. Now, she cannot say the word, but she thinks it all the time, repeating it in her head until it momentarily loses its meaning, making her think that she has conquered it, but then she opens her mouth to say it and cannot even get the first syllable out. 'My daughter is d . . . My daughter is de . . . My daughter is . . .' she will stutter and then just give up.

'I understand,' says Detective Anderson. 'Why don't you take a few deep breaths? Cynthia and I have as much time as you need.'

She does take a few deep breaths, and uses the time to look at Cynthia—as he has called her. She is about the same height as Anna, with curly brown hair tied in a messy bun. Her breasts strain a little at the blouse she is wearing, drawing Anna's eyes to them. 'She looks too young to be in here, too young to be a detective,' she thinks. There are no lines on her face, only a few freckles. *Pretty. Too pretty. Look how pretty my detectives are.*

This morning, in the mirror, Anna had seen how the grey circles under her eyes have become more obvious because she is so pale and her face is so much thinner. Her skin is now dry and flaky. She cannot seem to moisturise it enough.

Detective Anderson clears his throat.

'I can't seem to stop crying,' says Anna. She has no idea why she has said this because it is not strictly true. She has moments when she is not crying, moments when she is not even sad; moments when she feels nothing. But those moments are overwhelmed by all the other ones where she finds herself in the grip of violent, debilitating emotion, and looking at Detective Anderson, she does feel as though he might understand such a thing.

'I keep thinking that eventually I'll get it together or . . . I don't know . . . dehydrate or something, but that's not happening. Do you think I'll ever stop crying?'

Chapter Two

Caro is running late. Geoff offered to drop her off but she didn't even bother answering when he first made the suggestion. She didn't when he suggested it twice more either.

'I don't think you should be driving,' he stage whispered to her in a final attempt to convince her to accept his offer of a ride.

'Oh, fuck off, Geoff,' she said in reply while unloading the dishwasher this morning.

He had sighed because Lex was in the room and he never swore in front of her, and then he had taken his briefcase and Lex had taken her school bag and the two of them had slunk out of the kitchen, their heads bowed under what Caro assumed was the collective weight of their disappointment in her.

She had smashed a mug after they'd left. It was the last thing she had removed from the dishwasher, coinciding with the sound of the garage door closing, letting Caro know that she was now truly alone. She had watched, fascinated, as the mug exploded into shards. It had not been as cathartic as she'd thought it would be.

She had smashed it into the sink because she knew that she would have to clean it up afterwards. Only as she was picking up the pieces had she realised that the mug was an old favourite, large enough for a generous cup of coffee, with a silly picture of a dog decorating the outside. It had been a gift from a great-aunt who was no longer living and Caro had always treasured it.

'Sorry, Gertie,' she had said, looking up at the ceiling, then muttered, 'Just fuck, fuck, fuck,' as she picked the pieces out of the sink.

Her thoughts had turned to Gertie's funeral. Keith had been away on business, so Anna had come with her. They had sat together in church, and Anna had kept her arm around her friend's shoulders the whole way through as Caro sobbed messily and embarrassed her mother. Afterwards, as they were making their way back to Anna's car, two women from Gertie's nursing home had stopped them and enquired if they were lesbians. Caro and Anna had howled with laughter the whole way home. Then Anna had joined Caro for a gin and tonic, so they could toast Gertie, who always said that her longevity was due to the gin and tonic she had every day at exactly five o' clock. 'If

I were a lesbian,' Anna had said, 'you would definitely be my first choice.'

'No I wouldn't,' said Caro. 'I don't think I'm anyone's first choice anymore. I'm so fat.'

'Don't say that,' Anna had said. 'You're gorgeous and I would do you in a second.'

'Anna McAllen, what would your mother say?'

'She'd say . . . oh, who cares what she'd say.'

'That's right,' said Caro, 'who cares what anyone says. Let's run away together to an island where they serve wine and tea and all we're required to do is read books and be lesbians.'

'God,' said Anna, 'I'll take that any day of the week.'

Caro picked the last piece of the mug out of the sink, pressed the sharp sliver against her thumb and wondered how much pressure it would take to draw blood, but hadn't been brave enough to try to actually hurt herself.

After that, she'd had a cup of coffee and then another cup of coffee, and then she had given into her craving and had a vodka and orange. 'Look at me celebrating,' she said as she raised the glass to the empty kitchen. She had wanted one more but knew that she had to drive. 'Too little too late,' she thought as she forced herself to return the vodka to the freezer. The orange juice was just for colour.

The alcohol stopped her hands shaking, and allowed her to shower and dress. 'On a bender' is a phrase she has heard for years but never really paid attention to. But, as she finished her drink, she had acknowledged to herself that she was, indeed, on a bender. It was a phrase that conjured up out-of-control celebrities, giving it an edge of glamour. The edge wore off quickly after the first lot of vomit that didn't quite make the toilet.

Two weeks and counting. She has become attached to her breakfast drink remarkably quickly. Before this, she had been quite capable of making it to midmorning most days.

'I think you should have a lawyer with you,' Geoff had said to her last night.

'I'm only helping them with their enquiries,' she said. 'If I take a lawyer with me, it looks like I'm guilty.'

Geoff had looked at her and slowly raised one eyebrow in a move she's pretty convinced he practises in the mirror. It's a lot more effective now that he's bald, but also makes her want to laugh at him, which, she imagines, is probably better than spitting at him.

'I know,' she had said in response, 'I know you think I'm guilty and I just don't give a fuck, Geoff. I've tried to explain what happened and you don't want to hear it. That's fine, but you don't get to judge me, because you weren't there! You've already made up your mind because you always make up your mind against me.'

'I'm just trying to protect you, Caro—I don't want you to go to jail.'

'You are not,' she had said slowly, 'doing anything of the sort. You want me to walk in there with my lawyer so I look like I have something to hide. Having me in jail would solve all of your problems.'

Geoff sighed. 'How much have you already had to drink, Caro?' he asked. She'd opened her mouth but no answer had come out. In the last two weeks, she has spent a lot of time not answering him, believing silence was better than an argument. Instead, she left him sitting in the living room and locked herself in their bedroom. This time, it had taken everything she had to remain upright as she walked away from him, the room tilting from side to side. Once she was in the bedroom, she managed a shower and a night of black sleep, untouched by bad dreams. She had woken at dawn to throw up, much as she had woken the day before, and the day before that.

In the police station, a small group of people are standing in front of the counter. They seem to be protesting about something because Caro hears one man say, 'It's a bloody disgrace that it's allowed to go on,' and then the rest of the group murmurs, 'Yes, yes . . . bloody disgrace.' To Caro, they all look about five hundred years old, and she seethes at how long they are going to take now they have the attention of the policewoman behind the counter. Caro has parked half a block away, so that she can create the illusion she walked or was dropped off. She had hurried along in the heat and now feels sticky and irritated; even more irritated than she was this morning. She doesn't think they'll want to breath test her but isn't sure. It's not like she's ever been in a situation like this before. Caro watches the disgruntled group, thinking, 'So, this is your life, Caroline—what do you think of that?'

'And I'll tell you something else . . .' says a man dressed in a crisp three piece suit, stabbing his finger on the counter, 'we're not going to . . .'

'Excuse me,' says Caro loudly and the group falls silent as they all turn to look at her. A few of them would give Geoff's raised eyebrow a run for its money.

'I'm here for my interview,' she says quickly. 'I'm Caroline Harman.'

The request to come into the police station had finally come yesterday from a woman named Isabel Dillon who'd identified herself as, 'the case manager'. Caro had no idea what that meant, but she'd been waiting for a visit from the police for two weeks. Now that it was here she was terrified and strangely relieved as well.

The policewoman smiles politely at the group in front of her, checks her computer and says, 'If you'd just give me a moment. This way, Mrs Harman,' she continues, indicating that Caro should follow her through a door to the back of the police station. As she walks past the group, Caro hears one of them mutter, 'Well, I never,' and she also thinks she hears the words, 'Wasn't she . . . ?'

She lifts her chin higher as she feels their eyes burn her between her shoulder blades. 'They don't know me,' she thinks, although she knows that it is very possible they know of her. The accident was two weeks ago and had been reported on television and the internet. There were no pictures of her, but Caro knows that her name was out there for everyone to see. What she had assumed would be old news by now is still fodder for the media. 'Screw you all,' she thinks as she follows the policewoman, 'don't you dare fucking judge me!' She would like the story to be old news by now, to feel that the whole country has moved on from this particular tragedy but it doesn't feel possible.

She and Anna haven't moved on, and at odd moments in the day, Caro catches herself realising that she will never, ever, move on. She is as trapped as if she were already in prison.

'Do I have to come in?' Caro had asked Isabel Dillon.

'No,' she had replied, 'but it would be better if you did. We can only ask that you come in to help us sort out what happened. You are free to wait until you are charged with an offence.'

'What offence?'

'Mrs Harman, I am sure that the detectives who will be interviewing you will be able to explain everything. Shall I tell them to expect you?'

'Are you going to be interviewing Anna as well?'

'That's not your concern right now.'

'So, yes,' said Caro. Isabel Dillon was silent. 'I'll be there,' Caro had said as she made her way to the freezer, 'I'll be there.'

Caro follows the policewoman along a corridor until she gets to a room at the end. 'They're waiting for you,' she says, and then opens the door, turns and walks away. 'Thanks so much,' Caro replies to the policewoman's back.

A man and a woman are sitting in the small room that has a table and three chairs. There are no windows and, almost instantly, she can feel herself getting edgy and claustrophobic, although she knows that may be from the vodka wearing off.

'Mrs Harman, thank you for coming in. I'm Detective Sergeant Susan Sappington and this is Detective Sergeant Brian Ng.'

The woman stands up and holds her hand out for Caro to shake. Caro surreptitiously wipes her own hand against the leg of her jeans before she takes the detective's, which is as cool and dry as Caro had known it would be. Detective Sappington is dressed in a grey pantsuit, which would lie perfectly against her thin body if not for the gun holstered at her side. Caro smooths her hair, pushing behind her ears the pieces that are escaping. She wonders if the detectives can see the grey in her black hair. She's very overdue for a colour. She pulls her shirt down a little, wishing she'd thought to wear something loose and cool instead of her slightly too tight black T-shirt. She didn't know what people were supposed to wear to be inter- viewed by the police but, in the end, she'd just chosen clothes that fitted.

Detective Sappington smiles and indicates that Caro should sit down.

She is perfectly polite, even though Caro is at least half an hour late. Despite her plan to be guarded, Caro finds herself beginning with an apology: 'I'm sorry I'm late.'

'Please don't worry about it.' Detective Sappington sits down and Caro does as well. The other detective just nods at her and she understands immediately who's in charge.

'Is it okay to start?' says Detective Sappington and Caro nods. Detective Ng turns on the camera they have set up at the end of the table and Caro feels sweat collect at the base of her spine. 'This is really happening and I am really here,' she thinks.

'It is eleven-thirty am and this is the West Hallston police station. Attending are Detective Sergeant Susan Sappington and Detective Sergeant Brian Ng.

'To begin with, Mrs Harman, I want to let you know that we are recording the interview. Do you give us permission to do so?'

'No, I don't,' says Caro, hating the idea of her face being on camera.

'Mrs Harman, whether we use a tape recorder or a video recorder or we manually record the interview doesn't matter. It will be recorded in some form or another. Using a video recorder does tend to shorten the process.'

Caro looks at the small camera set up on a tripod. She thinks about having to wait as the detectives write everything down and she says, 'Okay, fine. You can record it.'

'Thank you. I also want to let you know that you do not have to say or do anything, but if this does go to court and you attempt to use information that you have not given us in this interview it may not be accepted into the record.'

'Do you think this is going to court?' asks Caro, feeling her stomach flip with panic.

'I have no idea,' says Detective Sappington. 'I also want to let you know that you have the right to let a friend or relative know where you are and you have the right to request a lawyer.'

'Do you think I need a lawyer? What on earth would I need a lawyer for if I haven't been charged and you don't know if I'm going to be?' Caro feels her heart speed up as she acknowledges to herself that Geoff was right and she should have had someone with her. 'I need a lawyer,' she rehearses in her head but the words don't come out. She feels like her guilt has already been decided, but knows that if she gets up and leaves now, they will be convinced that everything was her fault. She wants to be able to explain things to them; she needs to be able to explain, so they understand. A lawyer may tell her that she cannot say anything, that she must keep what she knows to herself.

'Would you like a lawyer?'

'I . . . no.'

'Are you happy to answer some questions about the night of the accident, Mrs Harman?'

'Why are there two of you here?' Caro hears the sharpness in her voice and congratulates herself. She feels like she has taken an important step and now they know she won't be pushed around. *The best form of defence is a good offence, or something like that.* She crosses her arms over her chest.

'I'm going to ask you some questions, Mrs Harman, and Detective Ng is going to observe.' Detective Sappington's voice is pitched perfectly to calmness, but instead of relaxing, Caro finds herself even more irritated.

'Fine, whatever,' she says. 'I just want to go home. How long is this going to take?'

'I'm not sure. Do you have children who need to be picked up? If so, I can get you a phone, so you can call someone to let them know.'

'No, I don't have children who need to be picked up,' she says and remembers Lex's bowed head from this morning. 'Keep quiet,' she thinks but Detective Sappington relaxes in her chair, waiting for Caro to continue, so, without having meant to, she says, 'I only have one child and my husband drove her to school this morning. My mother . . . yes, my mother is going to fetch her.'

'Right, so now—' says Detective Sappington, but Caro speaks over her even though she doesn't mean for the words to be heard by anyone but herself.

'She won't get in the car with me.'

'Who won't?' asks the detective.

'What?'

'Who won't get into the car with you, Mrs Harman?'

Caro looks at the wall behind the detective and shakes her head.

'You're doing an excellent job of putting your foot into your mouth,' she can almost hear Anna say.

'Lex, my daughter,' she says. 'Lex won't get in the car with me because of the accident. She doesn't understand.'

'What doesn't she understand?' says Detective Sappington.

'That it wasn't my fault,' says Caro, meeting the detective's gaze, 'she doesn't understand that none of this is my fault.'

Chapter Three

Anna shreds the tissue in her hand and sniffs. The detectives watch her. She closes her eyes for a moment, feeling herself back in Maya's room, where she had spent the night. She hadn't meant to stay there, had only gone in for a look, to feel her child, but she had sat down on the bed, the room spinning a little from all the wine she'd drunk. Then she had rested her head on the pillow, and covered her face with her arm, the way Maya used to do when she slept.

'Why do you do that, Maya? Why do you cover your face when you sleep?' Anna had asked one morning, knowing she would never get an answer, but asking anyway because she couldn't keep to herself all the questions she had for her daughter.

Maya had picked up her iPad and touched the word 'jump'. She had only been seven at the time.

Anna had smiled at her. 'Do you want to jump?'

Maya had touched the word again and again, until Anna had gently taken the iPad away from her. 'Jump then, Maya; if you want to jump, jump.' Anna had jumped up and down to show her. 'Let's jump together, Maya—jump, jump.' But Maya hadn't wanted to jump. She shook her head and touched her eye. She pointed at the iPad, and when Anna gave it back, she touched the word 'jump' again.

'What did you expect?' Anna had thought. 'Let's do your writing exercises,' she had said, pushing on with the day, but Maya had begun to scream and thrash. It had taken seconds for her to go from sitting calmly on the couch to becoming a screaming, raging dervish.

'Oh, not today, Maya; please, not today,' Anna had said but it was too late. Chaos had reigned for hours.

Lying on her daughter's bed, Anna had relived that day, trying, as she always did with days like that, to work out what had set Maya off. She had touched the word 'jump' on her iPad but hadn't wanted to jump, so why had she touched the word?

And then she had touched her eye. '"Jump", eye; "jump", eye,' Anna had muttered to herself. *What had Maya meant? What had she wanted?* Anna had taken her arm away from her face as a car turned in the road outside. Its lights flashed through the gaps in the closed curtains and Anna instinctively covered her face again. '"Jump"; eye,' she thought. The lights flashed into the room again as the car drove off.

'Oh,' Anna moaned, feeling her stomach churn with nausea. 'Oh, Maya. It was the lights, the lights from the cars outside,' she whispered, sitting up. 'That's what you were trying to say. The lights made your eyes jump, so you had to cover your face. I get it, Maya, I understand now. It was the lights.'

She had curled up on the single bed and let herself cry once again. 'I get it, Maya, I get it now,' she said. It was so clear, so obvious, what her daughter had been trying to say, that she had been answering the question. As she had drifted off to sleep, Anna had another thought: *What else did I miss?*

When she had woken up, only hours later, she had found herself covered with a blanket. 'He's trying so hard,' she thought as she gulped water, and had experienced a sharp stab of sorrow for her husband, who just wanted to take care of her.

'Okay, Anna,' says Detective Anderson, forcing her back into the present, 'I know this sounds silly but, just for the purposes of keeping an accurate record, I'm going to need you to state your full name and date of birth.'

'Anna McAllen, twenty-first of February 1976,' says Anna and it occurs to her that she's forty. She hadn't even thought about it on her birthday but she has reached the Big Four-O. She recalls being twenty-five when Sophie, her boss at the graphic design company where she worked, turned forty, and feeling sad for her.

Sophie had a husband and two children to go home to,

and didn't want more than half a piece of cake because she was watching her weight, and at the time it seemed to Anna that Sophie's life was almost over.

'All I want to do is get to bed early and have a full night's sleep,' Sophie had said. 'Just wait until you girls have kids. You'll know what I mean.'

'Imagine being that old,' Anna had whispered to Melanie as they sipped champagne out of plastic glasses.

'Hideous,' giggled Melanie and then she threw her hair back over her shoulder, attracting everyone's attention. Anna and Melanie had worked on many projects together and knew some of the older men in the office called them 'the beauties'. Watching Sophie pick at her cake, Anna had been sure that even when she was forty, she would be young and beautiful, still attracting attention with her long blonde hair and perfect smile.

'Having children won't do that to me,' she had thought and then quickly took another sip of champagne because it was the same thought she had had about her own mother.

'I only wish you have a daughter just like you,' Anna's mother had spat at her during an argument over doing the laundry.

'Well, she certainly will never have a mother like you,' Anna said in reply.

'I'm not sure about having kids,' Melanie said as the party broke up. 'They don't seem like much fun.' She and Anna had lost touch after Maya was born. Melanie might still be single, for all Anna knew.

Anna had not had a party to celebrate reaching the milestone birthday, although Keith had brought home a large chocolate cake with a 'four' and a 'zero' painted in white butter-cream icing, which Maya shouldn't have been allowed to eat. She had let her daughter blow out the candles, and then grab the icing roses off the top and snatch a whole piece of cake with her hands, making a mess of everything. She didn't really feel like having a piece after that, but she can still remember the smile on Maya's face as she tasted the rare mouthful of pure sugar. Joy is always easy to see on a child's face, regardless of who that child is. Anna touches her cheek, and realises she is crying again and that both detectives are watching her.

'Sorry, can I get another tissue?' she asks.

'The box is empty, Walt,' says Detective Moreno and she stands up quickly. 'I'll go and get another one. Would you like a drink, Anna? Some tea or coffee, or water?'

'Thank you, Detective Moreno. Yes, I would love some tea—strong, with no sugar.'

'I'll take a coffee,' says Detective Anderson without even looking at Detective Moreno.

'I'll be back in a minute, and please call me Cynthia, and Detective Anderson, Walt. We want you to relax and we'd like to make this as easy as possible.'

Once she's gone, Walt stands up and walks over to the camera, checking it, Anna assumes. He has large hands with the ragged fingernails of a worrier.

She wonders what it would be like to lie next to him, to have him touch her. She closes her eyes briefly and imagines the scape of a rough nail against her skin.

'What kind of a husband would he be?' she thinks. 'What kind of a father?'

Since Maya was diagnosed, she has often found herself looking at other men and thinking about how different her life would have been if she had chosen someone whose faulty genes had not mixed with her own faulty genes and created Maya.

'There must be something wrong with me to think like that,' she had said to her therapist when she found the courage to confess these thoughts. The therapist, an older woman named Mollie, had taken her usual minute to ponder a question from Anna before she said: 'It's an idle thought, Anna. I'm sure other parents in your situation wonder the same thing from time to time.'

'Is there a way to test for that? Like, I mean, is there a way to find out if one of you is carrying the gene?'

'No, Anna; I don't think there is a way, not yet. If there was, would you feel better knowing that the gene came from Keith or that it came from you, or that it was recessive from both of you?'

'I don't know,' Anna had said.

'There is no one to blame, Anna. We've talked about that. It just is, as some things just are.'

'An aphorism, Mollie, really?' she had said.

'It's the truth, Anna. No good comes of such speculation.'

Anna had suppressed the urge to leap to her feet and stamp her foot like a child. 'I don't like it,' she wanted to say. 'I don't like it.'

In the last nine years, Anna has seen at least five different therapists, none of whom has ever managed to make her feel better and now it doesn't matter anymore. *Or maybe it does? Would a therapist help her explain what had happened? Would a therapist understand it?*

Right now, Anna can think of nothing to say to a therapist, or for a therapist to say to her. There are some things that cannot be reasoned with, some events that cannot be reframed so as to be more acceptable, and no positive thinking that would bring Maya back, so what would the point of a therapist be?

'You need to talk to someone,' Keith, her mother, her mother-in-law and her sisters-in-law have all said to her.

'You're one to talk,' Anna had said to her mother when she suggested seeing someone.

'I'm only trying to help, Anna,' Vivian had said, a wounded look crossing her face as she became aware other people were listening. Her mother was always particularly self-conscious in front of Keith's mother and his sisters, knowing that Anna often turned to one of them first when she needed someone to talk to. 'Keith's mother says ...' Anna would quote when speaking to her own mother.

'So you've already spoken to her,' an aggrieved Vivian would say.

'Of course I have,' she would reply. It is, Anna knows,

an unnecessary and unkind thing to do but she had never been able to stop herself from doing it.

'I'll think about it,' she had said to her mother-in-law, because there was never a reason to be rude to Keith's mother.

'I have nothing to say,' Anna has told Keith because that, in the end, is how she feels. She has nothing to say and she would prefer to have nothing to think either.

Cynthia has left behind her a light smell of musk perfume and, without filtering the comment, Anna says to Walt: 'She's pretty. Is she your girlfriend?' It was his coffee order that had alerted her—there was no please or thank you, just an assumption that the other detective would be happy to get him coffee and would also know exactly how he liked it. It might be because they are work partners but Anna senses something else. She can remember the thrill of knowing exactly how Keith liked his coffee, of feeling like she knew him better than anyone did. Now, she can't remember the last time she'd actually made Keith a cup of coffee.

'Um . . .' says Detective Anderson and the tips of his ears colour a little. He goes from man to boy in an instant, and Anna feels a streak of jealousy towards the lovely Cynthia. 'Who are you?' she thinks. She doesn't know where her thoughts are coming from anymore. Maya, and everything to do with Maya, took up most of her conscious thoughts, and it feels like now she's not here Anna's brain is in some sort of freefall. She finds herself biting her lip a lot to prevent herself saying awful things.

'I can't believe I just asked you that,' she says. 'It was very inappropriate, I'm sorry. I feel like I've said that word a million times in the last two weeks. I keep apologising.'

'It's all right, Anna. It's been a difficult time; a really difficult time. You don't have to keep apologising,' says the detective, but he doesn't look at her.

'I feel like I should. You were so nice the night of the accident. I remember that, you know. Even though I don't remember much, I remember how lovely you were. You were so patient with Keith. I wanted to smack him.' Anna bites her lip even though the words are already out. 'Oops,' she thinks.

Walt doesn't say anything. He looks up from the camera and focuses his gaze on her, and she feels more stupid words trip off her tongue. 'I shouldn't have said that but I did want to give him a slap. He was so . . . so . . . so Keith, really. I suppose it was a reaction to what had happened, but when he was sitting next to me and just wailing like a child, I wanted to hit him. "Why has this happened? Why has this happened?" he kept saying; do you remember that?'

'Yes, Anna. I do remember.'

Anna shifts in her chair. Walt doesn't take his eyes off her. She thinks that perhaps her discomfort is exactly what he's hoping for. She looks past him at the wall behind his head as they wait for Cynthia to return.

Keith has shed more tears than she has, but then, he has always cried easily and is unself-conscious about shedding tears in front of others, unlike Anna who always feels faintly ridiculous when crying, as though she is performing rather than feeling anything. She has cried alone in the shower, in Maya's room with the door closed, at the bottom of the garden at night. Today is one of the few times she has cried in front of people and she thinks it odd she should have picked two strangers. Keith thinks her reticence is peculiar, but he's found a lot of things not to understand about her over the last eleven years, making Anna believe that he never really understood her at all. Maybe she never really understood him either but he seems a simple enough man. She should have known, knowing who she was, that Keith was not the man for her.

If she looks back at the beginnings of their relationship, she can see that Keith came along at exactly the right time for her to fall for him. She had just ended a relationship with an advertising man, Max, who commissioned work from her agency. He was tall, with hair that looked ginger in some lights, and dark green eyes, and he was into extreme sports. Even when he was sitting at a desk, he looked ready to leap, to run, to fly. He spoke quickly and his laugh boomed across whatever room he was in. He took Anna kayaking and mountain climbing, and coaxed her into parachuting out of an aeroplane. He was exhausting and sexually insatiable, and almost violently jealous if Anna even glanced in the direction of another man. The excitement of the first few weeks with him gave way to fatigue as Anna felt herself constantly on her toes, anticipating his next move. She ended it when he suggested bringing another girl into bed with them. 'What fucking century are you from?' he said when she turned him down.

A week later, she met Keith at a party Melanie had taken her to. He was in computers, was only slightly taller than she was, and had a relaxed, easy laugh. On their first date, he took her to a romantic comedy and she caught him quickly wiping his eyes when the movie ended. He was kind and sensitive, and always pleasant to be with. He was polite to her mother and got along with her brother, and before Anna knew it, she was Anna-and-Keith, not just Anna.

Getting married was the next step, and only in moments of stress did she question if she had simply been borne along by the tide of her relationship or had been actively steering her way forward.

'Are you going to interview Keith as well, Detective Anderson?' she says. She wants to call him Walt but it would feel strange to do so.

'We will speak to him but today we're primarily concerned with you and Caroline. You were the only two there at the time.'

'I don't call her Caroline. It's odd to hear you say her full name. I call her Caro.'

'How long have you known each other?'

'It feels like forever, but it's only eleven years—well, nearly twelve now. We met when the girls were a year old. They were both so little then, it was hard to imagine them ever sleeping through the night or feeding themselves. It was hard to imagine that they'd ever be . . . real people,

I suppose, but it happened. They changed and they grew; well, I suppose Lex changed more than Maya did.'

Anna places the two girls side by side in her mind and compares, for the thousandth time, their differences. Lex, at eleven, is tall and has the slightly gangly look of a child who's been stretched. Her arms are a little too long and her legs seem sticklike, but her burnished hair and brown eyes make her beautiful, and Anna knows that, one day, she will turn heads as she walks by. Maya was taller than Anna and already in large adult sizes. Even on her special diet, she managed to get bigger and bigger. Food—at least, the food she liked—was everything to Maya, and when she was eating, she was happy and quiet.

'It's her one pleasure,' Anna always thought, 'why deny her?' By the time Anna realised that thought was a mistake, it was too late to change Maya's eating habits. She could go through two packets of rice crackers in ten minutes. She hated all fruit except bananas and could eat three at a time. She loved peanut butter on gluten-free toast and could eat six slices at breakfast.

'You need to take control of her diet,' the paediatrician told Anna the last time she had a check-up. 'I can't control her,' Anna wanted to say but instead had nodded like she understood. The paediatrician was a lovely man, well into his sixties and looking forward to retirement. Visiting him mostly made Anna feel like she was talking to her late grandfather and he was rarely stern with her. She didn't really need to see him, because Maya had so many other doctors taking care of her, but she liked him. He listened more than he talked.

She had kept nodding, even though what she had wanted to do was tell him about what had happened when she'd locked the pantry door so Maya couldn't get to the food inside. Maya had tugged at the lock for a few minutes while Anna tried to pull her away, and then had turned around and pushed Anna hard, slamming her into the kitchen island, causing her to drop to the floor. Anna had heard herself whimpering because of the pain that had surged through her back. Maya had walked out of the kitchen and retuned with her iPad. She had touched the button for 'open' again and again, until Anna had scrambled to her feet and unlocked the pantry door.

'I'll try,' Anna had told the paediatrician.

'Maya and Lex were very different,' she says to Detective Anderson, and thinks now it's peculiar to acknowledge that, while she has imagined her friend's daughter growing up, she never imagined her own child in adult form.

'It's strange to think that Caro woke up to see her child this morning and I didn't wake up to see mine,' she says. 'I hate to sound like Keith, but it's all so bizarre that I have to wonder how it is possible for something like this to happen.' Anna covers her mouth with her hand. She has said very little in the last few weeks except 'thank you'. 'Thank you for coming, thank you for the card, thank you for the casserole, thank you for the cake, thank you for your tears, thank you for knowing that my daughter is . . . gone and my heart is broken. Thank you.' Now the words seem to be pouring from her, as if being shut in this room with this man who is a stranger has somehow freed her tongue.

'I don't . . . I don't . . .' says Detective Anderson.

Anna can see he has no idea what to say to her. Most people feel useless in the face of someone's grief. They utter phrases they've heard and say stupid things but they don't mean to offend. It's because they have no idea what to say. In moments of anger, Anna directs her fury at people who've told her that Maya is in a better place or that everything happens for the best; but when she is calm and quiet, she understands that it is difficult to be comfortable with silence. Everyone feels they have to say something, say anything. Human beings are not programmed to just be, and while the idea of someone holding her hand without saying anything is appealing, she knows that it's unlikely to happen.

She imagines the police are given manuals on dealing with grief-stricken people, but whatever the manual says is probably useless in the face of raw emotion. She wonders if this detective joined the police force for action and excitement but now finds himself dealing with very different situations. She feels sorry for him and then wants to laugh at herself. *You feel sorry for him?*

He opens and closes his mouth a few times as he looks at her, and she can feel him sifting through a list of phrases he must have in his head. Finally, he simply opens his arms wide, as if to tell her, 'I don't know what to say,' and she forgives him for that because she appreciates his silence more than she would words. She has no idea what to say either—not even to herself.

'It was so quick,' says Anna. 'One minute she was fine, and the next, she was lying in the road and I was screaming. I only realised the ambulance had been called when the paramedics shoved me out of the way so they could get to her. Time slows down, you know, just like it does in the movies. Seconds seem to take hours, and sound doesn't get through. All I could hear was my heart beating, and then, suddenly, Keith was there and he was shouting, and Caro was pulling me away, and then we were in the car, following the ambulance. I don't remember getting into the car, but I remember the flashing lights of the ambulance. I thought,' Anna leans forward and covers her eyes with her hands, 'I thought—where is that ambulance going?'

'It's okay, Anna; it's okay,' says Detective Anderson, and Anna takes another tissue from the box Detective Moreno—Cynthia—has just placed in front of her.

'Are you sure you want to do this today? It really doesn't have to happen now. We can wait, we really can,' he says.

'No, I don't want to wait. I want this done.' It is about the only thing she is sure of. She wants this over with, so that she can lie on her bed and close her eyes for a whole day; for a whole week, or month, or forever. She had had no idea how much time grief takes up, how many things there are to do, how many forms there are to sign and conversations to have. 'We have a beautiful pink coffin that we can use, if you'd like,' the woman from the funeral home had said. Anna had looked at her, wondering if the woman was mad, wondering if she was mad. It didn't matter. None of it mattered. Her mother organised the food to be eaten after the funeral. 'Lots of people will come,' she said, and Anna nodded like she understood what she was saying, but what was she saying—*who on earth could eat?*

After today she doesn't want to have to talk ever again about what happened two weeks ago. She just wants it done. She sits up straight in her chair and takes a sip of tea. It is scalding, just the way she likes it, and the burn in her mouth centres her. She nods at Walt—she will call him Walt now that she has said so many other things to him— letting him know she is ready to go on.

'All right then; let's go back to when you and Mrs Harman met. Where did you meet?' he says, no doubt hoping that an innocuous memory will allow Anna time to get herself under control. She has a feeling that the hard questions will come soon but, right now, Walt doesn't seem to want to push her. He has no idea, after all, of how much she can take. It feels like they are playing a strange game, she and her two detectives, and that she needs to be careful what moves she makes.

'We met at the clinic. We'd brought the girls in for their twelve-month check-ups on the same day. I was sitting in the waiting room, flicking through one of those parenting magazines—you know, the ones filled with articles about how you should only feed your child organic food?' Anna shakes her head. 'Those stupid, stupid, articles. Anyway,

I wasn't really reading, I was just looking at the pictures of all the perfect mothers with their perfect babies, and she just started talking to me. She was so . . . I don't know what you would call her . . . so honest, I guess.'

'Honest?

'Yes. I was just sitting there in the waiting room, watching Maya. She was in her pram, playing this little portable DVD player. She was watching a video of a hand putting shapes into one of those shape-sorters. Do you know what that is? Do either of you have kids?'

'I know, Anna,' says Cynthia, and Anna turns to look at her. She has freckles across her perfect little nose, making her look impossibly young to have a child.

'You don't look old enough to have children,' Anna says, and is about to apologise again but bites her lip a little instead. She wishes that she looked like someone who had not been worn down, worn out, worn through, by having a child.

'I have two boys,' Cynthia says and a smile makes its way across her face. Anna recognises that smile; she's seen it on so many mothers. She knows that she had one of those smiles when Maya was a few days old. She knows that she walked around with that same smile for a few weeks after Maya was born—at least, until things got difficult. She can remember wanting to touch every person she saw and say, 'Did you know about this? Did you know that you can love another human being this much?' Cynthia's smile speaks of a secret, deep love, of exclusive membership to the greatest club in the world.

I will never have that smile again, Anna thinks but it doesn't make her feel sad. The love that smile signified nearly destroyed her. In her case, it had been a temporary feeling, an infatuation that was blown away by the reality.

'I think we must have about five different shape-sorters around the house,' says Cynthia. 'You must have seen one, Walt, they're a standard toy for any kid.'

Anna thinks about the relationship between the two detectives. They are not married and only one of them has children. She assumes she must have been wrong about them but still senses something between them. An illicit affair, perhaps?

'Yeah, of course I have,' says Walt. 'I think I gave my niece one for her first birthday.' Anna catches a lightning-quick look between Walt and Cynthia, and understands that Walt has seen the shape-sorters at Cynthia's house. She doesn't know if she can see this because the two of them are quite transparent or because she is looking for it. She has spent the last eleven years looking down at Maya and has only looked up in the last two weeks, to find her senses heightened as though she'd just learned to see and hear again. Well, that's what Maya was doing,' says Anna, forcing herself to concentrate. 'She liked to watch the video over and over again. She even knew how to press the rewind and play buttons to get it to go again. It only lasted about a minute. I think she liked that the same thing always happened. She is . . . she was . . . a big fan of routine. The triangle shape went into the triangle hole, and the same thing with the square and the rectangle. When she rewound it, the same thing happened but backwards. She liked things she could predict, she liked things to be the same. She would just sit and watch it over and over and over again.'

'At twelve months. That's pretty advanced,' says Cynthia, and Anna swallows to stifle a laugh she can feel building up inside her. Her reactions are all inappropriate but there is nothing she can do about it.

'Yes, that's what Caro said,' she replies. 'She sat down in the chair next to me and put Lex—Alexa—on the floor and just stared at Maya.'

'And you two started talking?'

'Not right away. For a few minutes, she watched my child and I watched hers. She'd put Lex on the floor, and Lex had crawled over to one of the chairs in the waiting room and pulled herself up to stand, and then she cruised around the room, holding onto whatever she could to keep herself up and walking. Every time someone else walked through the clinic door, she turned to look who was there. She smiled when another mother put her child on the floor next to her. She pointed at a picture and looked at Caro, and tried to say something. She was very . . . very different to Maya.' Anna stops talking. It was so obvious to her, watching Lex, that what Maya was doing was not normal. Maya never lifted her eyes from the screen. She didn't care where she was or who was there; all that mattered was the screen, and the shapes going in and out of the shape-sorter. It was obvious to Anna when she watched any child the same age as Maya that her daughter was different.

By the time Maya was twelve months old, Anna had read and re-read at least five books that detailed milestones her child should have reached, searching for an answer as to why Maya was doing things so late or not at all.

'All children are different,' her paediatrician told her. Anna had felt comforted by his age, by his lack of concern. 'He must have seen hundreds and hundreds of babies in his time,' she had thought.

'Stop comparing her to other kids,' Keith said.

'I'm sure you were the same,' her mother said.

But the idea that everything was not right gnawed at her all the time.

'Something is wrong,' Anna wanted to yell whenever someone else placated her. 'Can't you see? Don't you see it?'

She feels her stomach churn a little and takes another sip of tea. Two weeks ago, if she had been asked to describe motherhood in one word, it would have been 'anxiety'. It was all she felt, all she had felt for Maya's whole life. Now she has many more words; like 'despair', and 'grief', and 'failure', and 'broken'. She feels untethered now that there is no reason to feel anxiety. Untethered, unmoored, about to drift far away.

'Those clinics feel like heaven when you have your first child. I wanted to take my clinic nurse home with me,' says Cynthia, and Anna is drawn back into the little room with the two detectives. She sips her tea again and tries to behave appropriately.

'Why are you here?' she wants to say to Cynthia. 'I wasn't talking to you.' Instead, she smiles at the other detective, trying to make her expression as natural as possible, and is rewarded with a smile from Cynthia.

'How long have you been a detective?' asks Anna.

'Oh, um . . . just a few months now,' says Cynthia, and Anna sees her cheeks colour a little. Anna smiles at her again, and Cynthia smiles back but more uncertainly this time.

'Cynthia has great instincts, even though she's new to being a detective,' says Walt, and Anna notes how Cynthia ducks her head a little and enjoys the praise. She cannot remember the last time Keith complimented her or said anything nice about her at all. 'Don't think about that now,' she tells herself.

'The day I met Caro felt a bit like heaven,' says Anna. 'I didn't have any friends who were mothers. I'd tried a couple of mothers groups but they didn't . . . didn't really work out. After Caro had been watching Maya for a while, she said, "How old is she?" and I looked at her for the first time—I mean, at her and not her child. She and I are the same age but she looks a lot younger than me. She always says that's crap but I think she does. She's always had a bit of a weight problem and I—well, obviously I don't. Keith calls me a stick insect.'

'That's not . . .' says Cynthia, and then she is quiet. Anna can see that she wants to leap to her defence, to the defence of another woman shamed for her body, and she wonders if Cynthia's curvy body has ever been a source of mean-spirited comments from someone close to her. She cannot imagine this of Walt.

'Oh, I don't mind. I *am* skinny,' says Anna. 'I know I am, but since Maya was born, I've never managed to keep weight on.'

'So, you and Caroline—Caro—started talking?' asks Walt, and Anna can hear an edge of impatience in his voice.

'Yes, sor . . . I'm getting distracted. Yes, we started talking. She looked like she had just thrown on whatever clothes she put her hands on that morning; you know that look?'

'Ah, not really.'

'Well, you must know it, Cynthia.'

'I do, I remember it well.'

'She was wearing a pair of jeans that looked like they could still be her maternity jeans—you know, the ones that have that panel in the middle—and she had on a big, loose T-shirt, and her hair was clipped up with three different kinds of clips and there were some curls hanging down her back. She looked a complete mess, but the moment I saw her, I envied her.'

'You envied her?' asks Walt.

'Yes . . . because she looked like her clothes—loose and relaxed. I saw she was tired—I mean, everyone with a baby is tired—but she smiled at me and her eyes lit up when she looked at Lex, and I just wanted to be her.'

'Why?'

'Why?' says Anna, and then the laugh she had managed to suppress comes bubbling out. Walt and Cynthia look at each other, and Anna knows they think she is laughing because she's hysterical and because it's better than crying, but she does genuinely find it funny when she pictures herself and Caro at the clinic the first time they met.

'I didn't mean to laugh,' she says. 'I think if you'd taken a picture of the two of us that day, you would have seen two such completely different women that you would have automatically assumed that we would never even exchange a few words, let alone become best friends. I was already back in the jeans I had worn before I got pregnant with Maya—in fact, they were a little loose—and, while Keith held Maya, I had spent at least half an hour getting ready to go to the clinic. My hair was perfectly straight and I was wearing make-up. I'm sure I looked like I was on my way to a party but I was sitting there in the clinic, absolutely certain that if I relaxed, even a little bit, I would slip into a coma. I was completely and utterly exhausted. Not just tired but physically, emotionally and mentally exhausted.'

'Babies can be hard work,' says Cynthia. 'My boys are five and nine now, but I remember what it was like at the beginning . . . especially when my husband . . . ex-husband . . . slept through the baby's cries.'

Anna takes in Cynthia's smile and her bright blue eyes, and she knows that if she were not sitting in a room with her being interviewed, and Cynthia were not a detective, she would yell at her. She briefly imagines the things she would say, the epithets she would hurl at smug little Cynthia, who knows how hard babies can be. Because if she has two average kids growing up doing everything they were supposed to do, then she really has no idea at all. Anna takes a deep breath before she speaks, and reminds herself that she knows nothing about Cynthia. It could be that the detective is struggling under the weight of her own problems as well. She has an ex-husband, as she has inadvertently told Anna, and it could be that her children are not average; it could be that she is just trying, as many mothers will, to form a connection with another mother, but Anna knows she needs to help her understand so that Cynthia will choose her words more carefully next time.

'Yes, all babies are hard work,' she says, leaning forward to engage Cynthia, 'but Maya was harder than most. I lost all my baby weight in the first couple of months after she was born. I felt like I was on the stress diet. I never had time to eat, and when I did, I had to force myself to swallow.'

'It can be a very hard time for a lot of mothers,' says Cynthia and this time Anna sees Walt give her a quick look. He has heard something that Cynthia hasn't—or hasn't wanted to.

Anna doesn't know why she needs Cynthia to recognise what she was dealing with. It serves no purpose now but the need to explain won't go away. She wants Cynthia to know that while all mothers sometimes have to look deep inside themselves to find reserves of strength and compassion for their children, some mothers have to look deeper than that. Some mothers have to look past regret and dislike and fear, and find love for their child. It's not an easy task. She wants Cynthia to understand it because she can never actually use words like 'regret' or 'dislike' or 'fear' when she talks about her child. When she *talked* about her child. She has to keep reminding herself to think in the past tense when it comes to Maya.

If you say the words, you are faced with the full glare of society. If you think the words, all you feel is guilt and self-loathing; but to say you are anything less than totally in love with your child, is considered almost criminal.

Anna tries again. 'It can be, yes, but for some mothers it's harder than you could ever imagine. Maya wasn't your average baby. For the first two weeks after she was born, she was just an angel, slept all the time, hardly ever cried, and Keith and I even thought that she was already smiling, and then it was like she changed overnight. One morning, she woke up at around seven because the house next door was being knocked down. The sound of the bulldozers woke her and she started screaming; not crying, just screaming. We had no idea what had happened. I mean, I understood about the noise. I had expected it to wake her and I had planned to go out for the day, but the noise didn't seem to just bother her, it seemed to terrify her. She screamed like she was in pain. I thought something had bitten her or she was sick. I undressed her and checked her whole body but I couldn't see anything. I tried to feed her but she just arched her back away from me and kept screaming. I got her out of the house as quickly as I could, thinking she would be fine if I could just get her away from the noise, but it didn't stop her screaming. I went to my mother's house for the day, but no matter what I did or my mother did, she wouldn't stop screaming. My mother isn't the best with babies but she did try.'

'What on earth have you done to her?' was what her mother had said when she opened the door to Anna and a red-faced, screaming Maya.

'I haven't done anything. I don't know why she won't stop crying. Why won't she stop crying?'

'I don't know if I can deal with this noise all day,' her mother said after trying to bounce Maya up and down for ten minutes. 'This is too much,' she said after pushing her in the pram for an hour.

'Help me,' said Anna. 'Don't you know anything that can help me?'

'Why would I know?' her mother had yelled and, minutes later, Anna had heard the sound of her car reversing up the driveway.

'Eventually, I got her in to see the doctor at around four in the afternoon, but by then she had exhausted herself into sleep and the doctor couldn't find anything wrong with her.'

'Was something wrong with her?' asks Walt.

'Nothing that could be seen, not then. She never really went back to the way she had been. She stopped sleeping for more than a couple of hours at a time at night or during the day, and the only way she would stay quiet was if I bounced her up and down. I don't mean that I just had to bounce her to sleep. I mean I had to keep bouncing her or she wouldn't stay asleep, until she was really deeply asleep. And if she was awake and not feeding, I had to bounce her so she wouldn't scream. One day, she screamed for sixteen hours straight.'

'Wow,' says Cynthia, and Anna sees the light of acknowledgement in her face.

'Yes, wow,' she answers.

Chapter Four

Caro rubs her nose. There is a stale smell and she wishes there were a window to open. She tries to focus on the pale grey walls of the room, which suddenly seems smaller than she first thought.

In her neat pantsuit, Detective Susan Sappington looks like a primary school teacher. Caro can just see her peering at a small child and reducing it to tears for some misdemeanour. She has her hair wound tightly in a bun, and is wearing glasses with red rims that keep slipping down her nose. Caro wants to laugh at her but can't. Detective Sappington doesn't look like the kind of woman you laugh at. She probably never leaves her kitchen in a mess at night or goes to bed with the washing up undone, or . . . or drowns her sorrows in half a bottle of vodka. She looks like a woman who has her life under control.

'Okay, Mrs Harman,' she says. 'I know this may seem strange but, just for the record, can I get you to state your full name and date of birth.'

The reasonable way she says things irritates Caro. It would be better if the detective were a little aggressive, but she isn't and Caro can feel her own irritation beginning to choke her. She should not have to be here in this small, stinking room.

'But you've got all that in front of you. I gave them all my information two weeks ago. It's already written down.'

'I know but the interview is being recorded, so I just need you to state it for the camera.'

Caro pushes her hair behind her ear again, wishing she had tied it back properly instead of just using some of Lex's hairclips. She can feel her hands shake and wonders exactly how long she is going to cope. She can see herself leaning forward and throwing up on the floor. It would not be the first time she has vomited in a public place; or the second, or the third. She has a humiliating vision of herself in the ladies toilet at the shopping centre last week. She had missed breakfast in favour of her vodka, and then she had gone to the shops and stumbled on a wine-tasting at the liquor store. Caro had made the young man doing the bartending pour her tiny glass after tiny glass of wine, making sure to remark on the taste and colour each time. She had imagined that she sounded like a connoisseur. She thought people were watching her because she sounded like she really knew her stuff. She pointed out to the elderly man standing next to her the wines she considered to be good, and was offended when he didn't listen to her and instead turned and walked away. After an hour, the manager had come up to her and whispered, 'If you don't leave now, we'll have to call the police.'

The shop was filled with people and Caro had straightened her shoulders to protest that she was being treated unfairly, and then seen the look in the manager's eyes. It wasn't aggression or anger, but pity. She had left quickly but, after about five minutes, the nausea hit and she had made it to the ladies toilet just in time. While she vomited, she had heard other women coming in and out, the tap of heels on the tiled floor, the whoosh of the hand dryer, and when she was done, a collection of voices whispering about something being wrong. She had wanted to call out to them that she was fine, but once she had finished throwing up, she hadn't been able to do much for a minute except slump on the obviously filthy floor and rest her head on the toilet seat. When she had finally emerged, it had been to find two women in almost matching skirts and sweaters.

'Oh, my dear, are you all right?' one of them had asked while the other looked concerned.

'Just fine,' Caro had replied. 'I'm in my first trimester; you know how it is.'

Yes, they had known how it was, and they had wished her luck and expressed their joy for her, and then they had left Caro staring at herself in the mirror.

'Mrs Harman?' says Detective Sappington.

'This room looks exactly like the one on television, the one that they use in that show about a woman detective,' says Caro.

'Mrs Harman, please—we really want to just finish the interview, so that you can go home.'

'Fuck, fine; Caroline Harman, fourth of July 1977.'

'Thank you. Now, before we go on, are you sure we can't get you anything? Some water or tea or coffee? I notice your hands are shaking. Are you all right to continue the interview?'

Caro clenches her hands into fists, hearing a slight edge of smugness in Detective Sappington's reasonable tone. 'Bitch,' she thinks. 'I'm fine,' she says, trying to moderate her voice, 'but I would like some water. This has been an awful couple of weeks, as I'm sure you're aware.'

'I'll get it,' says Detective Ng. He is dressed in jeans and a T-shirt, as though he's just the intern. Caro likes his smile, but knows already that he's not the one she has to worry about.

'Thanks, Brian.' says Detective Sappington. 'Are you sure you're okay?' she says to Caro.

'Stop asking me that and just bloody get on with it,' says Caro.

'I'm not trying to upset you; I'm just concerned for your welfare.'

'I've said that I'm fine. I don't want to talk about this anymore. Ask me your questions.'

Detective Sappington pushes her glasses back up her nose and consults her notes. Caro pushes her nails into her palms. She is pretty sure that Detective Sappington is trying to annoy her. 'Surely you've read those already?' she wants to say but keeps quiet.

If Detective Sappington wants to punish her for being rude, then fine—let her go ahead and do it. The silence grows in the hot room and Caro begins to understand why they don't have windows in the interview room. She is sure anyone confronted by a person as self-satisfied as Detective Sappington would have smashed the glass.

'Let's just start with how you and Mrs McAllen know each other.'

'We met at the clinic.'

'The clinic?'

'Don't you have children?'

'No, not yet.'

Caro nods her head. Now she understands. The detective in her neat, perfectly ironed pantsuit, still has the illusion of control in her life. Wanting children, having children, raising children makes most people realise that everything is random and chaotic and completely out of their control.

She feels a little more kindly towards Detective Sappington now. The woman has no real idea about life. No idea at all, and since she looks like she is well into her forties, it may be that she will never have children, and so she will most likely be able to continue with that illusion for the rest of her life. Caro thinks that her 'not yet' is a standard response that she must have been giving for years, and that there will be a terrible day when Detective Sappington looks in the mirror and realises that her 'not yet' has become 'never will'.

Caro wonders if she has ever wanted children, yearned for them and been denied that joy. She may have no interest in children at all, but then why not simply answer 'No'. 'Not yet' implies hope for the future.

'Every neighbourhood has one,' she says. 'You take your baby there to be weighed and measured, and to talk to the clinic nurse about anything that worries you. I was there for Alexa's twelve-month check-up and Anna was there for the same thing. Our daughters are . . . were . . . born just a week apart. We must have missed each other at the hospital by a day or two.'

Caro relaxes her hands a little, and takes a deep breath as she remembers those astonishing few days after Alexa's birth. Detective Ng returns with her glass of water and Caro takes a cautious sip. She had thought she would literally die during labour, which went on for sixteen hours, leaving her so exhausted that Geoff told her afterwards she asked him to 'Just let me die . . . please.'

She doesn't remember this. She doesn't remember much before the moment the midwife placed her squalling baby on her chest with the words, 'Here you go, Mummy.'

At times during her pregnancy, Caro had been worried that she would not bond instantly with her baby, that she would fail to fall in love with the squirming alien inside her body, but then her daughter was there. She had breathed in the smell of her child, and Lex had stopped crying and opened her eyes to peer at her, and then, seemingly satisfied that her mother was in control, she had closed her eyes and gone to sleep.

'Careful,' Caro had admonished the midwife as she took Lex away to be cleaned and wrapped. The love she felt for Lex instantly consumed her and she felt high for weeks afterwards. It was a magical time, despite the sleep deprivation and the loss of control, or maybe because of it. She just gave into it, into everything.

'So, you were both at the clinic on the same day?' says Detective Sappington, pulling Caro away from her dreamy recollection.

Caro sighs. 'Yes; you can just drop in on certain days and wait to see the nurse. I came in and put my name—well, Alexa's name—on the board, and then I put her on the floor to play and saw Anna. She was sitting alone flicking through a magazine without actually looking at it. Mostly she was watching Maya, her daughter; just staring at her as though she thought she might leap out of her pram at any moment. Maya was watching a video on one of those portable DVD players, and every time she got to the end of it, she would press one of the buttons to rewind it, and another to make it play again.

'I couldn't believe it. I mean, Lex was trying to walk, and she already had two words—"star" and "cat", I think—but Maya's fine motor skills were amazing. She was just sitting in her pram, watching this video. At that stage, if Lex was awake, she was moving. She barely even sat still to eat. I looked at Anna and she looked like she'd stepped out of a magazine, like she'd just come from hair and make-up. She was even thinner than she is now . . .' Caro stops talking. She hasn't seen Anna for a couple of weeks. She may be thinner than ever now; thinner than when they first met. Anna stops eating when she is stressed or unhappy. *It's a wonder she hadn't faded away altogether even before the . . . the accident.*

'Mrs Harman,' prompts Detective Sappington.

'Oh . . . yes, I was saying that she looked amazing. She was dressed in neatly ironed jeans, and a soft leather jacket and high-heeled boots. "Who dresses like that to come to the clinic?" I thought. I had barely made it out of my pyjamas, but Anna looked perfect. There wasn't a blonde hair out of place but there was still something about her that looked wrong.' Caro pushes her lips together. She has just gone on and on as the memory of meeting Anna assailed her. Her first glance of Anna had led her to look around the room for the nanny she assumed would be with the overly made-up mother and quiet, beautifully behaved child, but then she had looked again.

'Wrong?' asks Detective Sappington.

'Yes, wrong. She was holding onto the magazine so tightly she was crumpling it and her body was so stiff it looked like she was trying not to touch the chair.'

'So you started talking to her?'

'Well, not at first. There were a couple of other mothers there with their children and I recognised them and smiled at them but they didn't seem interested in getting into a conversation. I wasn't really friendly with them. I knew a lot of the mothers in my community by sight. I went to a lot of stuff with Lex then . . . mothers group and Gymbaroo and music time . . . but I'd never seen Anna anywhere. I thought that she may have just moved into the area and that she must be lonely.

'Geoff always says that I have a way of adopting lonely people and trying to help them, but I don't think that's true. I just felt for Anna when I saw her. I moved one seat closer to her and watched Maya, and then I asked Anna how old Maya was.'

Caro hadn't immediately started talking to Anna. She had felt the unwelcome possibility of rejection from the yummy mummy in tight jeans, and so she had tried to smooth her hair and pull her shirt further down over her maternity jeans. She was usually able to tell herself, 'Fuck it, I have other things on my mind,' when she felt she looked like she had just crawled out of bed, but for a moment, Anna made her wish she had started her diet three weeks before and that the gym membership Geoff had given her for her birthday wasn't lying unused in a drawer. But then Lex had pointed at a picture of a kitten on the wall and said, 'Meee', which was her version of 'meow', and Caro had smiled at her daughter and glanced quickly at Anna, and seen not another mother acknowledging how cute toddlers were but something else. Anna looked away from Lex, like she didn't want to see her. 'Odd,' thought Caro and wanted to know more.

'So you started talking and you became friends.'

'Yes. She told me that Maya was the same age as Lex, and I didn't believe that because Maya was just calmly looking at the video and making it repeat every time it got to the end. I mean, the girls were both around the same size, but Anna was so thin and small that I thought her child must be a lot older, and just small, like her.

'"Is she your first?" I asked her and she said, "Yes and you?" I told her that Lex was my first child and then we just sat in silence for a minute, and then, without thinking about it, I just said, "Fucking hell, isn't it?" And she looked at me like she'd never even heard someone use words like that, and then she sort of sagged against the chair, like the air was slowly going out of her. "Oh yes," she said, "it is absolute hell." The thing is, I didn't really mean it. I'd had a bad night with Lex, who usually slept from around eleven until six in the morning by then but had been up every two hours for no particular reason the night before, and I was tired but I was mostly happy to be a mother. I loved watching Lex changing every day and she made me laugh all the time, but for Anna, I think it literally was hell.'

'Why, Mrs Harman? Why do you think that?' asks Detective Sappington and she sits up straighter in her chair. It occurs to Caro that this is exactly the reaction she had wanted and exactly what she has come here to get. She wants to tell them all about Maya, so that they will understand that the child's death was not her fault, was not her choice. Her death must be blamed on Anna. But, as she opens her mouth to explain, she remembers Anna's pinched face on that first day and feels strangely protective of her—regardless of what she is now accusing Caro of.

'You know about Maya, don't you? I mean, you've discussed this with Anna?'

'No, Mrs Harman. I've been briefed about what happened but I haven't actually met Anna yet. I wasn't there that night. Detective Anderson attended the hospital—do you remember him?'

'Was he the tall one with dark hair? Yes, I remember him. I only saw him for a moment, after I had my blood test. I wanted to go up to Anna, but Keith didn't look like he wanted me anywhere near them, so I stayed away.'

She had desperately wanted to go to her friend, had wanted to wait with her for news of Maya, but she could see that it was impossible. Everything had changed, and she knew from the way Keith looked at her that she would never be welcome near Anna again.

She thinks about how simple the words she has just uttered—'so I stayed away'—are. They do not begin to cover what she felt that night. They don't touch on the horror and the confusion, and on how hard it was to keep herself from running to her friend and throwing her arms around her. They don't explain her own grief and guilt, or the shame that washed over her when Keith locked eyes with her and silently shook his head, warning her away. They are a few simple words that cannot even begin to describe that moment.

Caro closes her eyes and sees Anna rocking in the thin plastic chair at the hospital. She smells the stringent antiseptic in the air and sees again the look Keith gave her. She had been able to taste his hate in her throat, to feel his accusing glare bouncing off her body. It was bitter, choking. Her skin felt burned.

'I couldn't hear what Detective Anderson was saying,' she tells Detective Sappington, forcing herself to get on with what she needs to say, 'but I could see that he was helping Anna, was helping both of them, and then I left. The constable drove me home. I wanted to stay but I didn't . . . I had to get home.'

Detective Sappington sits back in her chair. She folds her arms across her chest but remains silent.

'He did seem nice,' says Caro as she recalls the large detective sitting next to Anna, murmuring softly to her. "He's very good looking, isn't he? You probably think I'm a bad person for noticing that but I'm sure a lot of people do. It's the black hair and the green eyes, I think.'

'Mrs Harman . . .' says Detective Sappington, and then she smooths her perfectly smooth hair and Caro knows that she has definitely noticed how good looking Detective Anderson is. 'Someone has a crush,' she thinks, imagining that police stations are like soap operas, with romances sizzling around every corner. She wonders how long Detective Sappington has been infatuated with Detective Anderson and if she has any chance of having her affections returned. Maybe they are in a relationship already but Caro doubts it. Knowing this secret about the person opposite makes her feel a connection with her. The poor woman is just like she is—wanting what she can't have.

'Look, you might as well call me Caroline, or Caro . . . I hate being called Caroline.'

'Okay, Caro. We were discussing Maya,' says Detective Sappington.

'Yes, Maya. The clinic nurse came out—I don't think I will ever forget her. Her name was Lucille. She was one of those women who'd been trained one way and refused to learn anything new. I think she was already in her sixties, and she wore a white uniform and had grey hair cut really short, and when she looked at you, you felt like you'd somehow done something wrong. She was very bossy with the mothers. She turned all of us back into children. Her favourite phrase was, "Well, I don't hold with all this new rubbish." No matter what I said, she always said that. I mean, she was very kind and really knew how to handle a baby, but when I asked her about introducing solids and told her that I wanted to wait until later, because Lex seemed to be doing fine on just breast milk, she gave me the "rubbish" line and told me I had to start solids that afternoon. I had this kind of love–hate relationship with her; she stuck to her own ideas but she thought every baby was just amazing. She loved them all, and would talk softly to Lex while she undressed and weighed her, and even sing to keep her calm. And she never forgot a child. She'd

see a name on the board and look around the room, and
recognise that baby or child immediately.

'The day I met Anna, Lucille came out of her office and
saw her there, and she kind of rolled her eyes and sighed,
and Anna sat up again and then pulled her fingers through
her hair, as though she were trying to make it look better.
I had never seen Lucille react to a parent that way. She
always said something like, "I hope you've been treating
Mummy nicely, Alexa; shall we take her into the examining
room?" But she didn't say anything like that to Anna. She
just nodded at Anna and wiped Maya's name off the board.
She looked really unhappy to have Maya in the clinic, and
when Anna picked up Maya, she dropped the DVD player,
and I found out why.'

'What happened?'

'Maya started screaming—not crying, but screaming,
like someone had physically hurt her. Anna picked the
thing up and tried to give it back to her, but the video
had finished, and when it dropped the screen must have
changed, because Maya's screaming only got worse. Her
body arched backwards, and she went from behaving like
a much older child to behaving like a much younger one.
It was weird. Anna followed Lucille into the office with her
head down, and Maya kept screaming and for the whole
appointment, she just screamed her head off. By the end
of it, I had a headache, and the two other mothers were
looking at the door to the office, with their arms folded and
that kind of smug, judgemental look that some mothers

get. You could almost see them thinking, "That would never be *my* child."'

'Caroline—I mean, Caro—I'm just not sure what this has to do with— '

'It has everything to do with it. You want to know what happened but I'm pretty sure you're not going to believe me, so I'm going to tell you from the beginning and that way, when I get to the accident, you'll actually understand what I'm saying . . . is that okay with you?'

'Yes, yes, that's fine. But I'm going to ask you again if you're okay. You really don't look very well.'

Caro feels her fists clench again. She would like to just get up and walk out, and keep walking until she reaches somewhere far away from here and the fucked-up mess her life has become but she knows—just like she knew that she would have to clean up the broken mug—she doesn't have that choice. She is a mother, and even though Lex hates her right now, she is still her mother and bound to her forever, and being a mother means that you can never run away or leave the mess for someone else.

'Susan . . . can I call you Susan? Yes, Susan, you're right. I'm not very well at all. I haven't had a drink today and I really need one,' Caro says, omitting to mention her vodka and orange this morning. She had showered and brushed her teeth before she arrived at the police station, so knows there is no trace of the alcohol on her, although Geoff tells her that it comes out of her skin. 'You're starting to smell like an old wino,' had been the exact words he used to Caro the week before. 'Sometimes I can smell you before I even walk into a room.'

'Sometimes I hate you before you even walk into a room,' Caro had replied. When she finally sobered up enough to remember them, she had hated herself for saying those words; but then, she always hated herself for the things she said when she was drunk, or maybe she just always hated herself.

Before Susan can say anything else, Caro raises her hand. 'I want to say this now, and I'm sure you know already, that I was not drunk on the night of the accident. I'd had a drink or two, that's true, but I wasn't over the limit.'

'Caro—Mrs Harman—I don't want to upset you, but I think you may need to face the fact that you were, indeed, over the limit at the time of the accident.' Susan says this in her most reasonable voice, like she is explaining something to an eight-year-old having a tantrum, and Caro is back to hating her again.

'You don't know that!' she yells, knowing that she's basically admitting her guilt by getting upset. 'Do you understand, you don't know that! The blood tests haven't come back yet. If they had, and if you had conclusive proof that I had been drunk, you would simply have arrested me, and you haven't done that. I'm here of my own free will because this was no ordinary accident, and you need to let me explain it before you simply decide that I was drunk.'

'Please don't shout at us, Mrs Harman. It really benefits no one at all,' says Susan.

'I need you to understand, that's all. Since the accident, I haven't driven at all and I know that my drinking has increased. I know that but . . .' Caro thinks about her car, parked far away from the station. It's not really her car, it's a rental. The police still have her car, although she's not sure what they think they're going to find. It was barely even dented and won't need to be fixed. Geoff hadn't wanted to get her a rental car but Caro had insisted.

'What if I need to get to Lex? What if something goes wrong while you're at work?'

'Caro, your mother and sister are picking up Lex from school, and I'm dropping her at school. You need to just take some time.'

'I need a car, Geoff,' she had said, and so he had relented and rented her one. It has mostly sat outside the house, waiting for her to drive it. Today, she had wanted to drive Lex to school, to take back some control before heading to the police station, to try to restore some sense of normalcy, and she knows that if Lex hadn't fought with her about it, then she wouldn't have needed a drink this morning.

'That's not true,' she hears someone say and looks around to see only the silent detectives.

'It was a very . . . very bad night,' she stumbles on, 'and it's been an awful couple of weeks. Geoff blames me and Lex blames me, and I know Anna blames me, I know she does, but no one understands, no one knows Anna like I do, and I know, I know, that the accident wasn't my fault. I know it.'

'If you weren't drunk, Caro, can you explain to me why you refused to take a roadside breath test?'

'I was upset. I didn't refuse to take it, I just couldn't concentrate long enough to do it. I didn't understand what he was saying. Everything was crazy. There was so much noise, and Anna was just screaming and screaming. I couldn't . . . I said I'd go to the hospital for a blood test with the policeman who was there and I did.'

'Perhaps you did that in the hope that by the time the test was administered, your blood alcohol level would have dropped? It's not the case, you know. If you were over the limit at the time of the accident, then it will show up in the blood test. Your blood was taken pretty quickly after the accident.'

Caro stands up and pushes her chair back with her foot. 'You know, I don't have to take this crap from you. I know my rights. I can get up and walk out of here right now and you can just bloody wait for those results, which will, by the way, show that I was not over the limit. I am certain of that.'

'Okay, Caro, okay; let's just all calm down a little,' says Susan. She has raised her hands and motions for Caro to sit down again. 'I'm not trying to upset you. Please sit down, please. Have another sip of water.' Caro picks up the glass and swallows the rest of the water in one gulp as Susan keeps talking. We will do this your way, okay? I want you to have the time to explain what happened. You're right, I have no idea what the tests are going to say. I'm sorry

I upset you. We're going to take this one step at a time. If you need to tell us the story from the beginning, then that's what you'll do. Will you be all right without a drink?'

Caro knows she is being handled. She can almost see Detective Sappington mentally flipping through the pages of her procedural manual and finding the page that says: 'What to do when your suspect gets aggressive'. Caro knows what's happening, but the detective's voice is even and she speaks slowly and, without meaning to, Caro relaxes a little. She understands that she doesn't actually have any choice about being there; knows that if she storms out of the interview room now, then the next time she's here it will be because she has been placed under arrest. The only real hope she has of staying out of jail is to give her side of the story and hope that it trumps Anna's side of the story. She doesn't think about the possibility of her blood test coming back with the wrong reading. It is not something she can let herself think about.

'I'll be fine,' she says as she returns to her chair, 'just fine but I'd like some more water; a lot more water.'

'That's fine, Brian . . . can you?'

'No problem, I'll be right back.'

'Just breathe, Caro. Just relax and breathe, and we'll get through this,' says Susan.

Susan slumps a little in her chair while Caro watches her warily, waiting for the detective to say something that's going to piss her off again. She is jittery and her eyes feel like they have small specks of dirt in them. She wants a drink. She wants to lie down. She wants to get out of this room shaped like a box. Susan takes a deep breath and then another, letting the air out slowly. Caro finds herself breathing in with her.

Susan rests her hands in her lap and breathes deeply, and watches as Caro, unthinkingly, does the same. They breathe in sync for a moment and Caro feels some of her tension release. The detective sneaks a quick look at her watch.

'Do you have to be somewhere?' asks Caro.

'No,' says Susan. 'I have as much time as you want. As much time as you need.'

'I need forever,' thinks Caro. 'Forever.'

Chapter Five

Anna can see that she's managed to make Cynthia understand what she's saying. She knows that she could have said,
'Maya was autistic,' and Cynthia would have understood,
but she feels the need to make the detectives understand
exactly what that meant to her, to her life, to their life as
a family. Everyone knows what autism is or, at least, they
think they do. Say 'autistic' to someone who has never met
an autistic child and they will automatically think '*Rain
Man*'. Anna used to think '*Rain Man*'. But *Rain Man* was
a movie and the actor in it was not autistic. At night, he
could stop holding his head to one side and being afraid
of cracks on the sidewalk, and go home to his wife. Even
after eleven years of knowing that her child was autistic,
Anna still had days when she would wake up and think

that Maya would have somehow been cured overnight, that she would magically be able to stop playing the role she was playing and just get on with being a little girl.

'Maya was autistic,' says Anna to the detectives, and sees the nod of recognition but is not grateful for it; only resentful that it comes with so little actual knowledge. She sighs, thinking about those first days after Maya was diagnosed, when she began researching the condition, and discovered everything that autism could mean and everything that it could not mean. What she remembers most was feeling overwhelmed and sad—very, very sad.

In one hour-long appointment at the developmental paediatrician, she had all her worst fears confirmed and, at the same time, lost the child she thought she was going to raise. It was devastating.

She has spent Maya's whole life explaining her to people and, now, sitting in the small, stale room across the way from the man who put his arms around her when the doctors admitted that Maya was gone, she feels the need to explain one last time.

'There are babies who cry more than others. I've read that you can go to any mothers group and always find one child who has colic or is really unsettled, but Maya was like nothing anyone had ever seen. I tried mothers groups a few times, but I think I made the other mothers uncomfortable. I had to bounce Maya the whole way through or she'd scream. And each time I went, there was one mother who said, "If you just put her down for a minute, she'll be fine," and inevitably I'd do just that because I could see the way they were all looking at me, and then Maya would start screaming and I could feel them judging me, judging her. They would turn their heads away from us and try to speak over the noise and eventually one by one they would get up and move away from me, from Maya. It was easier to get up and leave then, easier to be at home alone, so I could avoid everyone's stares. I don't think anyone really believed me about the screaming until they experienced it for themselves.

'One day, about two weeks after the screaming started, Keith's mother came for a visit. She's one of those women they call "earth mothers". It's like she was born to get pregnant and raise a large family. Keith has five siblings, three brothers and two sisters, and they all have kids. Nothing fazes Estelle. She bakes every day, just like she did when her kids were little, and when they were at school, she was always the class mother, and she helped with homework and sang while she did the dishes.' Anna shakes her head. 'It sounds ridiculous now when I say it, ridiculous that any mother could be so perfect, but it was the impression Keith gave me. He remembers this really idyllic childhood. According to him, his mother barely ever raised her voice. He and his siblings never fought, and the whole family just loved being with each other. They used to have game nights, where they all played Monopoly in teams, and they all went on holiday together for years and years, until the family was just too big. Like something out of a fucking sitcom . . . oops, I didn't mean to swear.'

Anna can vividly remember her third date with Keith, where they trod the well-worn path of their childhoods. They were in an Italian restaurant, and still wanting to tell each other everything, still excited to share every thought and feeling they'd ever had. Anna had started talking about her mother; complaining, really. 'It's like I was never completely sure that she loved me,' she told Keith. 'Even now, I'll call her to say hello and I'll get the feeling that I've interrupted her doing something more important. Do you know what I mean?' But Keith had no idea what she meant, and Anna could see that he was almost incredulous that she should ever question her mother's love.

'My mother calls me every day; sometimes twice a day,' he said.

'That's sweet,' said Anna because it had seemed sweet, and the more she learned about Keith's family, the sweeter it became, and she had found herself imagining scenarios whereby she became part of this big, loving family, and she was surrounded by her own children and her nieces and nephews, and Christmas was always wonderful chaos. Marrying Keith, she realised years later, had been partly to facilitate her move into this big, perfect family.

'Hope you're ready for everything that comes with being part of this family,' her sister-in-law Arla had said on the day of the wedding as she fussed over Anna's veil.

'Oh I am, I really am,' Anna had replied and she was. It was what she wanted, what she had secretly dreamed of whenever she and her mother fought, whenever she was left wounded by something her mother said.

But Maya hadn't fit into any of those happy-family scenarios. She was afraid of her cousins, or baffled by them, and they didn't understand her screaming, or her spinning, or her monumental tantrums. Maya hit and kicked and bit into soft flesh.

'You wouldn't be the first person to swear in here, Anna,' says Walt with a half-smile. Anna feels the urge to touch him again and wishes that she were Cynthia. She wishes that she could go home with Walt and just lie next to him.

'I imagine not. This is such a strange little room. I wish there was a window we could open.'

'Are you having trouble breathing?' asks Walt.

'No, I just feel . . . closed in. I suppose that's the point of all of this but don't you feel it as well?'

'No, I'm used to it, I think.'

'How long have you been a detective?'

'Oh, about ten years now. I've seen and heard just about everything, so you can say whatever you want to say. Don't worry about swearing or anything.'

'Were you raised very differently to Keith, Anna?' says Cynthia. 'Sorry, Walt, I didn't mean to interrupt.'

'Different? Yes, it was different.' Anna laughs a little, thinking about the word 'different'. It wasn't such a big word and it certainly didn't seem big enough to describe the chasm that existed between her strained childhood and Keith's idyllic one.

'I think my mother found children a nuisance. My brother moved to Canada when he was eighteen and he's still there today. It was only me and my brother but I always got the feeling that we were too much for her—that our noise and the mess we made, and the things we needed, were just too much.'

'What made you think that?' asks Walt. He leans back in his chair and puts his hands behind his head.

'She made it pretty obvious. She would take to her bed for days sometimes. My father would come home from work, and my brother, Peter, and I would be sitting on the sofa in the dark, and I'd hear him sigh as he walked through the door because he knew it had been another one of those days.'

'Why in the dark?'

'Cynthia!' says Walt and she bows her head a little. Anna knows that after this is over, she will be reprimanded for asking the wrong questions. Or maybe for asking too many questions.

'Sorry, Walt. Sorry, Anna; you don't have to answer.'

'I don't mind,' says Anna and she finds that she really doesn't. It's been years since she has told anyone about herself, about her childhood, about her likes and dislikes. Nearly all her conversations with her husband, her few friends and her mother have revolved around Maya. Her needs have superseded every other thing in Anna's life. 'I haven't told many people about my childhood,' she says, trying to pinpoint the last time she talked about it. 'Keith knows and Caro knows, but Keith never liked me to discuss it, especially after Maya was born, as though discussing my mother's failures would somehow transfer them to me. I could never explain to him that becoming like my mother was my greatest fear and that I needed to talk about her all the time to avoid turning into her.'

'If you hate her so much, if she was such a bad mother, then why do you still insist on seeing her? Cut her out of your life,' Keith had said when Anna complained that her mother didn't seem excited about her pregnancy.

'I don't want to cut her out of my life, Keith. I want her to be part of our lives, part of our child's life. I want her to be a good grandmother.'

'That's not going to happen,' said Keith. 'You've said so yourself. She doesn't like kids.'

'Maybe she'll like her grandkids.'

'Please, Anna. We have my mother and she's excited. Isn't that enough?'

'No, it's not,' said Anna. 'It's not.'

Anna realises that she's trailed off again. She needs to concentrate.

'Keith,' she says now, 'has a habit of hearing what he wants to hear. "That's all in the past," he would say whenever I brought it up, as though the past wasn't something that needed to be discussed. Not my past, at least. His endless family camping stories are always on the agenda.' Anna can hear the bitterness in her words and wonders if the detectives can hear it too.

'My mother was a better grandmother than a mother,' she continues, 'not that it took much for that to be the case. If I confronted her with something that happened when I was a child my mother would simply deny it rather than discuss it. Keith never wanted to talk about it and my mother pretended it hadn't happened, so my childhood was something I tried not to think about, but I've been thinking about it a lot lately. My mother was no advert for mothering but at least my brother and I are still alive. That's not something I can claim as a mother.'

Anna stops talking, and looks up to see Walt and Cynthia staring at her. She has just rambled on and on without thinking. She hasn't even answered the question.

'It makes us seem weird, so I just don't talk about it,' Peter had said about their childhood, when Anna went to visit him before she and Keith got married.

'It's my last single-girl holiday,' she had told him. 'I'm meeting friends in Europe but I want to see you too.'

She had spent a week in Canada reconnecting with Peter. One night, over a few too many cocktails, they had started talking about their childhood and that was when he had told her that he never discussed it.

'Lots of people have difficult childhoods, Pete; it's not like ours was the worst story you could imagine.'

'I know,' Peter had said, 'but I always felt like she just wanted me gone, like she wanted me to be as far away as possible, because she could only love me when I didn't need her.'

'She does talk about you a lot now.'

'Now she can love me the way she wants to—not the way I need, or needed, to be loved.'

Anna had always assumed that Peter had left for Canada because he yearned for adventure. She understood then that he could have lived in Australia and still been a ski instructor but had felt the need to place thousands of miles between him and his mother. It also explained his choice of a girlfriend—a loving, sweet girl named Judith, who taught kindergarten and gushed whenever she spoke about her students.

'Um, sorry,' she says. 'I was talking about my mother. She used to rage at us before she went to her room. There would be days and weeks where everything was fine, just normal, and then one day she'd walk into one of our bedrooms, or into the living room, and she'd see a toy on the floor or—later—one of my books and she would just go . . . go insane. "You are monsters," she'd scream, "you are blood-sucking monsters. You take and take and leave nothing for me. I tidy and I clean and for what? For what? I cannot stand the mess, the noise is too much. Every day I wish I'd never had you! Every day I regret it!" And then she would go to her room and lie down with the curtains closed, and Peter and I would just sit very still until my father came home. We thought that if we could be quiet enough when she was in one of her moods she would forget that she hated us, so we sat in the dark pretending that we weren't there. It seemed to work because after a day or so she would come out of her bedroom and normal life would resume. If either Peter or I asked her if she was feeling better she would look at us like we were insane, "I haven't been sick," she would say.'

'That must have been difficult,' says Walt and Anna nods. She thinks that he must allow Cynthia to talk about everything to him. She can see him listening and empathising.

'Yes, it was, but when I think about it now, I understand her frustration. Children take everything you have to give, don't they?'

'I . . . I guess some mothers feel that way,' says Walt but he sounds like he doesn't understand.

'Well, you wouldn't,' thinks Anna. 'Do you feel that way, Cynthia?' she asks.

'There are days when it feels like too much, but mostly that's when I'm tired from work.'

'Anna, I think we're getting a little off topic here,' says Walt.

'Yes, you're right. I'm . . . well, I'm not going to apologise again and I seem to have run out of tears at the moment. I was talking about Estelle. Keith had been telling her about Maya—well, complaining to her about Maya, I guess. He couldn't cope with no sleep and then having to be at work all day long, which I understood, but I couldn't cope either. I think that having Maya really freaked Keith out. She wasn't what he had come to expect from his nieces and nephews. She wasn't like anything we could even have imagined. The sleep deprivation got to both of us. It felt like we were slowly being annihilated, like everything we were was being destroyed. At least, I felt like that. All I thought about was sleep. I didn't want to eat or go out or talk to anyone. I just wanted to sleep. I used to stand in the kitchen listening to Maya cry, and fantasise about cool sheets and a soft pillow.

'At first, Keith didn't even want to admit there was a problem and then he kept saying things like, "You know, Hannah's kids slept through from six weeks," and "Arla's kids have never had sleep problems," as though he could somehow shift the blame onto me. I think he didn't want anyone messing with the picture in his head of what a family was like. I'm sure his family wasn't really that perfect but Keith had a way of editing his own memories, so that it seemed like it was. Anyway, he must have asked Estelle to help because she was really good with babies. She'd kind of stayed away in the beginning, probably because she didn't want to interfere.

'One day she arrived at the house just as I had finally managed to get Maya to sleep and had actually managed to put her down as well. The bell woke her, obviously, and I opened the door to find Estelle. I had picked Maya up, and I was bouncing up and down like a lunatic, hoping that I could somehow get her to go back to sleep, and, of course, I was in tears already at nine in the morning. I spent a lot of time in tears those first few months.

'"Well, this can't go on," she said, and took Maya from me and told me, "Go to your room and put a pair of earplugs in. Sleep, and I'll hold her for as long as it takes."

'I wanted to tell her that I was fine, but I so clearly wasn't. I handed Maya over, and went and lay down. Two hours later, Estelle woke me up. Maya was still screaming. I don't know how I hadn't heard her. I must have passed out, rather than just gone to sleep. "I can't do anything with her," she said and I could see that she was close to tears herself.

"'It's okay, I'll take her now; thanks for trying," I said and she left. She almost ran out of the door.'

'Anna . . .'

'No one could settle her,' says Anna, ignoring the interruption as she remembers the look on Estelle's face when she handed Maya back. It was a mixture of horror and confusion. Something spiteful in Anna had wanted to say, 'welcome to my life! Not much time for baking and singing with this particular grandchild is there?'

While Anna had been able to quickly forget the pain of childbirth she doesn't think she'll ever forget the exhaustion and despair of those early months with Maya. It feels like sleep deprivation has been written on her bones and she will never recover from it, like a person who has suffered from hypothermia and feels they will never truly be warm again.

Anna waits for Walt to interrupt her, but he doesn't so she keeps talking. 'The doctors could find nothing wrong. We had her tested for everything. We put her on medication for reflux, on sleep medication, on formula instead of breast milk and back again, but nothing worked. She reached all her milestones ... you know, like sitting and crawling. She reached them right at the end of what doctors considered normal but she got there and, because of that, everyone thought it was just because she was a first child and I was a nervous mother. I think a lot of women get fobbed off like that because we have no idea. You can read every baby book on the planet and still be completely unprepared for actually having a baby.'

'You are so right about that. I was a mess with my first one,' says Cynthia, and Anna knows that she can stop now, that she should stop now. She's explained it all sufficiently but she can't seem to stop. The words keep pouring out of her mouth and she has no more control of them than if they were being said by someone else. Images of doctors' offices appear in her mind, and she remembers that, after a while, the first thing she looked for was the magazines. Keith came with her to most appointments and if he was there, she could just sit and look at one. He loved being with Maya, despite the lack of sleep. When he held her, he seemed to tap into a reserve of strength and patience that Anna felt she had long been drained of. But then, he was at work all day and Anna was home, trapped in the house. Trapped with Maya.

'Anyway, the screaming continued,' she says, and a pained look flits briefly across Walt's face but she goes on. 'Some days it was worse—like the day it went for sixteen hours— and some days it was better, and she would sleep more and feed more and seem calmer, but it never really stopped. On good days, I'd be relieved that she had somehow managed to move out of her screaming phase, but then a day or two would pass and we'd have another bad day. She never slept for more than two or three hours at a time at night, even when she was six months old and all the books said she should be sleeping through. I thought I would never get a good night's sleep ever again and then we got the present from America.'

'From America?' says Walt. He is doodling on the pad in front of him. 'Pay attention,' she wants to tell him. 'This is my life we're talking about and you have to pay attention.'

'Yes,' she says aloud and then waits a moment until Walt looks up at her, 'from one of Keith's cousins. It was a late, late baby present and we had no idea what it was until Keith read the instructions. "What's it for?" I said.

'"I think it's to help a baby sleep," said Keith.

'"Well, it won't work on Maya," I said. I was standing in the living room, bouncing Maya up and down. She was about seven months old then and getting quite heavy. She was screaming, just as she had been screaming all day long. I think she'd been awake for twelve hours straight and screaming for most of that time. I bounced, and jumped from leg to leg, and Keith and I shouted at each other to be heard above the noise. By then, we'd already had the police out once or twice. Oh God, I remember that . . . it was hilarious.'

'Hilarious?'

'Well, not really, but they ran away as fast as they could as well, once I explained and they saw Maya for themselves, they couldn't get out of the house and away from the noise soon enough. I wanted to go with them . . . God, but I wanted to go with them. Everyone ran away from us then. So, Keith unwrapped this sleep machine and saw that it only had an American plug. "I've got a converter somewhere," he yelled, and he spent the next twenty minutes looking for the thing, and then when he turned the machine on, it was on the loudest possible setting and this static noise screeched through the house. It was louder than Maya's screams. "Sorry, sorry," Keith said, "I'll turn it down," but as he went to do it, I realised why the noise was louder than Maya's screams. She was quiet.

'I stopped moving and she stayed quiet. "Don't," I yelled at Keith. "Don't touch it . . . look." Maya was absolutely silent and her eyes were wide open. I felt her whole body relax in my arms, and then her eyes started closing and she went off to sleep. It was, and I don't use this word lightly, a miracle. It felt as though we'd been blessed. "Let's move this to her bedroom," Keith said but I begged him not to touch it. "Just get the pram and I'll try and put her down," I said. She slept for six straight hours. Six straight hours! I slept on the couch next to the pram. I turned the machine down a little bit at a time until it was a reasonable volume, and she stayed asleep.'

'I have one of those sleep machines but my boys never seemed to like it,' says Cynthia.

'Well, Maya loved it; the static noise calmed her down. It changed my life. She started sleeping through the night, and because she was getting sleep, she was able to deal with the day better, so she screamed a little less, and if she ever started again, I just turned on the machine and, even if she didn't go to sleep, she calmed down immediately.

'She still screamed at the clinic ... really, really screamed. She hated being touched by the nurse, hated being undressed. And I hated being looked at by the other mothers. I felt like a complete failure every time I went in there and it was no different on the day I met Caro. I think I vowed to never go back again, but then Caro helped me and it seemed like everything changed. I mean, Maya was still the same but I felt like I had someone I could call, someone I could share things with. I felt like I had someone.'

Walt stands up and stretches. Anna watches the movement of his muscles under his shirt and envies Cynthia again. She doesn't even know if they are dating, and yet, while she talks about Maya, there is a parallel story running in her head about Walt and Cynthia. She has constructed a whole life for them and it is perfection. She has become good at this, at playing a soothing set of images in her head. She had even managed to do it in the middle of one of Maya's tantrums once and had been surprised when she emerged from the story in her head to find Maya lying quietly in her arms.

Once Maya was diagnosed, Anna started reading romance novels at night. It was a way to tune out all the information on autism floating around her head. It allowed her to stop thinking, if only for an hour or so before she needed to close her eyes.

She had taken one of the books from a shelf at her mother's house on a whim and opened it hoping only to stop the treadmill in her head, but two pages in and she was hooked. She thought of nothing else until Keith called her to help him with dinner.

She would spend all day with Maya, researching what she could do to help her and taking her to all different kinds of therapies, and then, when she was finally asleep at night, Anna would read romance novels like she was gorging on chocolate. She read about warriors with giant hands, who carried the scars of battle and wrapped themselves in armour but whose hearts were pierced by women with flowing hair and perfect skin. She flicked quickly through the pages, rejoicing as every heroine was rescued by every hero. She bought them from charity shops, mindful that Maya would destroy them if she found them. They sat in piles by her side of the bed, causing Keith to make jokes about her 'fantasy life'.

'It's where I'd like to live,' she wanted to tell him but never did. They were the most beautiful escape, as long as she made sure to pick ones in which none of the protagonists had children.

'I knew something was wrong with Maya,' Anna says, looking at Cynthia. She is more interested in the story than Walt is. She is, like every mother Anna knows who has average children, thanking whatever god she believes in that she is not her. 'I kept saying it, and Keith kept telling me that I was wrong and I so wanted to believe him. But you can't bury your head in the sand, can you? One of Keith's sisters came over for tea and I was explaining the sleep machine and how it worked, and I was laughing and Keith was laughing because we were so completely relieved that we had figured out the problem, and his sister Hannah, who's a nurse, said, "Maybe this is something you need to look into?" And Keith said, "What do you mean, Hannah?"

'"I don't mean anything, Keith. I'm just saying that this may be something more than a sleep problem and it wouldn't hurt to look into it."

'God, Keith was so mad at her. He sat back against the couch and crossed his arms, and I actually saw him turn a little red. "There's nothing wrong with my daughter, Hannah, and before you say anything else, I think you should remember that you're only a nurse. You empty bedpans and take temperatures. You're not qualified to assess someone else's child."'

'That's pretty harsh,' says Walt. He has sat down again and slid a little further into his chair, relaxed. Anna can see he's just going to let her talk and talk, hoping that she says something he can use. Anna would like to tell him that she knows what he's doing. She would like to shut up and force the detectives to prod the story of that night out of her but she can't seem to do that.

'I know. I couldn't believe what he'd said to her. If I'd been her, I would have been really pissed off, but she just got really quiet and said, "Have it your way, Keith." It was really the first crack I'd ever seen in his relationship with one of his sisters. He didn't want to know but I knew. I felt it. I'd been trying so hard to pretend that Maya was fine, I knew there was something very not fine about her.'

Anna had walked Hannah to the door. 'I think you're right,' she had whispered to her, 'but I don't know what to do.'

'Oh ... oh, you know, maybe I'm just being over-cautious. Keith is right. It's not my place to comment. I'm glad you've finally got her sleeping,' she said.

'But ...'

'I'll see you later, okay?' Hannah had said and turned to go.

'But I think you're right, I need someone to help me convince Keith that we need to look into this.'

'Anna, I can't get between you and Keith, you know that. Maya's still very young, things change quickly at that age. I'm sure she's fine.'

Anna had known better than to continue to push her sister-in-law. They weren't close enough for that.

'She's still young,' was something Anna heard about Maya for months, for years. Until it was too late to use those words because they were no longer true.

Chapter Six

Caro feels like she has been sitting in the small interview room for days, but when she looks at her watch, she realises that it's only been a couple of hours. Her mouth is dry and she sits on her hands for a minute, hoping to make the shakes go away. She keeps talking quickly. She needs to get the story told before she begins feeling really sick. The shakes are bad but the nausea is worse, and she knows that it's possible things could get even worse. She knows how this works. She's done it before, and before and before. Some months, every Monday is supposed to be the beginning of a new self. She sympathises with hopeless dieters. Monday beckons from every regret-filled Sunday night.

It's never really been this bad before. She's never been this bad before. She hadn't meant to let things get this far.

All she wanted to do was block out Anna's screams, the sound of the ambulance, and the voice of the policeman telling her she would be tested in hospital. She needed to make it all go away for a few hours and then a few days, and now she is here and it's been two weeks, and she can't remember the last time she chose water over vodka before she was sitting in this room.

The two detectives sit quietly, looking as if they have nothing else to do other than listen to her tell her story.

Caro thinks of what Lex said to her last night, 'Fuck off and die,' and she wants to say it to them. It's a childish impulse that she knows comes from fear. She bites her lip, thinking about Lex's flushed cheeks and teary eyes. She had never sworn at her mother before and Caro knows her child was more shocked by these words than she was. Caro's first reaction had been to laugh, which had made Lex even angrier. Caro understands her daughter's contempt for her and even knows that she deserves that contempt. It had been during the argument about Caro driving Lex to school in the morning.

'I'm driving you whether you like it or not,' she had said to Lex. 'It's time for things to get back to normal around here.'

'I don't want you, I want Daddy.'

'Daddy has been late to work every day for the last two weeks, Lex. I'll drive you to school tomorrow.'

'I'm not getting in the car with you. You don't know how to drive. You hit Maya. You killed Maya.' Lex was brutally honest, and Caro could see she didn't understand completely the punch her words had.

Caro felt them hit her but knew she had to win this argument; for herself, if nothing else. 'Lex, I've explained that it was an accident. Everyone knows it was an accident. I didn't mean for it to happen. It's wasn't my fault. There was nothing I could do.'

'You were speeding.'

'No, Lex, I wasn't. You know I wasn't. Lex, please—I feel terrible about this. It's an awful, awful thing and I don't want to discuss it anymore. Please, let's just leave it now. I'll be driving you to school in the morning and that's final.'

'If it wasn't your fault, how come you have to go and see the police tomorrow?'

'Who told you that?'

'Daddy,' Lex said and she had folded her arms, triumphant at having bested her mother. Even as her child attacked her, Caro could not help but see her beauty. Alexa's big brown eyes dominated her face, and her copper-coloured hair was almost down to her waist. Caro still thought the same thing she had thought the first time she held her, the same thing she thought every time she looked at her daughter: 'How could I have produced such an exceptional creature?' And every now and again she thought, as she did then, 'How could I have produced a creature with such a capacity to wound?'

'Daddy should not have told you that, Alexa, and it really has nothing to do with you.'

'It has everything to do with me!' shouted Lex. 'They're going to put you in prison! Everyone will know my mother's a criminal.'

'No, they are not. What rubbish. Where did you even hear such a thing?'

'I read it on the internet. The news sites said you were speeding and drunk.'

'Alexa Robin Harman, you are talking absolute crap, and I've told you before that I don't like you being on the internet without permission! I'll throw that computer away if you can't stick to my rules!'

'You don't stick to any rules. You just do what you want. You shouldn't have been driving. It said so on the internet. Lots of people are talking about you on the internet. They're saying horrible things about you. You shouldn't have been in the car, and now Maya is dead and my mother killed her and everyone's talking about it at school.' Lex had burst into noisy tears, and Caro knew she needed to put her arms around her child and comfort her but she couldn't move.

Everyone was talking about it at school. Everyone was talking about it at school. Caro felt her cheeks colour as she imagined the mothers and children passing her name back and forth. She could hear the sniggers and the gasps of horror. She had been working so hard to keep it all at bay, to make the whole thing seem unreal. Even as she had discussed it with Geoff and talked to Keith on the phone, continually begging him to let her speak to Anna, she had been separate from it.

Each time Keith had told her that Anna wouldn't speak to her, she had been heartbroken but that wasn't the only thing she'd felt. She also felt relief, a relief so strong that it sometimes felt like her first hit of vodka, because what would she say to her friend, what words could she use? The daily phone call to Anna had become something she just did, and each and every day since the accident, she has pressed Anna's number on her phone and thought, 'I'll just have a quick chat,' and only when she hears the ringing of the phone has she realised what she's doing.

She thought about what happened like it had been someone else in the car, someone else who had felt the heavy thud of Maya's body against the metal. Someone else had watched Anna's mouth form a scream. Someone else had leapt from the car and stared down in stupefied horror at Maya lying on the road.

Caro had stepped away from it sip by sip and waited for it all to go away, but now they were talking about it at Lex's school and on the internet, which meant that it was everywhere. She had known that there would be an article or two but had assumed the story would disappear with the news cycle, but it hadn't. She could drink an ocean of alcohol and it still would not change the facts or alter the truth. There was no way to make it disappear. No way for it to somehow be someone else driving the car, someone else who'd hit a child. There was no way for it to be someone else.

Why hadn't she considered the internet? Whispers, rumours, speculation and accusations all found a home on it.

She understood now that she would never be able to walk through the school gates, or sit in a parent–teacher interview, or watch a school concert, without someone looking at her and judging her. There would be looks in the supermarket and at the petrol station, glances of recognition as people tried to place where they'd seen her face and what they'd heard about her.

She had been so wrapped up in the loss of Anna, and in her own pain and fear, that she had almost forgotten about the world outside her front door. That first night, she had left her car where it was because the police had told her she had no choice.

'You'll have to come with me to the hospital to be tested for drugs and alcohol,' the policeman had said. 'Is there anyone you'd like to call?'

'No,' Caro had replied because she needed to keep it secret, thought she could keep it secret. The policeman had dropped her home hours later, and she had stumbled into the house to find Lex on the couch, clutching her childhood rag doll, all the lights blazing, and Geoff pacing up and down with the phone in his hand. She had turned off hers while she waited to have the blood tests. She knew her family would be worrying but she needed to sit and think.

'Where have you been? What happened? You look . . . what happened, Caro?'

'An accident,' she had said to Geoff over and over again, and even as she spoke, she was pulling the bottle of vodka out of the freezer, filling a glass and drinking it down, trying to distance herself.

'An accident,' she kept saying. But that wasn't what everyone else was saying.

Everyone was talking about it at school. The accident had been on the news but she hadn't seen it, hadn't read about it. Geoff had passed on the details. Kindly? Cruelly? She had done very little since Anna screamed, 'You killed her, you killed my baby!' at her before Keith pulled her into the car with him. Very little except drink.

'I want to go with her,' Anna had shouted as Keith grabbed at her. He had arrived home at the same time as the ambulance pulled up outside their house. He always got home at six. He had pulled to a screeching halt behind Caro's car, the police car and the ambulance, and leapt out, leaving the motor running. Caro had been holding Anna, and she had watched the policeman pull Keith away from the paramedics and talk quickly, urgently, to him.

It was less than a minute later—less than, more than, Caro had no idea—that suddenly the ambulance doors were closed, and Keith was pulling Anna away and snarling at Caro, 'Get away from us!'

'I need to be with her, I need to be with her,' said Anna.

'They need room to move, Anna; just get in the fucking car.'

'I'll come with you,' Caro had said.

'Get away from us,' said Keith. The ambulance started its lights, its sirens and its race to the emergency department.

Once Caro was home from the hospital, she had felt a creeping paralysis in her body. She couldn't move, couldn't think. But what she could do . . . was drink.

And now everyone was talking about it at school. It shouldn't matter, it should be the least of her worries, but it did matter.

Caro had not wanted to continue the discussion with Lex. She had wanted her daughter to leave the room, so that she could pour herself another drink. 'I can't . . .' she had thought, 'I just can't.'

She had summoned the last of her energy, and stood a little straighter so that she could look down at her daughter. 'Alexa,' she said, lowering her voice, so Lex had to take a step or two closer to her and had to be quiet herself to hear what Caro was saying, 'I don't have to explain anything to you. It was an accident, and you'll get into the car with me because you have no choice.'

'Dad can take me.'

'Dad has to go to work; now, I'm not talking about this anymore. I'm the mother and I'm in charge! I'm fucking in charge, okay!'

And then Lex had sworn at her. 'Fuck off and die. I hate you!' She had whirled around and run for the living room door, sobbing as she went.

'What's going on here?' Geoff had said coming in from the kitchen, where he was cooking dinner. He hadn't even given Caro time to answer, running after his daughter instead.

The argument had tipped the balance in Lex's favour. Her father had driven her to school this morning.

'Mrs Harm . . . Caroline,' says Susan, and Caro puts any thoughts of Lex away for now and continues with her tale. The story of her and Anna meeting is a different, better place for her to be. The Caroline she was then is so different from the Caro she is now that she's sure she would have laughed if someone had told her how her life would look ten years in the future. 'That would never happen to me,' she would have said, 'I'm not that kind of person.'

Now she's not sure what kind of a person she is. Not sure at all. She rubs her hand across her forehead and starts speaking again. She needs to get this done.

'When Anna came out of the clinic office with Maya, she didn't look at me. I could see that she wanted to get out of there as quickly as she could. She put Maya in the pram—well, almost dropped her—and Maya screamed and arched her back, and Anna pushed her down and strapped her in. The other mothers in the waiting room didn't even pretend to be talking about something else. Their heads were together, and they were whispering to each other as they watched Anna. She was biting her lip while she forced the straps over Maya's body, and I could see she was going to hurt herself, or hurt Maya, but I didn't know what to do to help her. Maya was . . . was scary. She was so out of control.

'Finally I heard the click of the straps and then Anna stood up. She didn't look at anyone. She pushed the pram towards the double glass doors that led outside and then tried to use the pram to push them open. That obviously wasn't going to work but Maya was screaming so much that I don't think Anna could think straight. I don't think anyone could think straight with noise like that. Lucille called in the next mother, and I watched Anna bumping against the glass doors and got up and went over to help her. "Watch her," I said to the other mothers and pointed to Lex.

'Once Anna was outside, she turned around to, I guess, say thanks for the help or something but then she just burst into tears and, *voilà*, a friendship was born.

'I felt so awful for her. It was like looking at a drowning person and knowing they were about to go under for the last time. "Wait for me, we'll talk when I'm done. Go for coffee or something," I said.

'She started to shake her head but then she started nodding. "I'll wait," she said. "I'll walk her around and try to get her to watch the video again. I'll get her to calm down. I'll wait."

'I was the last one to go in to see the nurse, so Anna had to wait for me for at least half an hour, and when I came out, I was almost sure that she would have given up and gone home, but she was still there, walking back and forth in front of the clinic. Maya was quiet by then, watching her video like she'd never started screaming in the first place.'

'Mrs Harman—Caro —I'm just trying to work out why you're telling us all this,' says Detective Sappington and, to Caro, she sounds bored.

Sucked in, Caro wants to say, *you have to listen.* 'I'm telling you,' she says in the voice she used to explain things to Lex when she was a toddler, 'because, as I've already explained, you need to hear the whole story. You need to know that I was there for Anna from the time Maya was twelve months old and, believe me, it's difficult to be friends with someone who has a child like Maya. It's not as if we could just hang out in a coffee shop or a park, because she never knew when Maya was going to go off. Anna had this sleep machine at home that made a loud static noise Maya loved and that would instantly calm her down but it wasn't like she could take that out with her; and she had the DVD player but there was always a chance the battery would go flat, or that Maya would drop it and break it. She was only a baby. I think they must have gone through at least twelve of those things before she was two.

'So, when I tell you that I love Anna and that, after a while, I even loved Maya, you need to know that it's the truth, and you also need to know there's no way I would ever have done anything to hurt Anna, never ever.'

'And yet, she's blaming you for Maya's death,' says Detective Ng quietly.

Caro feels the weight of the words on her shoulders. She thinks about the bottle of vodka in her freezer. She swallows. 'I can't,' she thinks but knows she has no choice. Oblivion is not an option right now.

'I know, I know she's blaming me. Everyone is blaming me but I'm not the one who . . . who killed Maya. I was driving the car, yes, but I'm not the one who killed her. I know that what I'm saying is strange, that you can't understand it, but let me explain, let me keep explaining, and then it'll be your job to figure out who's telling the truth—me or Anna.'

'Yes,' says Detective Sappington. 'That's exactly what my job is.'

Chapter Seven

'Is Caro here?' Anna asks Walt.

'I don't know,' he says, but then he looks at Cynthia and Anna knows that she is.

'I bet she was late,' she says. 'She always runs late. Whenever we met up anywhere, I'd tell her to get there fifteen minutes earlier than I was going to be there, and then she'd phone me frantically when she thought she was already fifteen minutes late and I'd say, "Don't worry, I'm just arriving."'

Anna pushes her hand against her chest, where her heart is. 'I miss her so much,' she says, and she knows that Walt and Cynthia will assume she's talking about Maya, but she's not.

'Anna, would you like something to eat?' asks Walt.

'I . . . don't know. I'm not really hungry. How long have I been here?'

'Just a couple of hours but we can send out for some sandwiches, maybe take a break. You can come back tomorrow, if you like.'

'No . . . I don't want to wake up again with this hanging over my head. I want to finish this. I'd like to have the time to . . . to . . . I don't know, grieve, I guess. I just want some peace and quiet. I don't want to have to talk to anyone anymore. I don't want to have to explain how I'm feeling or what happened. I just want to be left alone.

'I never thought I would survive her funeral. I couldn't stand having to speak to everyone, having to say, "Thank you for coming," to every single person. You're not supposed to bury your child. Everyone says that, and when you do, it feels . . . it feels like one of those movies where the characters realise they're about to die because a tsunami is on the way, and there's nowhere to run and nowhere to hide. It feels like it is literally the end of the world. You're not supposed to survive the end of the world, Detective. I'm not supposed to be sitting here.'

'Anna, are you thinking about hurting yourself?' Cynthia asks quietly, as though she is making her way along a ledge towards her.

'Hurting myself? You mean, killing myself, don't you? Every day. I think about it every day.'

'Are you talking to anyone, to anyone who can help you?' she asks.

'As I just told you, I haven't stopped talking. I find myself comforting others without meaning to. My mother, who never really had much to do with Maya, has been over every day, and every day she sits on my couch and cries all day long. I think she enjoys it. And she's joined by my mother-in-law and my sisters-in-law. I make tea for everyone. Black tea for my mother, and green tea for my mother-in-law, and chai tea for my sisters-in-law. Lots and lots of tea. And, of course, there's cake and biscuits as well. My neighbour, Merle, dropped off a chocolate fudge cake. It was really good. I ate it at two o'clock one morning. I ate the whole cake.' Anna stops talking because she realises she is rambling; talking about nothing so she can think about nothing.

She is about to apologise again but doesn't. She is so sick of apologising. 'It's easier to be in the kitchen because when they see me, they crumble,' she says. 'I don't know what to say. I want to scream at them all to leave me alone but I think Keith prefers to have people around. It stops him from confronting me with accusations and blame.'

'Why do you think he blames you?' asks Walt. He had begun doodling again but now his hand stills. Anna can feel a change in the atmosphere. She has Walt's full attention now.

'Well, I was with her, wasn't I? I opened the front door to go out and get the post, and I left it open. I knew she was upset. I knew she liked to run when she was upset but I still left it open.'

'Why did you leave it open? I'm sorry, that's a hard question to answer, but I have to ask it,' says Walt.

'Why?' says Anna and she feels hot tears on her cheeks again. 'Here I go again. Just give me a few moments.

'I don't know why. I just don't know. I went to get the post. I didn't think. I was only going to get the post.'

'But it was Saturday, Anna,' says Walt quietly. 'The post doesn't come on Saturday.'

'I know that, Detective. I know that, Walt,' says Anna, emphasising the T at the end of his name. 'I hadn't managed to get out to the post box for a couple of days, and those circulars come all the time, you know. I went out to get whatever was in there. How hard can it be to walk down the front path of your house to the stupid chicken-shaped post box and get your mail?

'There have been moments over the last few years when I've forgotten exactly who Maya is and simply treated her like any other seven-year-old, or ten-year-old, or eleven-year-old child. I forget to be vigilant, to be afraid, and to watch.

'One day, when she was about five, I was standing in the kitchen and she was watching her space video and I was making lunch for her, and I looked over and she turned to look at me and gave me this little smile; so little, it almost wasn't a smile, but to me, it was like a small gift, and I wanted to touch her so much, I went over and put my arms around her. It was stupid of me but, for a moment, I forgot that she hated to be touched like that. She went ballistic. She started screaming and throwing things, and eventually she picked up a small plastic chair and threw it at the television, cracking the screen. It was only a hug, such a small thing, but it was the wrong thing to do and I forgot.

'That's what happened. I forgot. I wanted to clear out the mail box. I didn't know that Caro would be coming around the corner, on her way to visit me. She liked to do that. She's always liked to do that. The first time she just popped in, I was so embarrassed. I'd only known her for a few months, and I'd only invited her over when I was able to make sure that the house was tidy and that I looked like a normal mother with a normal child. She turned up one evening, and the whole house was in complete chaos because Maya had a cold, and even with her sleep machine and her DVD player, she still wouldn't settle. The doorbell rang, and I thought it was Keith and that he'd forgotten his key. I think it must have been close to the time he came home. "Thank God," I said out loud because I really needed some time out. I hadn't even made it out of my pyjamas. That's okay when you have a newborn but not when your child is nearly sixteen months old. I opened the door, and Caro was standing on the doorstep holding a cake box. I was holding Maya, who was screaming, and I had no idea what to say to her.

'"Bad day?" she said.

'"The very worst," I said.

'"Geoff offered to take care of dinner and bath time tonight so I can have a break. I found a new bakery last week and they're famous for their mud cakes."

'"The house . . ." I said.

'"Fuck that, just give her to me, and have a quick shower or something. I don't care about the mess."

'"She'll just scream," I said, and Caro laughed. "I think I can handle Miss Maya. Screaming doesn't frighten me."

'I knew that day we would be friends forever; I mean, I thought I knew it. She held Maya, and I heard Maya screaming but I didn't care. I can still remember how good that shower felt. I stood right under the hot water and blocked everything out. After I got out of the shower, Keith came home and he offered to drive Maya around. He had a CD of the static noise that she liked, and between that and the movement of the car, he hoped he could get her to sleep. Caro and I ate two slices of cake each. I was so happy to simply be able to sit still. By the time Keith returned with Maya, who was sleeping, I felt like I could go on again, like I could handle the night to come and all the days after that. I felt like she had saved me. Again. I felt like she had saved me again.'

'She sounds like a great friend,' says Cynthia.

'She is,' says Anna. 'I mean, she was. I didn't know she'd be coming around the corner. I didn't know she would have been drinking. I didn't know that leaving the front door open would lead me here. How could I have known? How could I possibly have known?'

'Mrs Harman's test results haven't come back yet. We don't know that she'd had too much to drink. She may very well have been below the legal limit,' says Walt.

'Caro was drunk. If she hadn't been drunk, she would have stopped. Even if it was dusk, she would have stopped. She would have seen Maya. She would have seen her! The speed limit in that street is like it is everywhere else, fifty kilometres an hour, and she would have seen her and stopped if she wasn't out of her mind. I don't care what your tests say. I am so tired of saying this, so tired of talking about this. I just want to be left alone!'

'Anna, please don't upset yourself,' says Cynthia in her quiet 'stop the person about to jump' voice. Anna feels an irrational flash of anger. She sees herself picking up the chair she is sitting on and smashing it over the table.

'Don't upset myself. Don't upset myself,' she says, hearing her voice rise. 'Whatever you do, Anna, don't upset yourself. Yes, I know. I need to remain calm. I need to be calm and quiet, and grieve politely.

'Do you know that at the funeral—well, after the funeral—we were all standing outside and everyone was coming up to tell me how very sorry they were, and a flock of white doves flew over the church. Everyone looked up. It was such a beautiful day; a perfect day. It was warm, but not too hot, like it is today, and for some reason, I could smell sunscreen in the air—I don't know why. My mother-in-law was standing next to me when the doves flew over. She was dressed in red because, she said, Maya loved red. I was all in black. "Why bother with what colour she loved?" I thought when Estelle told me why she'd chosen her dress. "Oh, look, Anna," she said when she saw the doves, "it's a sign, a message from Maya. She wants you to know she's at peace."

'I started laughing. It was so absurd. "Maya wouldn't have sent me a message," I said to Estelle. "She could barely speak. How would she have known what a white dove symbolises?" Estelle didn't say anything when I said that but she had this look . . . this look on her face, like she was seeing me for the first time and didn't like what she saw. I stared right back at her until she turned around and went to find Keith, no doubt to tell him she thought his wife was crazy.

'I upset her. I keep upsetting people because I don't listen to their platitudes and then act like they've made me understand what happened. I call people on the shit they sprout and no one likes that.

'It's all bullshit. There's nothing anyone can say to make it better. When someone dies after they've had a chance to live their life, to be an adult and get married, and have children and grandchildren, then you can say, "She lived a good life, she's at peace now," but you can't say that about an eleven-year-old child. There's nothing you can say about the death of an eleven-year-old that could make it easier to bear. Keith gets angry at me when I say that. "Everyone's only trying to be kind," he simpers at me. But I don't care about everyone else. I don't have the energy to accept people's sympathy.

'In the car on the way home from the funeral, we passed a church down the road from our church; a bride and groom were getting into a limousine, and I knew instantly that the doves were for them. I don't know who gets married on a Tuesday afternoon but there they were, off to begin their new lives. I was so jealous of them, my mouth filled with bile. I had to hold my hand across my lips because I was afraid I'd throw up in the car.

'Why did I leave the door open? That's such a good question, Detective. I'm sure I haven't thought about it or been asked it before.

'It's ridiculous I should have to be here. Ridiculous and cruel!'

Walt leans over and grabs Anna's hand. He squeezes harder than he needs to, making her focus on the slight pain he's causing and making her relax a little.

'Maya liked to be held tightly,' she says. 'I could never squeeze her hard enough but Keith could. It's a sensory thing with autistic children. If I tried to stroke Maya's hair, she'd pull away, but if Keith held her really tightly, she relaxed. She would wait for him at the end of every day. She knew that when the sun was setting in winter, he'd be home soon, and eventually I could explain the idea of time to her a little on her iPad. She knew what a six looked like and she knew that Keith came home at six, and she'd wait by the door and he'd come in and then fold her into this intense hug, and they would both just stand like that for about five minutes. I had to hold her tightly if she was having a tantrum but it wasn't the same thing.'

Anna is quiet for a moment as she remembers watching

her daughter and her husband. She is ashamed to recall her feelings of jealousy about their relationship. About the ease with which Maya seemed to relate to Keith, when she felt she had to fight for even the slightest acknowledgement of her existence. A smile from Maya would make her day but they were few and far between and mostly, mostly, it was all just one long battle, exacerbated by Maya getting bigger and lashing out at her. Anna knows that under the sleeves of her rosebud-print dress there are a few fading bruises left over from Maya's last major tantrum, and when they are gone, there will be nothing left at all.

Once Maya was diagnosed, once all the doctors had confirmed it and there was no other way to see things, Keith accepted it and then set out to become the poster parent of an autistic child.

It was a huge shift and difficult for Anna to accept. Even though she knew there was something wrong with her daughter and she kept pressing Keith to acknowledge what was being said about her, she also, secretly, clung to the hope that his denials offered. There was always a chance that Keith was right and there was nothing wrong with Maya.

'I don't want to be here,' says Anna.

'I know,' says Walt, and she knows he thinks she means in the interview room, 'and, believe me, I know it's not the best time for this conversation, but an accident like this has to be investigated, especially when there are two conflict-ing accounts, and the closer we are to when the incident happened, the more likely you are to recall the details. I know how hard you're finding this, Anna. I do know. Why don't we take a five-minute break and I'll get some food sent in?'

'Yes, fine. Fine, fine, fine,' says Anna. She is so tired, bone tired, dead tired. 'I would like to go to the bathroom and maybe call Keith, just so he knows that I'm going to be here for a little longer.'

'Follow me, Anna, I'll show you where the bathroom is,' says Cynthia, and Anna knots her hands together. She would like to scratch her eyes out.

'Oh, thanks, but I know where it is. I used it when I arrived.' She is lying, but she knows she can find the bathroom alone and the thought of having to make awkward conversation with Cynthia is too much to endure. 'I won't be long. Should I leave the door open?' She tries to keep her voice light—*nothing to see here.*

'Yes, thanks, but I'd prefer it if Cynthia could walk you over there.'

'I'm not under arrest, am I?'

'No, of course not.'

'Then can I just get a few minutes to myself?'

'Sure you can, absolutely . . . take all the time you need.'

'Thanks.'

Anna walks out of the room, then turns around quickly to ask if she can go outside and get some fresh air. Through the slightly open door, she sees Cynthia lean forward and squeeze Walt's wrist. She watches as he closes his eyes a little. It is a small gesture but so intimate that Anna doesn't want to interrupt, feels almost ashamed to have seen it. She knows she should walk away and give them some privacy but she hovers outside for a moment and watches Walt lean back in his chair, letting his shoulders sag a little.

'What's your feeling on this?' Anna hears him say to Cynthia.

'I'm not sure,' she says.

'Meaning?'

'I don't know. I wasn't there on the night, so you'd probably be in a better position to judge, but I find her a little strange.'

'Strange how?'

'Difficult to explain but I'm finding her a little distant.'

'Distant? I wouldn't say that. I think she's really emotional.'

'I know it seems that way, Walt, but even through her tears and her anger I'm still sensing a wall. She's hiding something.'

'About the accident?'

'About the accident, about how she really feels, I don't know.'

'Explain what you mean, Cynthia.'

'Maybe it's because I'm a mother that I can sense something. I'm sorry; I don't know how to make you understand.'

'Can you try?' says Walt.

In the corridor, Anna glances around her quickly to see if anyone is watching her but she is alone. She can feel her heart begin to beat faster.

'This is going to sound a little weird,' says Cynthia, 'but I think if it were me, all I would want to do right now is remember how wonderful my kid was. Maybe she's been doing that with her family but it doesn't sound like it.'

Through the slight crack in the almost-closed door, Anna watches Walt shake his head. 'That's right,' she thinks, 'she doesn't know what she's saying. Tell her she doesn't know what she's saying.'

'I don't quite understand,' he says.

'Do you remember that woman whose teenage son got himself killed speeding in a stolen car?'

'He killed his passenger as well didn't he? I remember, it was last month,' says Walt.

'Yes. I talked to the mother when she came in, and even though it was obvious to everyone that her kid had turned into a real drop kick ... she didn't see it. He hadn't been to school for months and was dealing drugs around the neighbourhood, and she knew all this about him but all she could talk about was what a good kid he'd been. She kept telling us about how he wanted to play the saxophone and how he used to tell her jokes. She knew he was no angel but he was still perfect in her eyes.'

'So, you think Anna should only be talking about what a wonderful kid Maya was?'

'No, especially not if she was difficult, but we haven't heard anything good yet, have we, and she was only eleven. I'm not looking for tales of what a delightful kid she was but the only time I've really seen Anna smile when she talks about her was when she was telling us how they finally managed to get her to sleep. I'm not thinking she should be going on and on about how great she was, but I'm waiting to hear something, anything, that tells me who Maya was beyond a child with autism.'

'I think you may be grasping at straws,' says Walt. 'It's too close right now. I think people need time to recover a little before they can look back and enjoy the memories of someone they've lost. It must be worse when it's a child; a lot worse, a lot harder.'

'Yeah, but . . . I don't know. I'm not making myself clear. It's a feeling more than anything else.'

'Well, it's something to think about and that's why I wanted you here today. I thought that having another mother in the room would be a good idea. I don't know why.'

'Maybe you can sense it too.'

'Maybe.'

'We should probably ask for those sandwiches,' says Cynthia, and Anna turns around quickly, silently making her way down the corridor. Behind her, she hears Walt come out and call to someone else, 'Hey, Sarah, could we get some sandwiches sent in? The usual mix. I'm not sure what she eats, but make sure there's a cheese and salad one for Cynthia . . . thanks.'

Anna can feel her heart racing as she asks a police officer at a desk for directions to the bathroom. She thinks about what would have happened if Walt had caught her listening and then shakes her head to get rid of the thought.

In the bathroom, she sits on the toilet seat lid with her head in her hands. 'It's not fair,' she thinks and hears her mother say, 'What right do you think you have to demand that things are fair? Are you a starving child in Africa? Are you fighting cancer? Are you homeless? You're one of the lucky ones, Anna, and life is never fair, so stop complaining.' Anna had only been twelve at the time and complaining about having to do three projects over the winter holidays, but she'd never again told her mother something wasn't fair. When they'd found out about Maya, she'd called her mother, and Vivian had said, 'Well, at least you know what it is, so you can deal with it. I'm sure there are worse things that a child can be diagnosed with.'

'I guess but it's going to be so hard, and it's already been so hard, and I look around me and I can't help seeing all the other mothers who just have to worry about toilet training, and thinking . . .'

'Thinking what?'

'Nothing, Mum. it's just going to be hard, really hard, and I think we're going to need a lot of help.'

'Keith's parents have a lot of money, don't they? Maybe they can help with therapists or carers, or whatever else you need.'

'I think we're going to need help from family, Mum.'

'Anna, you know I love Maya—I do—but I've raised my children. I have a life to live now.'

'I'm still your child,' Anna had whispered.

'I'll do what I can, Anna. You know I will.'

'Thank you,' Anna said. It had been hard to say the words when she had not felt thankful at all.

'I went shopping today and found a lovely top but I'm not sure it looks right on me. Can I pop over tomorrow and try it on for you? You're always so clever about clothes.'

'Sure, Mum,' said Anna. 'Sure.'

Keith's mother had called her the day after the diagnosis and said, 'We're all here for you, Anna. You know that, don't you? We will do everything we can to help. Hannah is going to speak to a specialist at the hospital and see if he can fit you in. We will help her be the best person she can be, Anna. Don't worry.'

It should have been enough that she had Keith's family. It should have been enough.

'Not fair, not fair, not fair,' she mutters into her hands in defiance of everything else she should be feeling. It is not fair that pretty Cynthia will get to go home to her children tonight. It is not fair that she gets to touch a man like Walt and have him respond to her.

Anna thinks about the night of the accident. Once the ambulance arrived at the hospital, Maya was whisked away, and she and Keith were told to wait and pointed towards a collection of plastic chairs.

'What do you mean, "wait?"' Keith had said. 'She's our child. We have to be with her.'

'Please, sir,' a nurse had said, touching Keith on the shoulder, 'the doctors are doing everything they can. They need to be left to do their job. Please sit down and wait.'

Anna had walked away from Keith and sat down on one of the chairs. She had sat up straight. She held her head high and just let the noises of the hospital wash over her. Keith came over and sat down next to her.

'What happened, Anna?' he asked. 'What happened?'

'Not now, Keith. I can't. Not now.'

'Oh God, Anna. Our baby. Our baby. What happened?' he said and then leaned towards her to touch her, but she held her body straighter and lifted her chin higher.

Keith put his face in his hands and cried, and Anna angled her body away from him. 'Shut up,' she wanted to say. 'Please just shut up.'

Sometime after they had arrived, Walt walked into the hospital. Anna didn't know who he was at first and only noticed him because of his height, but then she saw him talking to the constable who had brought Caro to the hospital and taken her . . . somewhere. The constable took off his hat and scratched his head as he talked to the tall man. He pointed towards Anna and Keith and then walked away.

'Mr and Mrs McAllen,' said the tall man and Keith nodded. 'I'm Detective Sergeant Walter Anderson. I'm so sorry about this. I'm here to help.'

The bathroom smells of lavender and antiseptic, the way most public bathrooms do. Anna hears someone else come in and she tenses up. She has been here too long. She resists the urge to raise her feet off the floor so no one can see she's in here and is relieved when the other woman leaves quickly.

Of course, Walt had not really been there to help. He'd

been there to find out what happened, and to find out who was to blame for what happened, but he had sat with them until the doctors came to get them. He had spoken to Keith quietly, calling him 'mate' and telling him that his tears were perfectly normal. He had gone to get coffee for the three of them and told Anna to just have a sip or two.

He had been there with them as their daughter fought for her life. Now, the idea that he was questioning her made Anna feel sick. The fact that he was listening to Cynthia, who had no real idea about anything, made her angry— no, not angry. It made her furious. 'How dare they?' she whispers in the empty bathroom. 'How dare they?'

She hears someone else come in.

'Anna,' says Cynthia. 'Are you okay in there?'

'Yes, fine,' says Anna, standing up and flushing the toilet.

Cynthia waits for a moment and Anna waits as well. She decides she is not coming out of the stall until Cynthia goes away.

'I'll leave you to it then,' Cynthia finally says and Anna hears her leave the bathroom.

She comes out and stands in front of the bathroom mirror, smoothing down her hair.

'I look just fine,' she says to her reflection, and then she leaves the bathroom and walks back down to the interview room.

'Ah . . . Anna,' says Walt when he sees her, 'all good?'

'Yes,' she replies and her mouth moves slightly as she tries, but fails, to smile. 'All good. All good.'

Chapter Eight

Caro has to keep swallowing to keep the nausea at bay. Every time she feels like this, every time she has a hangover that makes her want to squeeze the pain out of her head, she vows that she will stop drinking. It is a daily vow now, repeated often enough that she knows she doesn't even think about the words anymore.

Hangovers pass and nausea abates—the desperation for something to take the edge off goes on and on.

'Can I get some more water, and have a break so I can go to the bathroom?' she asks.

'Absolutely,' says Detective Sappington. 'Brian, will you ask Sarah if she can send us in some food? Caro, are you happy with a sandwich? Any preferences?'

'I don't care really. I haven't had much of an appetite.

Why do we need food, anyway? How much longer am I going to be here?'

'Really, that's up to you Caroline—Caro. You want to tell us the whole story and I'm happy to listen, but we need to talk about the accident, so we can hear your side. Before you go to the bathroom, I'm going to get Brian to see where Mrs McAllen is.'

Caro feels her stomach turn with the confirmation that Anna is here. She would like to run through the police station shouting her name until they are standing face to face, but if that happened she's not sure what she would say to her.

'Why? Are you worried we'll run into each other and compare notes? Or maybe you're worried that she'll try to kill me,' she says, shutting out the image of Anna hunched over Maya, shaking her and screaming her name.

'I'm not worried about anything. We just prefer our witnesses to remain separate until their interviews are over.' Caro hears the reasonable tone again. 'I'm being handled,' she thinks.

Detective Ng leaves the room for a moment and then returns. 'All good, they're back at it now.'

'Brian, can you walk Caro over to the bathroom, please?'

'And will he wait outside for me as well, just to make sure I'm a good little girl and don't try to escape?'

'You're not under arrest.'

'Well, it certainly feels like I am.'

'I'll just show you the way and leave you to it,' he says and Caro feels a small surge of gratitude.

'Thanks, Brian,' she says and follows him along the corridor.

'You doing okay?' he asks.

'I've been better.' Caro would like to tell him just how hideous she is feeling. She feels he might listen with a sympathetic ear, something she is not certain of getting from Detective Sappington.

'Have you been a detective long?' she says instead.

'Only about a year. I took a different route into the police force. I became a psychologist and then went into law enforcement.'

'That's an interesting change.'

'Not really. My thesis was on ice addiction, and after a while, I thought . . . you know, I might as well put some of that information to good use. My dad was in the police force and my brother is as well. It was kind of inevitable, according to my mother.'

They stop outside the bathroom. Brian smiles at Caro; his teeth are even and perfect. There is nothing threatening about him at all. She wants to keep talking to Brian. She wants to be away from the interview room and Susan as long as she can. She has a feeling that Susan can see exactly what's going on in her head. It's unnerving.

Brian turns to go but Caro stops him. 'Are you married?'

He looks at her and Caro flinches a little because she can see the pity in his dark eyes. He knows what she's doing. 'I am, yes; my wife, Lucy, is studying for her PhD in neuroscience.'

'Kids?'

'No, not yet. We both work pretty long hours. When she's done, maybe.'

Caro nods, feeling the nausea rise again. She bites down on her lip and concentrates on the pain.

'Is Susan . . . Detective Sappington . . . married?'

'No, Caro . . . she's not. Is there something else you want to ask me? Something else you want to say? It would be better if you said it in front of Susan, if that's the case. I'm sure you understand.'

'No . . . no, I don't have anything to say. I just wanted to know, that's all.'

'Caro,' says Brian, 'I know that right now this all feels completely overwhelming. I know that you've never been in a situation like this before and I want to tell you that we're here to help. We really are.'

'Oh really,' says Caro.

'Yes,' says Brian firmly. 'Really. Susan is the best detective we have. She's been a detective for over ten years and she became a police officer for the same reason that I did. We want to help. If you tell us what happened, if you tell us the truth, we can figure out a way forward for you. We are not the enemy. It's not our goal to put as many people in prison as possible. It's our goal to help as many people as possible. Do you understand?'

'It doesn't feel like that, and I'm trying to tell you the truth. I just need you to understand.'

'We're trying to, Caro, we are trying to. Why don't you take a few minutes and think about things? We'll have some food brought in for you and maybe that will help you feel a bit better.'

'I'm fine,' Caro wanted to say but knew she was kidding herself. Suddenly completely exhausted, she simply nods at the detective and goes into the bathroom.

She stares at herself in the mirror and is shocked to find that she looks even worse than she thought she would. Worse than she feels. Her hair is plastered to her forehead, because she's been sweating so much, and her skin is almost grey. She feels like she's in hell. The headache is tightening around her head with each passing hour. She leans forward and splashes water on her face, but it's tepid and doesn't make her feel any better. She wants a drink. God, how she wants a drink. One drink would make everything better. One or two drinks would allow her to think straight, and then she could get the story out. Just one or two drinks and everything would be okay. She could make them understand.

Her stomach roils and she thinks she's going to throw up, but after she's locked herself in a stall, the urge disappears.

'Please, God,' she whispers, even though she has not called on God for years. 'Please, God, help me.'

After a few minutes, she realises that they will come looking for her, and uses the toilet then makes her way back down to the interview room. Brian has told her to tell the truth and she thinks that's what she's trying to do. It's what she's trying to do in between wondering exactly what the hell the truth is.

'Hey, Caro,' says Brian when she takes her seat in the interview room, 'did you find everything okay?'

'Yes, thank you,' she says and flashes a small smile at him. He has obviously not mentioned their conversation to Detective Sappington and she's grateful to him for that. She feels like he may be on her side.

'Okay, Caro, can we get back to it?' says Susan, clearly impatient to be finished. 'Sarah will bring in some sandwiches soon. You were telling us about how you and Anna became friends.'

Caro shakes her head, 'Oh God,that feels like an entire lifetime ago. You know what phrase keeps going through my head? "How did I land up here? How the fuck did I land up here?" Not that I haven't thought that before this happened. It's something that runs through my head a lot.'

Susan looks at Brian and gives her head a small shake.

'Okay, I can see I'm boring you,' says Caro. 'I'll get back on track.

'Anna and I clicked immediately. It was as though she'd been waiting for someone like me and I'd been waiting for someone like her. I don't know if you've ever had a friend like that?'

'I have; I mean, I do have friends like that,' says Susan. Caro wonders if this is the truth. She cannot imagine Susan out of her pantsuit and in a pair of jeans at the weekend. She cannot see her having a drink with friends or sitting through a bad movie.

'I think being new mothers made it even more intense, especially with all that she was going through with Maya.'

'You keep mentioning that. What exactly was wrong with Maya?'

'I feel like I shouldn't say anything. She wasn't my child. It isn't my story to tell.'

'I think we're past that, Caroline, don't you? We need to understand what happened that evening, so you can move on with your life, and so Anna can begin to move on with hers.'

'Oh, I don't think that's ever going to happen. You don't have children, so you may not understand this, but there is no moving on from the death of a child. Your life feels like it stops, right there and then, and while you carry on doing all the things that you need to do to survive, you never really move on. Part of you is always stuck right there, waiting, wildly hoping, bargaining for the whole thing to have been a huge mistake.'

'I didn't realise you'd lost a child, Caro. I'm sorry.'

'I haven't lost *a* child, Detective. Technically, I've lost many, many children.'

'Technically?'

'Yes, technically. I've had six miscarriages. Of those, five were early, so that, really, they aren't even referred to as children by the medical professionals. They're called foetuses, as though that helps to lessen your attachment. As though you didn't name the group of dividing cells inside you, and imagine what they would look like and think about how nice a sibling would be for your living child. As if you just went, "Oh, I'm pregnant—good luck, foetus." And then got on with your day.'

Both detectives are silent. It's obvious neither of them knows what to say. Even Brian, with his psychology degree, has no idea of the correct words. Over the years, people have tried to find the right words to comfort her but they have all failed. They have all failed because the only words she ever wanted to hear were 'You will get what you want.' And no one could say those words, because no one knew what would happen.

After her third miscarriage, she had coffee with her mother and sister, and her mother was trying, really trying, to find the right words. 'It's nature's way,' she said, and when Caro hadn't responded, she had added, 'It's your body's way of getting rid of something that wasn't right. Imagine how much worse it would have been if you'd had a child that was deformed or disabled. It's a good thing.'

'Really, Mum,' Caro's sister, Melissa, said, incredulous.

'I've lost my baby, Mum,' said Caro. 'Do you understand that I've lost my child?'

'Of course I do, Caroline. Of course I do.'

Caro realises she hasn't said anything for a minute or two. She hates the way the memories all crowd together to wash over her. A drink always stops them from drowning her. This has been the case for years. Susan takes a look at her watch and Caro can tell that she had other plans for today. The detective has no desire to listen to Caro talk about her lost babies, but if she has to sit here and explain herself to them, then they're going to have to listen.

'I lost one baby who was old enough to be viable—do you know what that means?'

'I think so.'

'I do, Caro. It means that he or she was old enough to survive outside the womb,' says Brian.

'He,' says Caro, and she smiles at him and sits on her hands again. It amazes her that she can just say these things openly. That she can form the sentences and explain this horrifying phase of her life without the world shifting even slightly. How can there not be a sound of thunder? How can the world not crack in two?

It is a truism that time heals all wounds, and Caro supposes that the saying must be correct in some way because, otherwise, how could she sit here and talk about the babies who broke her heart and her soul? How can she mention them without everything turning dark? The thing is, time doesn't really heal, it just gives you distance. Anna screaming at her flashes through her mind. How much distance would Anna need? Would the distance of a month, a year, a decade, be enough? Would it ever be enough?

'You did that to her,' she says to herself but doesn't let the thought take hold. She breathes deeply, and talks about her loss and her grief because it has been many, many years and now she can.

'I lost a little boy at eight months. His name was Gideon. He should have been fine. We were so close to the end and he should have been fine, and when they placed him on my chest, I couldn't believe that he wasn't going to just take a breath. I stared at him, willing his little chest to move even a fraction. He was completely perfect and absolutely still. I wouldn't let him go. I think I thought that if I held on long enough, he would open his eyes for me. Eventually, after about a day, they had to sedate me to get him away from me. Geoff made them. He says he thought I was going a little crazy, but I think he just wanted me home, so he could go back to work and pretend it had never happened.'

'I am so sorry,' says Susan. Caro nods and looks at her. She can see the discomfort in the woman's face. She wishes she hadn't said anything now. The grief is too dark, too private. She shouldn't have shared it.

Every day, every single day, she did her best not to think about those years of darkness and every single day she failed. She wonders how many times she heard the word 'sorry' in the five years she had tried to have another child. 'I'm so sorry,' said her doctor. 'We're so sorry,' said her friends. 'Sorry the baby died, Mummy,' said Lex. *Sorry, sorry, sorry. It means fuck all.*

There is no reason for her to talk about her lost children, no reason at all, and she is sure that the two detectives have no desire to hear it, but she talks anyway. Geoff prefers not to discuss it, and even Anna, who is—was?—her best friend, could only take part in the conversation so many times.

'I shouldn't say that about Geoff,' she says, 'it's probably not fair of me. He would say that it's not fair of me. Gideon would have survived if he'd been taken out of my body but somehow he died, for no apparent reason. That was the only thing the doctors could tell me. They use a word, "idiopathic". And you know what that means? It means "We don't have a fucking clue." God, I'm thirsty.'

'What do you mean?' Geoff had yelled at the obstetrician when he told them they had no idea why Gideon had died. 'Just one of those things,' the obstetrician said and he looked at his watch. Maybe he hadn't looked at his watch. Maybe he had been kind and understanding and sympathetic, but in Caro's mind, he is heartless. It suits her better.

'Are you fucking kidding me?' Geoff had said, standing up and leaning over the large desk towards the doctor.

'Just leave it,' Caro had said, and stood up and pulled his arm, pulled him away and out of the office.

'I can't do it ever again,' she had said to Geoff in the car on the way home.

'I agree,' he said. 'It's too hard. We have Lex, let's be grateful for her.'

Caro had stared out of the car window with her fist in her mouth. She had wanted him to tell her that they would try again. She had wanted him to say that, next time, they would get it right.

At home, she had crawled into bed and slept. She had woken in the evening and Geoff had come into her room with a large drink. 'Here you go—vodka and orange, it will help and you might as well, now that . . .'

'Now that I'll never be pregnant again,' she said.

'I'll give Lex dinner,' he said. 'You relax.'

And she had relaxed—oh, how she had relaxed. The alcohol had gone straight to her brain, making her feel loose and liquid. She hadn't had a drink for years by then, afraid that even the tiniest drop of alcohol would make her question if the next miscarriage could have been prevented. That night, she had managed to get out of bed in time to put Lex to sleep, and she'd had a glass of wine with dinner and managed to feel grateful for all that she did have. 'From such small beginnings,' she thinks, shaking her head.

Caro realises that Susan is speaking.

'I'll get some more water and I'm sure Sarah has the sandwiches by now,' says Susan and looks meaningfully at Brian. He gets up and leaves the room.

'I don't think I can eat.'

'You should, Caro, you should try. It will help a little.'

'A drink would help a lot.'

'Do you want a drink?'

'Could you get me one if I said yes?

'It's not something we would want to do, but if it becomes medically necessary and will allow us to finish the interview, then I could do it. I would have to get permission but it could be done.'

'I'll try to get by without it, but it's good to know I have the option.'

They sit in silence until Brian comes back into the room, followed by a young woman Caro can only describe to herself as 'perky'. Her hair is in a high ponytail and it swings with each happy step she takes. Her grin is a mile wide.

'Oh, here we go; thanks, Sarah,' says Susan. The girl puts the sandwiches on the table, along with some paper plates and serviettes. The sandwiches are standard fare. Caro can see a cheese and salad one, and a ham and cheese, and even a vegemite sandwich, as though they are children. Susan stands up and looks the platter over, and then wrinkles her nose.

'I'm not sure if any of these are to your taste, Caro, but try to eat a little. I'm going to make a few calls, then I'll be back.'

When she is gone, Brian says, 'You should try to eat, Caro. It will help to settle your stomach.'

'How do you know I'm nauseous, Brian?'

Brian laughs as though Caro has asked an absurd question, which she realises she has. She has not managed to conceal the level of her distress; not even slightly.

'I know that you're going through withdrawal, Caro. Susan knows it and you know it too. How long has it been since your last drink?'

'I had something with breakfast.'

'I thought you said you hadn't had anything to drink today?'

Caro shrugs her shoulders. 'I lied, sue me.'

'It will get really bad tonight—the symptoms usually set in about five to ten hours after the last drink.'

'Fuck, don't you just love saying that? Aren't you just so pleased to be able to tell me exactly when I'm going to start feeling really shitty!'

'I'm not trying to—'

'To upset me, Brian? I know you're not trying to upset me. Is that in some book you people have all read? No matter how intense things get, just tell the person you're interviewing that you're not trying to upset them and everything will be just fine.'

'Feeling irritable is part of the process. If you eat something, it may help. I'm going to eat a sandwich; why don't you have one too?'

'You sound like you're talking to a child.'

'You're not a child.'

Caro feels some of the fight go out of her, leaving her drained. 'I'm really tired,' she says but she leans forward and takes the vegemite sandwich, hoping that the salt will help her stomach. She takes a bite, chews and swallows while Brian watches her. 'See, I took a bite and now I feel better. God, that's fairly horrible. I wish I was anywhere but here.'

'I know, but we just need to get through this and you can go home.'

'I'm not sure about that, Detective, not sure about that at all.'

'You're not sure about going home? Do you think you may not be allowed to go home?'

'Oh, Brian, I'm not stupid. I'm not afraid that I'm going to say something so that you arrest me and stick me in a cell . . . If I thought that, I would have refused to come in here without a lawyer. I know that I did nothing wrong. I know that, but when you talk about going home again, I feel like I have no real idea about where or what my home is. Sounds dramatic, I realise, but in two weeks, everything has changed. I mean, my life was no picnic to begin with, but now . . .'

'Now?'

'Now it's just . . . I don't know—just over. I had a best friend and now I don't. I had a child who trusted me and now I don't, and I had a husband who loved and supported me, and even though I suspected before all this that he was pulling away, that he has been pulling away for years, now I know for sure that he is.'

'I'm sorry to hear that. I really am.'

'You're sorry to hear what?' says Susan, returning to the room. Caro catches the faint whiff of chocolate. None of the sandwiches were to Susan's taste, obviously.

'Nothing, Suze, we were just talking. Did you get all your calls done?'

'Yes, all done. I got some Diet Coke for you, Caro. I'm not sure if you drink it. I could get something else.'

'No, that's fine. It's really cold; that's great.'

'Are you ready to get back to it?'

'As ready as I'll ever be, I suppose.'

'Do you think we can discuss the accident?'

'The accident,' says Caro and she rubs her hand across her forehead, 'when you call it an accident it sounds so trivial, so small. It doesn't sound like what it was, like it was the end of Maya's life.' She takes a tissue from the box sitting on the table and blows her nose.

'We know it isn't small or trivial Caro,' says Brian, 'and we know how you felt about Maya.'

Caro pictures Maya's face, sees one of her rare smiles, and feels her throat constrict. She has cried for many reasons in the last two weeks. There is a gap somewhere between her first and fourth drink of the day where she allows emotion to overwhelm her and gives into tears. The tears are for Geoff, who is bewildered by his wife, and Lex, who hates her mother, and Anna and Keith, who are so sad, and for herself because of how unfair she feels it all is, but she has never shed tears for Maya. Those tears would bring it all back, and before they come, she takes the next drink and steps away from the accident. But now she cannot take a drink, cannot make it all go away.

'Maya, poor Maya, poor kid,' she says. She sees Maya at four, when she first got her iPad, standing at the front door and pushing the 'hello' button again and again to greet Caro. She was so proud of herself, so happy that she could finally say something.

'Hello, hello, hello to you too,' Caro had said and had been rewarded by a rare giggle from Maya.

'I'm sorry; I don't mean to get stupid and weepy. She wasn't my child but I did love her—kind of. She was hard to love. I think she was very hard to love.'

'Even for Anna?' asks Susan.

'Especially for Anna. Especially for her.'

Chapter Nine

Anna swallows, forcing the last mouthful of sandwich down. It has been an uncomfortable few minutes as she and the detectives watch each other eat. It feels like they should all have gone to different parts of the station so they could eat in peace. The sound of chewing and swallowing is starting to drive Anna a little crazy but what can she say to the detectives? 'What are your plans for Saturday night?' They are all trapped in the stifling little room together and she's telling them . . . she's telling them everything about herself and her life and her child, and yet, they are complete strangers.

'Are you okay to start again, Anna? Have you had enough to eat?' asks Walt. Cynthia picks up the platter of sandwiches and their plates, and leaves the room.

'Yes, thanks, I'm fine; well, not *fine*, but fine.'

'Are you ready to talk about the night of the accident?'

Anna sighs. 'I don't know if I can ever be ready for that. How can anyone ever be ready for such a thing?'

'Anna,' says Walt, 'I want to tell you again that we can leave this and do it in a week or so, when you've had more time.'

'No, no, I want to do it now,' says Anna. 'I want to get it done. I wish it was over already. I wish I was a month into the future. A decade into the future. I wish I didn't have to feel like this for even one more hour.'

'I understand,' says Walt.

'No, you don't, because you can't,' Anna wants to say.

'Two days ago,' she says instead, 'I went into her room and someone, I don't know if it was my mother or my mother-in-law or Keith, but someone had tidied it. They'd tidied it so completely that any trace of who she was is gone. Like they wanted to make sure that when you walked into the room, it looked like it had belonged to any other eleven-year-old girl, as if that could make the memory of her easier to stand. They'd pushed her beanbag in front of the holes she kicked in the wall and they'd put all her clothes on the shelves, even though Maya preferred them to be in coloured piles on the floor. I used to tidy up her cupboard once a week, and every time I did it, I hoped that she would leave her clothes where I'd put them but she never did. She would come home and go into her room and then she'd come out and touch the words 'no' and 'mum' on her iPad and yank everything off the shelves again. "Just leave it like that," Keith said to me. "Do you want to cause a meltdown because you're a neat freak?"

'Her books had been put back on the bookshelves too, and now there's nothing in there that looks like her. She liked the books stacked in blocks of colour in front of the bookcase. I used to buy books for her only for their covers. I specifically used to look for covers that were in a single colour like red or blue or yellow. I was so angry about the books being put on the shelves, but I just didn't have the energy to find out who did it and knew it would do no good. I'm unlikely to forget who she was and how she was, anyway.'

'How was she, Anna?'

'She was . . . she was Maya,' says Anna, and realises that as she says this that it is the only way to describe who her daughter was. 'There are no typical ways for a child to be autistic, Walt. To start with, it's a spectrum. I met some children at Maya's school who were so ordinary, so normal, that I resented the fact they were taking up a place and, of course, those sorts of kids usually moved into mainstream schools quickly enough, but not Maya.

'Maya was extreme. She was severely autistic. It took almost two years of different doctors for us to get a definitive diagnosis. I took her to our paediatrician first, and then to a child psychiatrist, and then to an occupational therapist, and then to an audiologist and then an ophthalmologist. No one wanted to make a definite diagnosis, although by then, she was old enough for everyone to agree that there was something wrong. Maybe no doctor wants to be the one who dashes a parent's hopes and dreams.

'At first, when she was still a baby, I could see every doctor I went to thinking I was simply a neurotic mother, that I was watching my child too closely. Her paediatrician even suggested that I was suffering from post-partum depression. "Sometimes a lack of sleep and a huge change in lifestyle can make a woman think that she sees things that aren't there," he told me. "Maya is highly strung, and I can see that she is a little delayed, but we want to be wary of making knee-jerk diagnoses." But the difference between Maya and her peers got bigger and bigger, and, finally, the doctors started to see what I was seeing.

'Everyone we went to would run a whole lot of tests with Maya, and then they would sit Keith and me down at the end of the appointment and say something like, "Well, I do see some issues here." I remember how my heart used to skip a beat every time that happened. It was an awful feeling, and every time we left another doctor's office, I would look at Maya and think, "Her speech is severely delayed," or "Her cognition is poor," or "Her fine motor skills are lacking." I felt like I was eventually seeing a collection of problems, rather than my child, and because of that, I think I hated every doctor we went to see.'

Cynthia comes back into the room and sits down. She has reapplied her lipstick and put on a dash of perfume. She brings with her a smell of open spaces and flowers, and Anna thinks about a walk on the beach—something she has not done for years. Maya didn't like the feel of beach sand, and even when Anna was alone, she never went, because the beach was far from Maya's school and she was always afraid that a call would come, summoning her back.

As Maya got older, the calls from the school came more and more often. Maya had, at first, been well behaved at school, but the older she got, the worse her behaviour became. She would attack the other children on a regular basis. There were other students who could also become violent but, for the most part, the teachers seemed to have them under control. The problem was that none of their strategies worked with Maya. She would wonder over to a child working through a puzzle and slap him or her across the face, and when the teachers tried to discipline her for her behaviour, she would tantrum, falling on the floor, kicking and screaming and biting, and pulling hair and punching anyone who tried to come near her.

'We think she wanted to have a go at the puzzle and she just had no idea how to communicate that,' they told Anna.

'We're working on it,' they said.

'It's getting harder to have her in the classroom,' they began saying.

'She's become extremely disruptive.'

Anna was often called to come and get her, especially as she got bigger. Maya's teachers had bruises from their interactions with her, just like Anna did.

She doesn't let herself think about the final phone call from the school, the one that came right before the accident. It doesn't matter now.

'I can go to the beach now,' she thinks. 'I can go for a day or a week. There is no reason for me to be home anymore.' The thought is terrifying and thrilling at the same time.

'Go on, Anna,' says Cynthia. 'I didn't mean to interrupt.'

'I was talking about Maya, about trying to find out what was wrong with her. You know, I felt like such a fucking failure, like I had somehow messed up the one thing that every woman was supposed to be able to do. There were days, many days, over the course of her life when I didn't understand my child; didn't like her, even.'

'Sorry, Anna, you didn't like her?' says Walt.

'Oh, oh God, I didn't mean that. I mean, I just . . . I just meant that some days were really hard. Caro tried to help. She came over to my place all the time because she knew that then I could control Maya's environment. Once Maya started walking, it was difficult to keep on top of things. Whatever I did, she would follow me and undo. I know that most kids do things like that. They like to take the washing out of the basket and the pots out of the cupboard and then put everything back again, but Maya would throw things and rip things . . . she tore into books like she hated them. When she was older, she liked books for their covers, but when she was about two, it was almost like she had to destroy them. One of her therapists suggested that she didn't like the smell and feel of them. I took all the books away and put them up on a high shelf, and then I caught her trying to climb up the bookshelf to get them. I had no idea what she wanted. Now I know that she was just trying to find a way to communicate with me, but then it felt like I was raising a one-child army of destruction.'

'Anna, I know that you need to explain this and I'm going to let you do that, but it does feel like we're getting fairly off topic,' says Walt. 'The night of the accident is our main concern.'

'Yes, yes, the night of the accident. I know, I know.' Anna does know. She understands why she is sitting in a room with two detectives but she doesn't want to talk about that night. She knows that eventually she will have to discuss what happened, but in the back of her mind, she thinks that if she can just keep talking and talking, then, eventually, the detectives will give up and send her home.

'Do you know what I felt when I finally had a diagnosis for Maya?'

'What?' asks Cynthia, because Walt is looking down at his notepad. Anna can see he is getting frustrated with her but trying to keep his cool.

'Relief. I was so fucking relieved that I knew what was wrong.'

Walt sighs and leans back in his chair. 'Anna, please . . .' he says, 'we really need to get to that day. It's important that we hear from you about that day.'

'Walt, I think we can just let Anna talk.'

'Cynthia.'

'Please, I really don't want you two arguing because of me. I'm getting there, I really am. I need to explain who she was. I don't know why I have to do that. Perhaps it's because no one will actually talk about that anymore. When Keith spoke at her funeral, he talked about her being creative and having an infectious laugh. He said she loved movies and her friends, and I wanted to get up and shout, "No, that's not right. That's not who she was." She wasn't creative. She would take a whole box of crayons and draw lines, one after the other, again and again, until she couldn't move her arms anymore, and sometimes the picture that resulted would have a kind of beauty but it wasn't as though she were trying for beauty. And she didn't have any friends at school. There were kids she would play next to, or learn next to, but she never got past that. Most of the kids at her school were scared of her, anyway. I would drop her off and watch them move away from her, in case she was in the mood to pull someone's hair, or bite or kick. When Caro brought Lex over, Lex would try and talk to her, would ask her to play pretend or to play with dolls, and mostly Maya would ignore her but sometimes she'd look at her as if she didn't understand what she was. When she got older, she liked to watch a DVD about space. I don't know what she was seeing—maybe the colours or the way the planets were lined up—but she loved that DVD.

'One day, when the girls were around six, Lex and Caro came over for tea. Lex sat next to Maya and watched the DVD about space, but when it got to the end she didn't want to see it again and said, "This is boring," and she got up and ejected it from the machine. Maya went . . . went absolutely crazy. She grabbed Lex's hair and pulled it, and screamed and screamed. By the time we'd managed to get the two girls apart, Maya had pulled out a whole handful of Lex's hair. It was awful. Caro started crying and that made me cry and, of course, Lex was crying, but Maya was just screaming. I think it was probably the last time Caro brought Lex over but she didn't stop coming herself. She understood about Maya, she really did.

'We found a wonderful school for Maya, and I spent most nights researching diets for autistic children and new therapies for autistic children, and how to handle an autistic child. Keith and I both threw ourselves into that world. I think we thought . . .'

'You thought?' says Cynthia, leaning forward. Anna can see that Walt isn't really paying attention anymore. Perhaps he is thinking about being at the gym, or about the beer he's going to have after work, but he seems to believe that none of what she is saying is relevant to what happened. Cynthia is interested because Cynthia is a mother, and Anna can see that she knows how easily Anna's experience could have been her own.

'I think we thought that she could be cured, that she would get better, that there was a key we would find that would unlock our daughter, and we just needed to look hard enough. I suppose that's stupid.'

'Understandable,' says Cynthia.

Anna bites down on her lip. She wants to say, 'What would you know about it?' but knows the words would be aimed at the wrong person. She has heard every platitude in the book, every well-meaning piece of advice, every piece of information from an auntie's friend's friend who'd read of a cure. She's heard it all and she never wants to hear any of it again. Never, ever again.

'Understandable, but silly, really. If there was a way to cure autism, it would be headline news all over the world. I've read some freaky things on the internet by parents who say they've cured their child but I don't think they mean children like Maya. There were very few children like Maya, or maybe I just never met any of them because their parents, for the most part, kept them at home, hidden away, so they couldn't harm other children. I spent a lot of time at home with Maya, just trying to keep her calm.'

'That must have been so difficult,' says Cynthia.

'Not difficult,' says Anna. 'Impossible.'

She sees the detectives exchange a look but she doesn't care. She wraps her arms around herself and repeats the word.

'Impossible.

'Impossible.

'Impossible.'

Chapter Ten

Caro touches the back of her neck and finds that her hair is wet. It is boiling in the interview room but both detectives look calm and cool.

'I really think I'd like to go home,' she says.

'Caro, it would really help if we could get to that day, and then we can end the interview. You don't have to go into detail, just give us a general overview of what happened— what you think happened,' says Susan.

It sounds easy enough and Caro thinks that if she said she was done talking, then there would be nothing they could do to keep her at the police station, but there is also a bit of an edge to Susan's voice, something Caro has not heard before. Susan wants this information and Caro is not sure how far she will go to get it, how long they will keep her here, and if they would—if they could—simply place her under arrest to keep her here.

She drinks the last of her Diet Coke, feeling the cool drink settle in her stomach.

'Maya is . . . was autistic,' she says. 'Most people know what that is nowadays, especially since that idiot doctor who linked vaccines with autism, but I know a couple of autistic children and they're nothing like Maya was.'

'What do you mean?'

'Along with most of the usual symptoms of autism, Maya was mostly non-verbal and she had a temper. She wouldn't just get upset and throw a fit, she would rage. When she was little, it was okay because Anna could control her. I saw it happen a lot when I used to take Lex over there. Lex and Maya would be playing next to each other, and Lex would touch something, or move a certain way, or say something that upset Maya, and she would just go off. She would start screaming, and then she'd start kicking and pulling her own hair. It was fairly scary to watch, and I learned that the minute it started, I had to grab Lex out of the way. The last time I ever took Lex over there, I wasn't quick enough and Maya ripped out a whole chunk of her hair. Lex was terrified of her after that, so I never made her come with me again.

'When Maya was two and three, and even until she was about seven, Anna would grab her and hold her tight, really tight. Some would say too tight, but if Anna managed to hold her, and whoever else was around put on the sleep machine that made this hideous static noise, then Maya would calm down fairly quickly. At the end of any one of her tantrums, Anna would be completely exhausted and Maya would simply go back to doing what she'd been doing like nothing had ever happened.'

'That sounds pretty intense.'

'It was. It was heartbreaking to watch. Anna spent all her time trying to make sure that Maya stayed calm. If she'd had a good day the day before, then Anna would spend all the next day trying to make sure that it went exactly the same way—right down to the clothes Maya was wearing and the food she ate. Once Maya started school, it got even worse.'

'Even worse? Surely having her at school made things easier for Anna?'

'Maybe not, Susan. It meant that Anna couldn't control her days—am I right, Caro?' asks Brian.

'Yes, Detective Ng, you're right. Anna would pick up a fairly calm Maya from school, but once they got home, all hell would break loose. It was like Maya had to get out all her frustrations from school and the only person to take them out on was Anna. She started hurting Anna, really hurting her. She didn't mean to but she did.

'We used to meet for coffee some days, just before school pick-up, and Anna used to sit hunched in her chair, sipping coffee with her hands shaking. The problem was that the bigger Maya got, the more difficult it became to calm her down. She started hitting Anna, and not just hitting her—kicking her, scratching her, pulling her hair. By the time she was ten, she was doing real damage. It was hideous. Last year, Anna went to the hospital twice in a month—once, because Maya pushed her into a wall and she swung her arm out to protect her face and broke her wrist, and then again, because Maya pushed her down the stairs at home, and she twisted her ankle so badly, she thought she'd broken it. She was always covered in bruises. "I'm a victim of domestic abuse," she used to joke but it wasn't Keith who was hurting her. It was Maya.'

Both detectives are quiet.

'Couldn't anyone help her?' asks Susan.

'No, not really. Children aren't supposed to hurt their parents. Isn't it usually the other way around? I don't think anyone knew what to do, because Maya was so young and because it couldn't be explained to her, no matter how many ways they tried.'

'Sometimes,' says Brian, 'we do see cases of children lashing out at their parents. It usually happens when a parent has been abusive towards the child and the child finally gets big enough to fight back. Do you think that may have been the case here, Caro?'

Caro fights the urge to stand up and yell, 'You take that back!' at Brian.

Instead she says, 'You have no idea how off base you are. Anna would never have hit Maya, never. I watched her feed Maya lunch once and it took her seventeen tries just to get her to take the first mouthful. I would have gone insane, but once Anna knew that Maya was autistic, she tried to stay calm all the time. She never yelled at her, never even raised her voice a little bit, and when I asked her how she did it, she said, "It would serve no point. It's my own anger and frustration, and I'm angry and frustrated with her condition, not her."'

Caro doesn't tell the detectives that sometimes she found Anna a little too calm, almost as if she was zoning out. Her hands would repeat actions, and she would say the same thing again and again, but her eyes would be glazed. Caro put it down to Anna coping the best way she knew how. Now, she's not so sure.

'Wasn't there a way to control the temper tantrums?'

'I think calling them tantrums is . . . is minimising it,' says Caro. 'They tried different drugs and techniques. They tried everything, really, but sometimes Maya would just explode and then there was nothing for Anna to do but ride it out.'

'It sounds like you were pretty involved with Anna and her family,' says Brian.

'I was. We've spoken practically every day for the last ten years; except for the last two weeks, when we haven't spoken at all.'

'Anna is saying that you were drunk the night of the accident. Now, before you get upset, I just want to explore why you think she's saying that,' says Susan.

'She knows that I drink. I'm the perfect scapegoat.'

'Did you often drink around Anna? Did she know the extent of your drinking?'

'We spoke all the time, Susan. I knew about every step she took with Maya, about every up and every down, and she knew about me as well. She knew about all the miscarriages, about the lost babies. She came to see me in the hospital each time and she knew that a few days, and then some days, and then most days, and then every day, I needed a drink to help me through the rough patches. I'm not excusing it, I'm not explaining it. It just was and . . . is . . . what it is.

'Some nights, she'd call me after the girls were in bed, and our husbands were watching television or sleeping, and I would pour myself a glass of wine and she'd make a cup of whatever herbal tea she favoured, and we'd talk through the day. I'm sure there are a lot of women clinging to sanity because of a friendly voice on the other end of the telephone. Until you have a child, you have no idea how difficult it can be, no idea how your life will change, how isolating it is, how much it makes you question everything you thought you knew and understood about yourself.

'It was even worse for Anna, because she missed out on a lot of the joys of having a child. I used to try and keep my anecdotes about Lex to myself. I always felt awful for her because she never had many about Maya to tell me. She had progress reports and steps forward—or steps backward—to talk about but never anything cute or funny to report. By the time Lex was speaking in full sentences, Maya had just gotten her diagnosis. I did try to listen more than I talked. I did try to be a good friend to Anna.'

'It sounds like you were,' says Brian.

'I thought so,' says Caro, 'I really did. I tried to be there for her whenever she needed me, so when she called me on Saturday and asked me to come over I went. She needed me so I went.'

Caro watches Susan write down something on her notepad and wonders if anything she is saying is making a difference to what the detective thinks happened.

'When do you think your drinking habit changed to every day, Caro—how long has it been?' Brian asks. Caro sits back in her chair and folds her arms. She knows where this is leading.

'Are you allowed to ask me that question, Detective Ng? This isn't a therapy session. I'm not your patient.'

'You don't have to answer.'

'You know I went to a psychologist . . . actually, I went to many psychologists. After each miscarriage, I tried again, sometimes with the same one, sometimes with someone different, but in the end, they were no use at all. Anna and I used to exchange names, and laugh about how little they helped us . . . sorry, Brian . . . I don't mean anything by that.'

'That's fine,' says Brian. 'I don't take offence easily but I do wonder why you say that?'

'Because they didn't give me the answer I wanted. They talked about giving myself time to grieve, and allowing myself to feel angry, and communicating my feelings to Geoff, and blah, blah, blah. All I wanted to hear was that

I would have another baby; that I would go on to have as many healthy babies as I liked. None of them could tell me that, so, inevitably, I realised that they were basically all full of shit and had nothing to say that could help me.'

'So you thought alcohol was a better solution?' asks Susan.

'I'm sure that's not what she thought at all,' says Brian and Caro is pleased he's said something.

'I'm sorry, Caro; I shouldn't have said that.'

'I really need to use the bathroom again,' says Caro. She's going to throw up and she wants to get there in time.

Brian can obviously see what might happen because he leaps up from his chair and opens the door of the interview room.

'Okay, you know where it is,' he says, and Caro flees to the small toilet cubicle, where she hunches over and throws up her lunch. Afterwards, she sits on the floor, trying not to think about how dirty it might be, and waits for her body to stop shaking. The nausea is all consuming. It is worse than pain because there is no way to dull it. She closes her eyes and vows to leave the alcohol alone tonight, and then, because she knows herself, she changes this to a wish that she will only have one or two, and not keep going until she is unable to walk straight.

She thinks about a morning, a few months ago, when Lex found her in the bathroom on her knees, throwing up the two bottles of wine she had consumed the night before.

'What's wrong, Mum, are you sick?' she asked, just as she had done all the other times she had found her mother in the same position.

'Just a little, baby,' Caro had said as she stood up to rinse her mouth.

'You had too much to drink last night,' said Lex. She didn't shout it, she didn't cry, she just stated it like it was an obvious fact.

'No . . . no, I didn't. Why would you say that?'

'You drink too much every night,' said Lex.

'Did your father say something to you? Why are you saying this?'

Lex had studied her with Geoff's big brown eyes. 'I am eleven, you know,' she said. 'I'm not stupid.' And then she had turned around and walked away.

Caro had no idea what to say to her, no idea how to defend herself. She realised that Lex had known for a long time that the reason she threw up in the mornings was because she drank, and she only asked the question every time because, somewhere in her mind, as children did, she was hoping for a different answer.

Caro still doesn't know what to say to her, but it doesn't matter, because Lex has decided that she's not fit to drive her around anymore, and Caro knows that she is only a small step from deciding she's not fit to parent her anymore.

'How did this happen?' she thinks as the nausea rises again and she is forced onto her knees once more.

When she finally returns to the interview room, Brian

and Susan are sitting in silence. She can feel the atmosphere is a little charged, as though they've had an argument.

'I want to apologise again for my remark,' says Susan.

'It's fine,' says Caro, even though the apology has been anything but gracious. She can see the long day is beginning to wear on everyone, not just her.

'I'm not feeling very well,' says Caro.

'I can see that,' says Susan, 'but I think it's important that we keep going. You don't want to have to come back here tomorrow, I'm sure.'

'No,' says Caro, but as she says it, it occurs to her that the detectives don't want her to come back tomorrow either, because she may come back with her lawyer and all their questions will remain unanswered.

'Maybe I need a lawyer,' she says quietly.

Susan immediately scribbles something down on her notepad. Caro fights the urge to lean forward and rip the pad away from her so she can read all the things she's written about her. 'If you would like a lawyer, Caro,' says Susan in a neutral tone, 'you can simply tell us and the interview will immediately be over, but I have to tell you that bringing in a lawyer makes this a very formal situation, and formal situations lead to charges and trials. Right now, we're just talking but, as I said, it's up to you.'

'I don't know,' says Caro, feeling hot and flustered and nauseous again.

'I tell you what,' says Susan with a smile. 'Why don't I get us some coffee and biscuits, and maybe even some chocolate, and you have a think about it. I know I could really use some sugar and it will definitely help you feel better.'

'Um, okay,' says Caro but she is not sure it is okay—not sure at all.

Chapter Eleven

'I'm sorry I keep going on about this,' says Anna.

'It's okay,' says Cynthia. 'Take your time.'

Walt sits up straight and looks at his watch. 'It's getting late, Anna, and I can see that you're tired. I think we need to get to the day of the accident, so we can work through what happened.'

'I don't really want to—' says Anna.

'Anna,' says Walt, interrupting her, 'can you tell us why Maya was upset on the day of the accident?' He meets her gaze and Anna feels trapped.

'I didn't say she was upset,' she says, looking away. She feels a chill run through her. She hadn't said that, had she? She's been so careful.

'Yes, you did,' says Cynthia gently. 'Remember you said that you knew she liked to run when she was upset but you still left the front door open.'

'Would you like to see it on the tape?' says Walt, but Anna shakes her head. She doesn't know why she has let this slip, doesn't know how she is going to explain away the words.

'She was always upset,' she says, 'over one thing or another. She liked routine, but not just ordinary routine, strict routine. She preferred to eat the same thing every day, and wear the same thing, and do the same thing. Every morning, she woke up and had to have her toast cut into perfect triangles with the butter spread to the edges. She didn't like eating solid food but I'd managed to get her to eat toast for breakfast. If I didn't cut the triangles correctly, she wouldn't eat it.'

'Is that what happened on the day of the accident?' asks Walt.

'What?' says Anna. 'Oh no, no; I made the toast perfectly that morning. It was Saturday, so she didn't go to school, which meant I had to be really careful to stick to the Saturday routine, and I did, I did stick to it, but in the afternoon, she . . . she was tired or something and she just . . . got angry with me.'

Anna leans forward and rests her head in her hands. She knows what she did to upset Maya. She had been raising an autistic child for nearly twelve years and knew exactly what she had done to set Maya off.

Breakfast had been easy, and then she had switched on the television and Maya had watched the DVD about space. It was the same one she had been watching for ten years. When she was three, Keith had bought twenty copies of the same DVD. They were down to two, but he was going to get a friend of his to burn many many more. As she cleaned up the kitchen, Anna had watched her child. Maya's whole body was relaxed, a smile playing on her lips. She could actually see her breathing slow, as though she were meditating, which, Anna supposed, was exactly what she was doing.

Anna had wiped her cloth across the kettle and then stared at the face reflected back at her. She looked her age. 'Is this how my life will be ten years from now? Twenty years from now? Forever?' she remembers thinking. It was not a new thought. There had been many times since Maya's diagnosis when she had caught herself thinking the same thing. 'Take it one day at a time,' her therapists all told her. 'You can't worry about the future because it will drive you crazy.' But Anna had no idea how not to worry about the future. *Once Maya turned eighteen and left school, where would she go? What would she do? Who would take care of her if her mother and father weren't around?* She asked Keith these questions over and over again. 'We're a long way from that,' he always said. 'You never know what could happen. Maybe they'll find a cure, maybe we'll get through to her.'

The fact that after so many years, and so many failures, Keith was still hopeful usually gave Anna a level of peace.

It allowed her to hold onto her own hope for Maya's future; but that morning, as she stacked the plates in the dishwasher, she had realised that nothing would ever change for Maya. It was startling and shocking and it had stopped her in that moment, stopped her completely.

It had happened between her putting one red plastic cup into the dishwasher and reaching for the next red plastic cup. Anna had at least twenty of these cups, meant for small children with clumsy hands. Maya only liked to drink out of red plastic cups, and Anna thought idly that she would probably only like to drink out of red plastic cups for the rest of her life; and in that moment, she had stopped with the cup in her hand, unable to move and barely able to breathe, as she understood that this was, indeed, her life and always would be.

'Oh,' she had thought, 'oh no.' She had literally felt hope—the essence of it, the feeling of it, the idea of it—slip away. There was no more hope. There was only the reality of her life, this reality, this reality forever.

With this epiphany had come the understanding that she would never have a peaceful meal in a restaurant without worrying about how Maya was getting on with the family member who had volunteered to babysit. She would never be able to go back to work or to leave the country. She would never travel the world and see all the places she had dreamed of seeing. She would be tied to her child, her damaged child, until she, Anna, died. It wasn't as if she hadn't thought these things before but it was the first time she had understood them as the absolute truth. There was no way out and no way forward.

She had made herself a strong cup of coffee and drowned four teaspoons of sugar in it. She thought about the school reunion she had attended when Maya was nine. She had stood in the hall, filled with her old school friends, and had nothing to say. Everyone had jobs and multiple children. Everyone was juggling families and work, and there she had stood with only one child, and nothing to do when she was at school but wait for her to come home.

'So, what do you do when she's at school?' a woman named Marcie had asked. Anna remembered sneaking behind the gym with her for a cigarette when they were both in year twelve.

'Well, the washing and, you know, just generally tidy up. I don't have time to do anything when she's home because I need to be with her all the time.' She hadn't wanted to say, 'I prepare for her to come home. I sit quietly and get ready for what may come. I plan the whole afternoon and I try to rest, so that I'm ready. Sometimes I go out to a movie, and I sit in the dark theatre and eat popcorn, and check my phone every ten minutes in case the school is trying to get hold of me. Sometimes I walk around the block, just around and around, and imagine everything that could go wrong when my child comes home from school. Sometimes I get back into bed and cry for hours.'

What she hadn't wanted to tell Marcie was that mostly, even after all these years, she tried to find a way to be happy with her life. She had tried going to gym and yoga and meditation classes, and she knew that she should have been able to find some way to feel better about things but, no matter how hard she looked, she couldn't find acceptance and peace; she just couldn't.

'But she's nine,' said Marcie. 'My oldest is ten and I've already got her helping with the laundry.'

'Maya can't do that. She's autistic. She doesn't speak and she doesn't take directions. I'm working on getting her to bring her plate back to the kitchen after she's finished eating but . . .' said Anna, leaving the sentence unfinished. It was impossible to explain.

Maya had to be forced to brush her teeth because she didn't like the feel of toothpaste. She had to be forced into a bath because she didn't like to be undressed, and then, when she was in the bath and had finally relaxed into the water, she had to be forced out again. 'She is on the extreme end of the spectrum,' their developmental paediatrician had told Anna and Keith when Maya was five. 'As well, there are some other issues that are leading to delays in speech development and will always affect her learning.'

Anna had not had the energy to explain all this to the woman standing in front of her, holding out her phone with reams of pictures of her perfect children on it.

She had left the reunion early, placing her undrunk glass of wine on a table on the way out. She had called Caro instead and stopped by her house on the way home. 'Fuck them,' Caro had said. 'They don't understand. No one understands what it's like but you. Don't judge yourself against them. They have it easy and they just don't know it.' Caro had already worked her way through a bottle of wine and her words had been slurred but they had been a comfort to Anna.

'Maybe you should look into getting some medication,' Keith said every now and again when Anna tried to explain the gnawing anxiety about the future that gave her headaches and made her too wound up to sit still for long, but she was afraid of medication. She worried that it would dull her responses to Maya and she would miss something that led to a meltdown, or that it would make her feel tired or like her brain was filled with a fog she couldn't see through. But there was also something else, something she would never confess to a therapist or to Keith, or even allow herself to accept as a conscious thought. She hated the idea that medication would make it easier for her to deal with Maya, that she would be happy with her child and the way her life had turned out, because if she were happy and filled with gratitude and acceptance, then surely Maya would always be the way she was. If she just relaxed and accepted everything, it was possible that she would stop pushing Maya, stop searching for an answer, stop looking for a breakthrough.

That morning in the kitchen, she had realised that nothing she did or did not do would ever make a difference to how Maya was. In the same way that she had repeatedly gone back through everything she had done when she was pregnant and been reassured by doctors, over and over again, that there was nothing she could have done to prevent Maya being affected by autism, there was also nothing she could do to change who her child was. She had not only finished stacking the dishwasher, she had felt her world shift.

If she thinks about it now, she knows that while the red plastic cup triggered her realisation, it was not just that cup, and just that moment, that had done this. The day before, on Friday morning, there had been a call from Maya's school. After her diagnosis, Anna and Keith had spent hours researching schools, and had finally settled on one with a reputation for pushing autistic children to achieve the very best they could. Maya had been on a waiting list for two years, and on her first full day of school, Anna had felt giddy in the few hours of freedom she was allowed.

At first, Maya's behaviour at school was nothing out of the ordinary for the teachers, but the tantrums got worse as she got older, and her attacks on other children became the focus of other parents' complaints. Physically, Maya had become a threat to those around her.

That Saturday morning, Anna had stood in the shower and tried not to think about her Friday phone call from Mary, who referred to herself as the head facilitator. 'Anna, we would like you and Keith to come in next week so we can discuss Maya's progress here,' she had said casually. 'Oh yes, fine,' Anna said, 'but didn't we just have an evaluation?'

'Yes, but we feel we need to cover a few more things.'

Anna had felt her skin prickle. 'What things exactly, Mary?'

'Let's leave it for the meeting. Does Monday at two work for both of you? Can Keith get some time away from work?'

'I'll have to ask him.'

'Okay, let me know as soon as you can, because we want to have all of Maya's teachers there and her therapist as well.'

'I will,' Anna had said. 'I'll let you know.' She had not been able to do anything else for the rest of the day. 'They're going to ask her to leave,' she said to Keith when she called to tell him about the meeting.

'Don't go jumping to conclusions, Anna. It's possible they just want to change the way they're doing things. They might have some new strategies they want to try.'

'I picked her up early twice last week, Keith. She hit that little boy so hard, she nearly knocked out one of his teeth, and then she scratched Lila, who she usually gets along with, or at least plays next to.'

'Anna, Maya is not the only child there who has an issue with anger management. They know how to deal with these things. That's their job. It's why we're paying them thousands of dollars a year.'

'I think the other parents are complaining more and more, Keith. I think they're going to tell us that we need to homeschool her. I can't do that. You know how she gets with me. I won't survive it, Keith.'

'Anna, I have to go into a meeting now. We'll discuss this

when I get home. They're not going to ask her to leave, and if they do, we'll find another school.'

'Where?'

'I don't know, Anna; look, I really have to go now.'

Anna had spent the day googling schools but there was nowhere else for Maya to go. They would have to move interstate to get her into another school that could deal with her needs. She knew, without even having to think about it much, that she would have to homeschool Maya. She would be at home with Maya all day, every day. *All day. Every day.* She knew Keith would try to frame it as a good thing. 'Think of the money we'll save,' he would say. 'Think of all that can be achieved with one-on-one therapy,' he would say. 'Think of how easy it will be to control her environment,' he would say and all Anna would want to say in return would be, 'Think of me, Keith—think of me.'

On Friday night, she and Keith had not discussed the meeting. He had shut her down instead. 'Let's wait and see,' he had said. 'You always assume the worst.'

Anna had not pushed him, but in bed on Friday night, she had watched the numbers on her bedside clock click over again and again, and all she had been able to do was assume the worst.

The day of the accident had been a beautiful day, warm and cloudless. Anna had finished cleaning the kitchen and then gone to have a shower, secure in the knowledge that Maya would watch the video exactly three times. Anna had exactly fifteen more minutes to shower and dress. She had tried to let the hot water soothe away all thoughts of red plastic cups and phone calls from Maya's school.

Once she was dressed, she knew it was time for Maya to get on with her day, but for reasons she now cannot fathom, she tried to change things. What she had thought then, though, was, 'What difference will it make?' Because she understood now that the answer was, and always would be—none.

'Let's go outside to do your exercises,' she said to Maya. 'It's a beautiful day and we can sit in the garden in the sun.' She had picked up the book and the pencil they were using to work on Maya's grip. Her school was getting her ready to progress from drawing to writing. Anna had thought about a story Lex had written that had won her the writing prize at school. It was about a young girl who finds an old music box, and upon playing it, releases a ghost into her life.

'Where did she come up with something like that?' Anna had asked Caro.

'I don't know. She reads a heap and she's always had a great imagination. She was so pleased to win. We took her out for pizza to celebrate and she couldn't stop smiling.'

Anna knew Caro hadn't wanted to discuss it but she hated the idea that her friend had to keep her own child's triumphs a secret. 'I enjoy hearing about her,' she always told Caro, and she did, but every story about Lex hurt as well. Lex was everything Anna had imagined Maya would be; everything.

'Come on, Maya,' she had said, pointing to the garden, 'it will be lovely to be outside.'

Maya had looked at her for a moment and then swiped through her iPad until she found the word she was looking for: 'No.' The robotic voice made Anna clench her jaw tightly. She was so tired of that voice. None of Maya's therapists could figure out why she was still largely non-verbal. They had expected delays but not no speech at all aside from the word 'Dada', which Maya said whenever she saw Keith. She seemed to understand everything but still chose not to speak.

'Come on, Maya,' Anna had said, pointing to the garden again. 'Outside, outside in the sun.'

'No.'

'Maya, it's hot; please, let's go outside.'

'No, no, no, no,' the voice said.

Anna had walked over to Maya and taken the iPad out of her unresisting hands. 'Please, Maya, can't you just do this for me? Just this once? I want to feel the sun on my face. I want to sit in the garden with you.'

Maya had held out her hands for the iPad and Anna had stepped back.

'Say it, Maya. If you don't want to go out into the garden, say it. Say "No". Say it.'

Maya held her hands out again for the iPad. Anna could see her getting agitated but she didn't seem to be able to stop herself. Maya stood up and grabbed the iPad, and pressed the 'no' again and again and again. 'No, no, no,' said the robotic voice.

'Anna?' says Walt, and Anna raises her head from her hands. 'She broke her iPad,' she says to Walt. 'It was how she could speak to us. She pointed to words and then she could communicate with us, but she dropped it and broke it, and for some reason . . . for some strange reason . . . the other iPad wasn't charged or wasn't working or . . . something. She had to wait for it to start up, and the longer it took, the angrier she got.'

Anna hears the words come out of her mouth and, at the same time, sees her own hands grabbing the iPad out of her daughter's hands. She watches herself fling the iPad across the room, and the cracking sound it makes as it hits the floor is satisfying. It feels right and she turns back to Maya in triumph. 'Now you can't say anything,' she says. And that's when the screaming began.

'I tried to get the other one to start, but it wouldn't, and Keith was at work because he'd gone in to finish a few things, and Maya had a complete meltdown. She screamed for at least an hour, maybe longer. A baby screaming is hard but an eleven-year-old doing it is a lot worse. Every time I came near her, she kicked me or pulled my hair or hit me.'

'That must have been very difficult for you,' says Cynthia.

Anna laughs. 'Yes . . . difficult. It was very difficult.'

'So, what happened then?' asks Walt.

'Eventually, she calmed down and I managed to get the iPad working, but it threw everything off for her and meant that she was edgy all day.'

The detectives sit back in their chairs and Anna shrugs her shoulders at them. She does not know if they believed her or not, but there is no way she's going to tell them that after an hour of screaming, Maya had exhausted herself just enough, and Anna had managed to come around behind her and grab her, pinning both the child's arms against her sides. She had dragged the heavy weight of her, kicking and screaming louder than ever, into her bedroom, where she had thrown her on the bed and then left the room, locking the door behind her.

The screaming had continued for another fifteen minutes before Anna had heard another sound. It was a slow *thump, thump, thump*, and she knew it meant that Maya's throat was aching and she was physically spent. She would be sitting on the floor in front of the pink wall in her bedroom, and rocking back and forth, thumping her head gently on the wall each time. It was never hard enough for her to really hurt herself but it did sometimes give her a bruise. Anna had known she should have gone into the room and sat down next to her daughter, and rocked with her, so that they could reconnect and Maya could understand that she loved her, that she wanted to help her, and then they could both get on with the rest of the day. Instead, she sat down on the couch and flicked on the television, and had a thought she had never had before: 'I can't do this anymore.'

'Okay, so she was edgy all day, and then you went to get the post and she just ran?' asks Walt.

'No . . . I mean, yes. I went to get the post and she just ran out the door, and I had no idea there would be a car and that it would be Caro. I started running after her but it was too late. It's not the first time she's run out onto the road. Once, she managed to open the door herself when I was in the shower, and she ran out into the street. The next-door neighbour was coming home from the shops and saw her in the road and stopped, and then she brought her home.

'Caro should have stopped. Maya is tall—I mean, was tall—taller than me already, and there was no way that Caro could have missed her. She was drunk, so she didn't stop. She didn't stop and now Maya is gone, and I'm tired of discussing this.'

Anna looks down at the table. She is done speaking to these people. *Done. Done. Done.*

'Anna, I'm going to get myself a coffee and maybe some chocolate. I could use some sugar. What about you?' asks Cynthia.

Anna looks up at Cynthia and can see what she's thinking. She's afraid that Anna is finished talking to them, afraid that they're going to have to let her go home, leaving them with no real explanation of what happened.

'I want to go home now,' says Anna, although her mouth fills with saliva at the thought of some chocolate.

'I know, Anna, but you did say that you wanted to finish today,' says Walt. 'We just need to get a few more details, if you could bear with us for another half an hour or so. Cynthia will get you some coffee or tea. It's nearly over now and I'm sure you'll feel better if you're able to put all this behind you. Let's keep going, so that we can all move on.'

'I think I've told you everything,' says Anna.

'I think you haven't,' says Walt, and for the first time that day, Anna hears a sharp edge in his voice and she feels a prickle of fear. She looks at Cynthia but she is looking down at her shoes. She thinks about standing up and just walking out but then wonders if she will be allowed to go. 'Do they know something?' she thinks. 'Has Caro said something to them? Has this whole day been about them waiting for me to tell them what they're already sure of?'

'Coffee or tea, Anna?' asks Cynthia.

'Um . . . coffee, please, with three sugars.'

'See,' says Cynthia smiling, 'I knew you needed a sugar hit. It'll be easier after you've had that.'

'What will be easier?' thinks Anna. She looks at the camera, hating the feeling of being watched.

'I'll grab some chocolate as well . . . our vending machine has the best stuff. Anything in particular you'd like?'

Anna feels the way she had when her mother told her that people would need food after the funeral: *How is it possible to eat right now?*

'I don't care,' she says to Cynthia.

'I'll grab a selection then . . . Walt?'

'Yeah,' he says looking at Anna, 'the usual.'

Chapter Twelve

Caro takes the bar of chocolate Brian offers her, opens it and divides it up into squares. She can hear Susan talking to someone in the corridor.

'Who's she talking to?' she asks, putting one of the squares on her tongue. It immediately sticks to the roof of her dry mouth and she has to take a large gulp of water to dislodge it, exacerbating the nausea.

'Just another detective,' says Brian.

'Are they talking about me?'

'I don't know. Why do you think they'd be talking about you?'

'Because I've been here the whole day, because Anna's here as well—at least, I think she's still here. Maybe she's talking to the detective interviewing Anna.'

Brian shrugs his shoulders.

Susan comes back into the room and sits down. She looks like something is bothering her. She flips back through her notes, and then nods her head, as though she has cleared something up for herself.

'Sorry to go back to this, Caro, but I just want to make sure of something,' says Susan. 'You said that Anna knew you were coming over, because she'd called and asked you to come.'

'Yes,' says Caro. 'She called me at around five and asked if I was busy. She often did that at the end of a bad day.'

'Often?'

'Yes, especially when Keith was at work. He tried to be home at exactly six every night, because Maya would wait for him, but that meant he got behind. So, every now and again, he would go in on a Saturday to catch up but it meant that Anna was alone with Maya the whole day. If she had a bad day on a Saturday, she'd call and ask me to come over, or we'd just talk until she felt better. It was the same in the holidays. Maya was not an easy child to spend a whole day with. Sometimes, I could go over there and just, you know . . . be there until Keith got home. Lately, I haven't been over much . . . Maya in full tantrum mode can be a bit scary . . . well, more than a bit . . . but I did try to talk to Anna as much as I could. Geoff used to tell me that I was neglecting our family in favour of Anna and her issues—that's what he called them, "issues". I felt bad for staying away so much, so on that Saturday, when she asked me to come over, I did. Lex and Geoff were at the movies, so I was alone anyway.'

'Yes, I understand that. I just want to make absolutely sure that Anna did call you; that you didn't just decide to go over there for a visit.'

'Susan, I've already answered that question. She called at around five. She said that Maya had broken her iPad earlier in the day and that the replacement one wasn't working properly, and Maya had been difficult all day. She asked me to come over and sit with her while she waited for Keith to come home, because he had another iPad with him, and because he worked in IT, he knew how to fix the stupid things. She said . . .' Caro closes her eyes and tries to remember the conversation. What had Anna said and would it explain what had happened? Had she missed something in her friend's voice? Had she missed it because she wasn't really concentrating, because she was focused on sounding completely sober despite the alcohol she had consumed? She can't remember exactly how much she'd had to drink that afternoon. It's all a blur. Everything that happened that day is coated with the alcohol she has been drinking steadily ever since. She's never been as out of control as she has been in the last two weeks. She hates not being able to remember, not knowing exactly what happened, but more than that, she hates thinking about the facts she does know.

Caro can't say this to the detectives. She bites down hard on her lip, trying to replace the nausea with pain.

'Anna was upset, really upset,' she says. 'She said, "It's been a bad day, Caro." And I said something like, "Poor you" or "I'm sorry," I can't really remember, but then she said … she said … oh God, I remember, she said, "No, Caro, you don't get it, it's not like all the others. This has been worse, Caro; it's been the worst day of my life."'

Caro is surprised she's recalled the words. They were different, not the words Anna always used. It was not a typical day and Anna hadn't even sounded really upset, more as though she were just stating an ordinary fact. 'I missed it,' thinks Caro, knowing that she'd heard but not heard, like she always did when she had been drinking.

In the same way she'd heard but not heard Lex telling her about the school excursion she'd be late home from and then spent the next afternoon sitting outside the school, frantic that Lex had not emerged. In the same way that she'd heard and not heard her sister telling her that her nephew, Mark, had to have his tonsils out and then had to apologise profusely because she hadn't called to ask how he was. In the same way that she heard and didn't hear Geoff telling her he couldn't deal with her drinking anymore.

There were so many things people said to her, asked her and explained to her that when they were said she thought she'd never forget, but sometimes the memory of a conversation came back too late, just like it had now. Anna had been trying to tell her something and she hadn't heard it.

'I missed it, and now Maya's dead and they're going to blame me,' she thinks.

She knows that the conversation she had with Anna is the key to getting the detectives to understand. That's all she can do now. She can't think about what kind of a friend she was on that Saturday, can't wonder how things would have gone if, instead of getting into her car, she had said, 'Tell me why, Anna. Tell me what you're feeling.' If she had just been able to think straight.

'So, she was pretty upset,' says Susan.

'Yes, but not only upset, it was more than that. She was . . . I don't know—defeated? Yes, that what she sounded like, like she couldn't go on anymore, and that's when she asked me to come over, and she sounded so bad that I said I would. I knew it wouldn't be for long, because Keith would get home soon.' Caro wrings her hands. She hadn't thought that at all. What she had thought was, 'Fuck it, I don't feel like this tonight.' That's what she had thought.

The memory of that thought comes back clearly because there had been many times over the years of her friendship with Anna that she had not wanted to deal with her friend's bad days. It wasn't as if she could ever say to her, 'Things will get better,' because they weren't getting better. Maya, if anything, got worse the older she got. She was more delayed and more violent, more frustrated and stronger, with each passing year. Anna was stranded in the long, dark tunnel of raising Maya and there was no light at the end.

Sometimes it was too much for Caro. If Anna had been a different kind of person, it would have been easier, but Anna could not focus on Maya's triumphs, on the moments of joy she experienced, because they were overshadowed by her child's failures and tantrums, and by Anna's inability to accept her life. Sometimes, Caro wanted to grab her and shake her, and say, 'Just accept it, accept it and make the best of it,' but she understood she didn't have that right. The fact of her child, her beautiful, intelligent child, meant that she had no right to tell Anna how to feel, because she had no real idea what she was dealing with.

'Okay,' says Susan. 'And how many drinks had you had by the time Anna called you?'

Caro is silent. She unfastens one of her clips, smooths her hair and clips it up again. In the back of her throat, she can taste the chocolate she's eaten. She cannot lie, she knows that, but maybe she can round down, as the test results aren't back yet. The thing is, she doesn't really know, but she assumes the fuzziness of her memory about that day means she'd had a lot. 'I'd had about two or three glasses of wine,' she finally says.

'Over what time period?' asks Brian.

Caro closes her eyes again—it's easier not to look at the two detectives. 'About two hours,' she says and then opens her eyes.

Brian shakes his head a little but says nothing. 'Bullshit, bullshit, bullshit,' she can see him thinking.

'I prefer to drink at night. I don't drink much during the day—at least, I didn't until the accident. I have a child to take care of, you know.'

'Yes,' says Susan quietly, 'we know.'

'How far away do you live from Anna's house?' asks Brian.

'It's exactly seven minutes by car. We measured it once, just as a joke, because we'd been seeing so much of each other. I used to tell Anna that it was harder for me to come to her, because I had to cross a main road with a bit of traffic, but she could go the back way, down a one-way street, to get to my house. Of course, if she had Maya, I always went to her, because Maya liked to be in her own environment, but we did see each other during school days. So, one day we measured it. It took me exactly seven minutes to get to her house and it took her five to get to mine. Why am I telling you this again?'

'Oh, no reason,' says Brian, 'just interested.'

'Caro, why do you think this accident was Anna's fault? I think you've had enough time to explain things and I still don't understand why you think it was anything more than an accident.'

'But don't you see?' asks Caro. 'I've explained it all. She knew I was coming. She asked me to come over and then she was out in the street with Maya.'

'Okay, so she was out in the street. Maybe she wanted to get out of the house for a bit? Or maybe they were taking a walk? People are allowed to be outside their houses, Caro, and sometimes they do walk out into the road. Kids run into the road all the time. That's why we have speed limits,' says Susan.

'Yes, but Maya wasn't supposed to be outside—'

'Yes, Caro, but she was, and any other child in that street could have been outside as well. Now, you were not travelling very fast, according to our investigators, so you had to have seen Maya, to have seen them both. You could have stopped, so what I want to know is, why? Why didn't you stop?'

'I did!' shouts Caro. 'I did stop but I didn't stop soon enough. I wasn't speeding and I wasn't drunk. I saw them and I slowed down, but suddenly Maya was right in the middle of the road.'

'Did she jump out in front of your car?' asks Brian.

'No, she was . . . no, she . . . she did . . . yes, she did, she jumped in front of the car.'

Brian and Susan look at her. Even to her own ears, what she has said sounds like a lie.

'Caro, I'm sorry,' says Susan, 'but I don't believe you're telling us the truth. You don't even sound sure of the answer yourself.'

'I am sure. She jumped out in front of the car . . . that's what happened. It's just because I'm not feeling well and I . . . I've been drinking a lot . . . and my memory . . .' Caro leaves the sentence unfinished. 'I really fucked this up,' she thinks.

'Shall I tell you what I think happened?' asks Susan, and Caro finds herself sitting back in her chair. Susan's tone is no longer reasonable. There is a hard edge to it.

'You don't know . . . what happened,' says Caro and she tastes the chocolate again. She holds her hand across her mouth and swallows hard. 'I need to go,' she says, standing up.

'Not right now,' says Susan. 'Sit down!' It's a direct order. Caro sits down.

'I think,' says Susan, speaking slowly and clearly, 'that you were sloshed. You got a call from your friend, and instead of telling her that you'd had too much to drink, you got in your car and drove over there, because drunk people have a habit of making stupid decisions, and an inability to think through consequences. When you got closer to her house, you saw Anna and Maya outside, and maybe you even saw Maya run into the road, but because you had so much alcohol in your system, you couldn't stop in time. Alcohol slows down reaction times. That's an undisputable fact. It's why you're not supposed to drink and drive. It doesn't matter how well you think you can drive when you've been drinking, because you're not thinking straight.

'So, you saw Maya run into the road and you pushed down on the brake, but because you were drunk, you didn't push down hard enough or fast enough, and you hit and killed your best friend's daughter.'

The words are a slap and Caro feels their violence. Susan's lips curl and her eyes squint. She looks like she hates Caro, who can feel the change in the air. They are going to blame her, and they are going to send her to prison, and she will never see Lex again.

'No,' she says quietly. 'No, no, no, that's not what happened,' she continues, beginning to shout. 'You don't understand how difficult Maya was. Anna was so unhappy, so sad. She was afraid of her own child. You don't get it.'

'Then tell us,' says Brian. 'Explain what we don't get!'

'I saw her,' says Caro and she swallows again. 'I saw them fighting, and as I drove towards her, I saw her push Maya into the road. I saw Anna push Maya in front of my car. I saw her push her—she pushed her.' Caro stands up and looks wildly around the room, and then pushes back her chair and grabs the small metal garbage bin. She vomits everything in her stomach while the detectives watch.

She vomits and vomits and everything comes out.

Chapter Thirteen

'Explain it again, Anna,' says Walt.

Anna touches her wrist. She can feel the blood rushing around her body. There's a pounding in her head. 'Careful,' she thinks. She would like to put her arms up over her head to protect herself.

Walt is leaning forward, pen in hand. He is waiting for her to slip up and then all of this will be over. Anna's focus narrows; all she can see are Walt's beautiful green eyes but they seem darker now. He doesn't wear the gentle smile she saw two weeks ago. Now he is just a cop. Anna feels pursued. She fights the urge to leap out of her chair and run until she's out of the building.

'I think I'd like to come back tomorrow,' she says. 'I'm too tired to finish this today.'

'That's fine,' says Walt. 'But before you go, I need you to tell me again why you lied about calling Caro to come over.' He has asked this question four times already, four different ways.

When he'd left the room Anna had heard him greet a woman. She'd heard them speaking but their voices were too low for her to hear anything. Now she knows that he was speaking to the detective interviewing Caro. Walt had come back from talking to the other detective and crooked his finger at Cynthia to join him outside. Anna had heard some urgent whispering but been unable to make out what Walt was saying to Cynthia. They had both come back into the interview room and he had said, 'Oh, just checking, Anna . . . you said Caro just popped over to see you, right? You had no idea she was coming?'

'No, I didn't know she was coming,' Anna had said. 'She often just popped over for a chat.' She had not been concentrating as she said the words. She hadn't noticed the way Cynthia and Walt were looking at her.

'Well, Anna,' Walt had said slowly, 'that's not what Caroline Harman says. She says you knew she was coming over. She says you called her and asked her to come over, in fact.'

Anna had been unable to prevent a small gasp.

That small detail, that tiny detail, was something she had not thought about at all.

She had tried to deny it at first, to turn it back on Caro, but that hadn't worked.

'No, I . . . I . . . I didn't. I didn't call her.'

'She says you did, Anna. She's very clear about that, and what I would like to know is why you told us she was just dropping over for a visit if you actually knew she was coming?'

'She's the one who's lying,' Anna had said. 'She knows she's going to go to jail for this and she's trying to find a way to make it all my fault.'

But Walt had not accepted this. He had sat back in his chair and folded his arms over his chest. 'Try. Again. Anna,' he had said and Anna had felt a chill at his words. She was fourteen again and trying to get out of detention for not finishing her homework. She was seventeen and lying to her mother about sleeping at a friend's. She was a child caught in an adult world that she didn't know how to navigate.

'Maybe I forgot that I called her,' she said and had been relieved when Walt nodded. She'd said the right thing, but then he'd continued to badger her about why she had forgotten, as though he'd missed everything she'd told him about that day. And now, ten minutes later, he was still asking the same questions.

'Did you lie about calling Caro and, if so, why?'

'Can you tell me any reason why you'd lie about calling Caro to come over?'

'Is there some reason why you felt the need to lie about calling Caro to come over?'

'Explain it to me again. Why did you lie?'

'I told you,' says Anna, frustrated still to be answering the same question. 'I forgot! I didn't lie, I haven't lied, I don't lie! I just forgot. It had been a long, bad day and I just forgot. Okay?'

'Not really,' says Walt.

Anna tries again. 'I've told you what a bad day it was. I've explained about how difficult she'd been. I just forgot, okay?'

'No, not okay, Anna. According to what you've been telling us, you forgot you'd called Caro to come over, and you forgot to lock the door behind you so Maya wouldn't run out of the house. Are you usually such a forgetful person?'

'I . . . no . . . it was just a . . .'

'I know, Anna, it was just a bad day. But no matter how bad a day it was, some things are not adding up. If you knew she was coming over, you knew that a car would be coming and, judging by how close your houses are, you knew she would be coming soon. Why had you allowed Maya outside the front of the house if she didn't understand that she shouldn't run into the road?'

Anna opens her mouth to speak but Walt holds up his hand to silence her.

'I don't think you forgot. I think you've known all this time that Caro didn't simply pop over for a visit. You wanted her there. What was the reason, Anna? Why did you want her there?'

'I didn't want her there. I never . . . I never asked her to come.'

'You did, Anna, you called her to come over, and now you're lying about that, even though you've just admitted it. Why are you lying?'

'You can't keep saying that!' yells Anna. 'It wasn't a lie. I'm not lying. I just forgot. I must have made the call when Maya was quiet for two minutes, and then she went off again and I forgot.'

'If she went off again,' says Cynthia, 'then why did you leave the front door open to go and get the post? Surely if she was hysterical, you wouldn't have chosen that moment to go and get the post?'

Cynthia's voice is still soft and her body is still relaxed. 'Good cop, bad cop?' thinks Anna. 'How fucking stupid. I'm not an idiot.' She feels a surge of anger—*How dare they?*—but behind that is her grief pushing forward. Always pushing forward.

'She was . . . she . . . I don't know . . . okay. I don't fucking know because I can't remember, because I've forgotten everything that happened that day except for the sound of the car hitting my child's body. That I can remember. I can describe it for you, if you like. I can tell you exactly what metal hitting flesh sounds like because that's the one thing I will never forget. I can explain about the crack I heard as her head hit the road, and how I knew even as I cradled her body that it was too late. I've seen what happens when a head hits the pavement, I've watched on the news what happens. So, would you like me to explain that to you? Do you want me to describe it in every detail, because it plays over and over in my head all day long? I won't forget that. Never, never, never!'

Anna puts her head down on the table and gives into the despair that always follows her around. She doesn't care about keeping it together, she just wants this to be over. She doesn't cry quietly, she sobs, and can hear herself almost howling. Part of her is ashamed of her lack of dignity but she can't seem to stop. The agony goes on and on.

Cynthia and Walt sit in silence. They say nothing and do nothing, and part of Anna wonders at their cruelty. Surely they should be trying to comfort her, but neither of the detectives moves, and, as she grows calmer, Anna realises that they are waiting for her to lift her head and confess everything to them. *They think they've broken through her defences, that they've found a way to get to the truth, but they've done no such thing.*

When her tears have stopped, she keeps her head down, not wanting to look at either of them. 'I'm going home now,' she says.

There is another moment of silence. Anna can almost feel the conversation between the two detectives that must be taking place in gestures and signs. She knows Cynthia will be telling Walt to back off ... she's the good cop, after all.

She thinks about getting a lawyer. She sees herself returning tomorrow with a man or woman in a sharp suit, who will sit by her side and say, 'She's not going to answer that,' every time Walt asks her a question. The thought is a comfort, even though she has no idea how to even go about finding the right kind of lawyer.

'You'll have to come back tomorrow,' says Walt. 'I'm sorry, Anna, but we do have to discuss this again. We do have to have the truth.'

'Fine,' says Anna and lifts her head. She is sure she must look terrible. She wipes her cheek and sniffs.

'It'll be all right, Anna,' says Cynthia softly. 'Get a good night's sleep and we'll start again tomorrow.'

'Yes,' says Walt, and he leans forward and pats her hand, like he hadn't just badgered her until she cried. 'Get a good night's sleep and we'll start again.'

Anna nods and stands up. She leaves the interview room silently. 'That's what I was trying to do,' she thinks as she walks out into the late afternoon sunshine. 'I was trying to start again.'

Chapter Fourteen

Caro lies in the dark, staring at the ceiling. She curses the fact that she is awake, sweating, shaking and nauseous. Her skin is itchy, and she is hot, and cold, and hot again.

She should never have chosen Roman blinds for the windows—they allow the light from the street to come in. She and Geoff have owned the house for twelve years, and decorating it, making choices about paint colours and carpets and curtains, made Caro feel like an adult for the first time in her life.

She had painted one of the spare bedrooms pink and one blue, in preparation for the perfect family she would have. It had never occurred to her that something as simple as having children would turn out to be so complicated.

'Idiot,' she sometimes says to herself as she walks past the empty blue bedroom.

Geoff doesn't understand why she has a problem with the small cracks of light but Caro likes it to be too dark for her to see her hand in front of her face. She fantasises briefly about getting out of bed and ripping the blinds off the window, which would, she knows, be counterproductive, but she wants to rip, tear, shred . . . something.

She would like to smash her fist through the window, or pick up a chair and throw it through the glass. She would like there to be noise and turmoil, to hear the tinkling of broken glass and the crack of demolished wood. She wants something to happen that others can see—something that would demonstrate what was going on inside her, something that would show the destruction, because that is how she feels: destroyed. She cannot fathom a way forward for her life.

She turns on her side, and then covers her face with her hands as she relives the horror of throwing up in front of the two detectives. The shame of it is unbearable. The lack of control, the churning of her insides and the smell come back to her. She moans.

It had certainly ended the interview. Caro had sat back in her chair, heaving and sweating, and seen the unmistakable disgust on both detectives' faces. 'Fuck you,' she had wanted to say but had not had the energy. Detective Sappington had nodded at her and said, 'We'll pick this up again tomorrow.' She had left the room quickly, leaving

Brian to offer water and tissues, and organise for her to get home. Everyone in the station had turned to look at her as he led her out—everyone including a man holding a mop and bucket to clear away the evidence of her humiliation.

She hadn't bothered saying that she could drive. She could barely walk.

A uniformed policeman had driven her home. Caro had not been able to talk to Lex or Geoff, who were sitting in the kitchen sharing a pizza.

'I was so worried,' Geoff had said when she walked in but he hadn't moved from his place at the table. Instead, he had put his hand on Lex's shoulder, as if to remind Caro that she was sitting there.

'What happened?' he asked.

'Nothing,' said Caro. 'I'm not done. I have to go back tomorrow. I need to sleep.'

She had dragged herself upstairs, thrown up again, and then managed to get herself into the shower and into bed. She thought briefly about taking herself downstairs again to get a drink—a sweet, relieving drink—but she couldn't face Geoff and Lex again, and so, had turned on her side and closed her eyes.

At some point, hours later or minutes later, she had heard Geoff open the bedroom door, knowing that he wanted to speak to her about the interview, but she had made herself lie absolutely still so that he would not bother her. She had dropped gratefully into the black hole of sleep, but it hadn't lasted long.

Now she is awake. and desperate, desperate, desperate for a drink. She looks over at her bedside clock and calculates it's been fourteen hours since her last drink. Too many hours.

She hasn't gone fourteen hours without a drink for the last two weeks, and before that, she hadn't gone twenty-four hours without a drink for at least two years.

'Alcoholic,' she thinks but the word sounds stupid. She is not an alcoholic. Alcoholics live on park benches. They don't have houses and children. They don't do the grocery shopping and the washing, and clean the house. Do they? Could she be an alcoholic, and if she wasn't an alcoholic, then what was her body doing if it wasn't withdrawing from alcohol?

'It's just because I've had so much to drink in the last two weeks; that's all,' she comforts herself.

'Liar,' she hears someone say, and she takes her hands away from her face and switches on the bedside lamp, looking around wildly for the person who has spoken. No one is there.

She switches off the lamp and lies down again.

It had happened so gradually that she cannot pinpoint when it went from a glass of wine every night to a bottle of wine every night, to more than that. It had been a slow creep, one mouthful at a time.

She is fascinated by American television shows about grossly overweight people, watching them obsessively, wondering how on earth a person allows themselves to get to a size so large they cannot even walk or get out of bed. She has made the connection between her drinking and those killing themselves with food but only briefly before she denies it. 'I am in control,' she has always told herself. 'I don't drink until after five,' and then, 'until lunchtime,' and then, 'until Lex is at school.'

And now she has to admit that she doesn't drink until her body cries out for it, which it does earlier and earlier each day. 'How did that happen?' she thinks now. She had never been much of a drinker when she was younger, preferring to remain in control of herself. No one in her household drank much at all. There were always bottles of alcohol left over from Christmas and New Year, and other family occasions, filling up cupboards and getting in the way.

'No one likes to see a drunk woman,' she remembers her father saying at a family barbecue where a cousin's girl-friend had overdone things and ended up falling asleep on the couch.

Even at university, Caro hadn't indulged much. She had only ever walked past the university bar to get to the vegetarian restaurant, and she can remember wondering what all the students sitting there were doing drinking in the middle of the day. She was judgemental towards girls who got drunk at parties and allowed themselves to be taken advantage of. 'A lady is always in control of herself,' her mother told her and her sister over and over again. Caro and Melissa heard constantly about all the things a lady was and was not, but mostly what Caro heard was that a lady never opened herself up to shame and scandal and judgement.

'Keep yourself above reproach,' was how her mother put it. It had only taken a few moments one afternoon for Caro to reveal herself to the world as guilty of all of what her mother considered the greatest sins. In the dark, she covers her face again, imagining reporting her behaviour to her mother. She can see how her thin lips will purse and her nose twitch as she considers what an embarrassment her daughter is.

Melissa wouldn't understand it either or, rather, she would understand it but Caro knew that her sister would almost have to cover her mouth with her hand to prevent the words, 'I told you so,' coming out. Mentally, Caro lines up all the people who have commented on her drinking, made allusions to the amount of alcohol she gets through on a Friday or Saturday night, or judged her for her lack of dignity. Geoff is there, and her mother is there, and her sister, and even Lex, who is too young to know anything. Only Anna has never said anything, even when Caro could see that she wanted to. Anna has been a safe and accepting haven for Caro, and in the dark, she touches her mobile phone on the bedside table, wondering if Anna would pick up this time. 'You won't believe the day I've had,' Caro hears herself saying. But Anna has probably also had a bad day, the worst day. 'Oh God, Maya,' whispers Caro.

'I don't understand,' her mother had said when Caro explained about the accident.

'There's no way to explain it, Mum.'

'No way to explain it? Caro, it's been on the news. I've had friends call me about it. You should have called me when it happened. It wasn't fair of you to let me hear it on the news. That's not the kind of family we are. You should have called me or, at least, Geoff should have called me. How on earth could you keep something like this from your family?'

'It only happened two days ago, Mum. I was going to call but I just . . . I was just trying to think about it by myself for a day or two. I don't know how to explain it. It's been so hideous and Lex is so upset. I can't even explain how I feel. I can't even think about it.'

'Caroline, I'm going to ask you a question now and I would like an honest answer. I read on the internet that you were taken in for drug and alcohol testing. Were you drunk, Caroline?'

'It's standard practice, Mum. They do that with every car accident.'

As Caro had spoken, she had heard the squeal of her brakes again, felt the jolt of her car as it hit Maya, seen Anna launch herself into the road and the look of horror on her friend's face.

The images and the sounds had returned hour after hour in those first days. They were there when she woke up and went to sleep, and when she stood in the shower. *Squeal, jolt, Anna, horror. Squeal, jolt, Anna, horror.*

It was a song she could not get out of her head, a thirty-second loop that played over and over.

'What's going to happen? Are they going to arrest you?' asked her mother as the loop started again.

Caro had taken a sip of her vodka. One sip slowed down the loop, two made it slower still. Half a bottle of vodka made the loop fuzzy, and a full bottle made it disappear altogether. But it came back. It kept coming back, and only a drink, or two, or ten, could stop it.

'Help me!' Caro wanted to scream at her mother. *Help me. Help me. I killed someone. I killed a child.*

'I don't know what's going to happen,' she said, instead tipping the glass and feeling the ice on her teeth. 'I just don't know.'

'Should I go to the funeral? I didn't know her well but I think I should go, don't you?'

'No, Mum. Anna doesn't want me there. She doesn't want anyone from my family there.'

'That poor woman. How could this have happened, Caro?'

Caro had stood up unsteadily and made her way to the kitchen. Geoff was at work and Lex was at school. Someone . . . someone . . . was bringing Lex home. She had poured a full glass of vodka, sweetened it with juice and lifted the glass to her lips again and again, and her mother's questions had blurred and disappeared.

She had not yelled or cried. She had remained calm and answered. She had restrained herself, just like her mother told her a lady always did. She didn't need to know that by the time the conversation was over, her daughter couldn't walk straight. Caro was a master at concentrating just enough so the person she was talking to thought she was paying attention.

Over the years, the comments about her drinking have gone from mild, 'You had a bit much at that party last night. Maybe you'd better take a week off from the booze, just to give your liver a break'; to the more pointed, 'You're drinking too much. It's not good for you'; to ultimatums, 'Give up the booze or lose Lex and me.'

Her mother had begun with, 'I think you may be over-doing it with the alcohol, Caroline. You're not setting the best example for Alexa. This is really not how a lady should behave,' and moved on to, 'I don't know who you are anymore, Caroline. We do not drink, our family does not drink like this'; and only weeks before the accident, she had said, 'You need to check yourself into rehab, Caroline. Your drinking is out of control. I'm sorry to tell you this, I really am, but Melissa and I have agreed that someone needs to say something.'

But every time anyone has said something, Caro has thought two things. The first was, 'They have no idea what they're talking about—a few drinks never hurt anyone.' The second thing was, 'What's the point in giving up?' Because there was no reason for her not to drink anymore, and it made her feel better, made her feel grateful for what she had, and able to view the third, empty bedroom in her house as just a room, instead of as the profoundly sad evidence of her failure to produce a second child.

She was never going to carry a child or nurse a child again, so if the alcohol helped her get through her sister telling everyone she was pregnant for the third time, or when some actress had twins at forty-six, or when Lex asked her why she couldn't have a brother, then why give it up? She still functioned, albeit sometimes a little less than completely effectively. 'They're all neurotic,' she's told herself. 'It's not really a problem.'

Lying in bed, Caro takes a deep breath and admits to herself for the first time that it is a problem. Her drinking is a problem. *It. Is. A. Problem.*

She lets the words settle. She breathes them in and out again.

The thirty-second loop of the accident assaults her senses. It has been playing all day long and there is no way to stop it now. Caro moans again. She has a problem with drinking, and realises that perhaps everyone knew—has always known—how much of a problem it is. Everyone except her.

It is only eleven but she's been asleep since eight. Now she's awake. She knows that Lex is asleep and Geoff is probably also asleep, in the guest room, where he has been living for the last couple of years. It is actually his study but they have managed to squeeze a single bed into it as well. 'Daddy snores, Lex, and Mummy needs to sleep.'

'Why can't I have the blue room?' Geoff asked when they made the decision to sleep apart.

'I don't know,' Caro had said, 'Why do you *think* you can't have it!' And then she had needed to make it better, less painful, easier to bear.

'I could go downstairs now,' she thinks. *Squeal, jolt, Anna, horror. Squeal, jolt, Anna, horror.*

There would be no one around to witness her nocturnal failings if she did get up and make for the freezer and the relief it holds. She pictures the bottle of vodka, lying next to the carton of chocolate ice-cream. She knows that the minute she has her hands on it, the nausea will disappear and the shakes will stop. Her heart will slow, and she'll be able to breathe properly for the first time in fourteen hours, because it's been fourteen hours since her last drink.

The loop will slow down and stop, and then it will disappear.

'Don't do it,' she whispers to the ceiling. 'Don't do it, don't do it, don't do it.'

'I can give it up whenever I want to,' she has always told Geoff.

'Then give it up.'

'I don't want to.'

'You should want to, Caro; for Lex, for me, for yourself.'

'Leave me alone, Geoff, I'm not your child.'

In bed, she turns the pillow over and has a frightening thought: 'What if I can't give it up?'

She thinks about getting up and going to see if Geoff is awake. She would like to tell him what happened today. She would like to tell anyone what happened today. She would like to describe the torturous loop. She would like to tell him that she literally feels like she is dying for a drink. She pushes the covers off her body. She is sweating profusely but is almost instantly freezing again and pulls them back on. She is itchy, but when she scratches at her arms, they burn. She would like to crawl out of her own skin.

'Don't do it, don't do it, don't do it,' she says again.

She wasn't going to say that Anna pushed Maya—at least, she doesn't think she was going to say it. She was going to say that Maya jumped out in front of the car and that it was Anna's fault for allowing the child to be outside. That was the plan. She is sure that was what she was going to say, but then she was so sick, so badly in need of a drink and so tired, that somehow the truth had come out. But now she is not sure what the truth was. She can't remember exactly what she'd had to drink, or how much she'd had to drink, so how can she be sure that she saw Anna push Maya?

Maybe Maya did leap from her front garden into the road?

How much had she had to drink? She has gone over it in her head again and again. She knows she had some shots of vodka, knows she had some wine, but she doesn't know how much. It's fairly likely that she shouldn't have been driving but she hadn't felt drunk. She'd felt sober, she'd felt fine.

Geoff and Lex had gone to see a movie that afternoon. 'Come with us,' said Geoff.

'No,' she had said. 'I don't feel like it. I'll just chill here. You guys go and have a good time.'

'Please, Caro, please come,' Geoff had said and then had put his hands on her shoulders. He wanted her out of the house, away from booze, safely inside the cinema, where the only thing she could overindulge in was popcorn. He knew that she liked to go hard with drinking on a Saturday afternoon. 'It's the weekend,' she always said. 'I don't have to drive in the morning.'

'But why do you need to have so much?' he asked. 'Why not just have one glass, so we can go out to dinner or out with friends?'

'Oh, give me a fucking break,' was her usual reply.

Going out with friends was easier if she'd had half a bottle of wine and a couple of shots. Then she could smile while Heather talked about her three boys and the chaos they caused, or she could nod in sympathy at Emma, who was juggling part-time work with twins. She could act like being the stay-at-home mother of one child was exactly the plan she'd had for herself.

She knew that she could have gone back to work, that she should have gone back to work. She had been good at her job as a preschool teacher. She'd loved the kids she worked with and only given it up to have her own family. But each time she thought about being surrounded by preschoolers all day she found the concept untenable. Babies were everywhere at the preschool. They came along in the bellies of pregnant mothers, and in strollers to fetch older siblings, and sat on hips at school concerts.

'I don't think I can love other people's children anymore,' she told Geoff.

'Do something else,' said Geoff.

'That's like asking me to be someone else.'

'Get a hobby. Paint, draw, write; anything, for fuck's sake.'

'You can't solve me like I'm a work problem, Geoff.'

Caro pushes the blankets off and then pulls them up again. Her whole body is shaking. Her thoughts return to that Saturday two weeks ago, and she remembers the look on Lex's face when she said she didn't want to go to the movie with them. It hadn't been disappointment. It had been relief.

'Just leave it, Geoff,' she had said when he asked one more time.

'Yeah, Dad, let's just go,' said Lex, and Caro can remember thinking, 'She sounds so old. When did she start to sound like that?'

She had tried to stay away from alcohol after they left. She had really tried. She had cleaned the kitchen and then, because she knew that she needed to keep herself busy, she even cleaned the pantry, but eventually she couldn't think about anything else. The first shot of vodka was always the best. It went down quickly and burned all the way to her stomach. She felt like she could breathe again, felt her lungs fill with air.

'Right,' she had said out loud. 'No more for me.' And she had meant it, had really meant it, but Caro knows by now that she means it every day. Every day she starts again, and really, really means it when she promises herself she will not drink. She looks over at her bedside clock. She hasn't had a drink for fourteen hours and thirty minutes. She pictures the bottle of vodka in the freezer again. It would be beautifully ice cold to the touch.

There was a stage, maybe four years ago, when Geoff would buy all the alcohol in the house. Every few months, he would buy a selection of wine and spirits, and that would last them until the next time they had guests over or saw they were running low, but Caro buys her vodka and wine herself now. She uses cash, and picks the cheapest brands available because some weeks she can get through two bottles of vodka and four bottles of wine. And that doesn't include the gin, and the cooking sherry she found at the back of the pantry last month.

She sits up and swings her feet to the floor. 'Just one, so I can get back to sleep,' she thinks.

The red numbers on the bedside clock change again. She hasn't had a drink for fourteen hours and forty-five minutes. She stays sitting on the bed. It is a king-size sleigh bed and Caro had loved it the minute she saw it. At the time, she and Geoff had been sleeping in the bed she had inherited from her grandmother. It was mahogany, and heavy and dark, with carvings of cherubs in the head-board. Both she and Geoff hated the bed but Caro didn't want just any replacement. She wanted something special, and special meant expensive, and so she had waited. Once she had seen the sleigh bed, she had visited it every month, waiting for it to be sold or go on sale. It finally went on sale, and Caro admired the curves and the light-coloured wood every time she got into it. She wasn't supposed to be in it alone, though. That had not been part of the plan.

Fourteen hours and fifty minutes.

She is stuck. She cannot lie down because her hands are shaking and her heart is racing and she's hot, so hot, but she cannot get up because she knows where she will go if she gets off the bed. Out of the corner of her eye, she sees movement, turns her head quickly and sees Maya in the room. She is standing in the corner and staring at Caro. Her long blond hair is loose, not tightly plaited, like Anna keeps it. *Kept it.* 'Oh,' says Caro but barely any sound comes out of her dry throat. Maya turns towards the wall and disappears. Caro touches her chest and her rapid heartbeat reassures her. The nausea is getting worse, though. 'Hallucinations,' she thinks. 'It's part of detoxing.' She has read about this, deleting her searches, as though she were looking at porn or talking to men on the internet.

She knows she has a problem. Every morning, when she promises herself that today she will stay away from alcohol, she knows she has a problem.

She begins to shiver again. There is a reason why she gives in each and every time. Her brain is too dependent and fights to be given what it needs.

The red numbers on the clock turn again. She has not had alcohol for fifteen hours. It is too hard, too hard, too hard. She stands up, hoping that her legs will support her weight, and moves towards the bedroom door. As she reaches for the handle, the door opens and Geoff is standing in the passage. He is illuminated by the small nightlight they have left on in the passage since Lex was born. His body and his smell are familiar and completely strange at the same time.

'Are you okay?' he asks.

She has no idea what has made him come to her room. He never does anymore, not since a few months before, when he'd tried and she had shoved him, swearing and slapping at his back, out again when he said that he thought she needed help.

Caro would like to think that, even in the dim light, her husband of fourteen years can see that she is not okay, that she is lost and alone and sick. But he doesn't know, because for the last two years, Caro has done everything she can to push him far enough away that he can't know. With every drink she has taken, she has pushed him away, not wanting him to get between her and the only thing that has made her feel like she can get through the day.

An image of the two of them on their honeymoon, in a cheap motel near the sea, flashes through her struggling brain. They had barely been able to leave the bed, so enamoured of each other's bodies were they. They had not touched each other like that for two years. If anyone had told Caro then that she would give up sex for alcohol, she would have laughed. She would have laughed so hard, she would have cried. Once or twice a month, she thinks about sex but dismisses the idea *It's not like it's going to get me what I want*. Caro realises that since Gideon died, she's been waiting for Geoff to tell her that they need to try again, that he wants her to get pregnant; that this time they will succeed. She has been waiting for Geoff to say it because she believes that if she says it, she will jinx herself with another failed pregnancy. She has been waiting and waiting, and with every passing month he has failed to say the words, she has drowned her sorrows, stuffing them down and throwing alcohol on top.

She feels close to death as her legs work to hold her body up. Her brain is fighting itself and she doesn't know how she will even get through the next five minutes, let alone the next few hours and days, but she has a moment of clarity as she looks at Geoff. He stands still and quiet, as if he almost understands what is going on inside her, and she focuses on the stubble on his cheeks and on his slightly rounded stomach. Her legs start to give way, and he steps forward and grabs her.

'Caro?' he says and then, 'talk to me. Please talk to me.'

'No,' she says. 'I'm not okay. I'm . . . not . . . okay.'

Geoff holds her up and she lets him take her weight, remembering how strong he is. He leads her back to sit on the bed.

'Tell me,' he says.

Caro's mouth is a desert and her stomach is heaving, but she squeezes her husband's hand tightly and is grateful that he squeezes back equally hard.

'I'm in trouble,' she says.

Chapter Fifteen

Anna flicks through the television channels again, knowing that she will find nothing to hold her interest. If she had the strength, she would dip into her collection of romance novels, but she is tired and fizzing with energy at the same time. She knows she won't be able to concentrate. She should be asleep. It is past twelve and she will be exhausted in the morning, and she knows that she needs her wits about her when she goes back to the police station.

She sips her chamomile tea, tasting the honey she put in it. Everything she eats or drinks needs to be sweet. There is a bitter taste in her mouth that she cannot seem to get rid of. 'Maybe you have an infection in your mouth,' Keith said when she told him about it but Anna knows that's not the case.

She cannot get used to the absolute silence in the house. For nearly eleven years, she has gone to bed every night with the static sound of Maya's sleep machine in the background. She is tempted to turn it on now but is afraid that Keith will think she's going mad. She could take some of the pills the doctor prescribed her but she is afraid of the dreams that come with them. It's better to stay awake.

She is used to sleeping very little and very lightly. Maya would sleepwalk sometimes and Anna would open her eyes to find her daughter staring at her. It had been terrifying at first but Anna had gotten used to it. Once she'd worked out what it was, she would take Maya gently by the hand and lead her back to bed. She was strangely pliable at these times, and even allowed Anna to tuck her covers tightly around her and smooth her hair back from her face. It was the only time that Anna could touch her without having to worry about a reaction. She would have loved to have been able to ask Maya why she did it, what she saw and where she thought she was going, but she would have loved to have been able to ask Maya anything.

Anna had refused Cynthia's offer of a lift home. 'I'll be fine,' she told the detective. Cynthia had touched her on the shoulder, and told her again and again that everything would be okay. Her soft voice and gentle hands had soothed Anna more than she wanted to admit. Being comforted by a stranger was somehow easier to accept than being comforted by her mother or by Keith. She had wanted to put her arms around Cynthia and just let go but she had managed to pull herself away.

She needed to be alone in her car. She had sat in the car for a few minutes, saying, "I'll be fine; I am fine, fine, fine, fine," until she started to irritate herself. Driving home, she had mentally gone over the interview, trying to work out where she had let herself down, had opened herself up to questions and suspicions, but the whole day was a blur.

'I think they're going to charge me with murder,' she had said to Keith as she walked through the door. She had enjoyed the momentary look of shock on his face but he had recovered quickly.

'Don't be fucking ridiculous, Anna. Jesus, what's wrong with you?' Keith had said.

He thought she was making a sick joke.

'I mean it, Keith,' she said. 'They think it was my fault.'

'It wasn't your fault. There is no way they'd think that, Anna. You've had a long day and you're tired. I'll make you something to eat and we can talk about it.'

'You weren't there, Keith. I know what they're thinking. You shouldn't be surprised, it's what you've been saying all along.'

'It's not what I've been saying, Anna.'

'You don't say it directly, Keith, but I know what all those questions are about.'

'What questions, Anna?'

'"Why did you leave the door open, Anna? Why did you need to get the post right then, Anna? Why didn't you have the back-up iPad working, Anna? Why did you let her get so upset, Anna? What did you do to her, Anna? Why would you let her go outside, Anna? Why didn't you call me sooner, Anna?"'

'Enough, Anna; enough now,' Keith said.

But Anna couldn't stop there. She was on a roll, as her years of failures and perceived failures with her child came spilling out. '"Why don't you hold her the right way, Anna? Why do you need her to speak, Anna? Why don't you just love her for who she is, Anna? Why aren't you more involved in the autistic community, Anna? Why aren't you a better mother, Anna? Why, Anna? Why, Anna? Why, Anna?"' Her words became bullets, ricocheting around the room.

'Stop it!' Keith had yelled. 'For fuck's sake, just stop it. What is wrong with you? Why are you being like this? We've lost our child. We need to pull together, not tear each other apart.'

'You pull your way, Keith, I'll pull mine.'

Keith had grabbed her hand, holding it too tightly for Anna to pull away. 'Look,' he said, 'it was an accident. I know it was an accident and it's only my grief, my loss, making me say what I say. I'm sorry. I know you just made a mistake. I know you didn't mean it.'

Anna can hear his mother in his words. Estelle had been over every day, she and Keith taking long walks together, and Anna knows that Estelle is counselling her son to forgive his wife her greatest and final failure.

'Come with us,' says Keith but Anna cannot stand the platitudes anymore. *People go on and on, and they say the most stupid things.* 'Time heals,' is the one she hates the most.

'What the fuck does that mean?' Anna had asked Peter when he called from Canada. She had shocked her brother into silence for a moment.

'I don't ... I don't know; I mean, I just ... I just want you to know I'm thinking of you, I'm thinking of you and Keith, and I hope that, in time, it gets easier.'

Anna had felt a twitch of remorse. 'Don't worry about it,' she had said. 'I know what you mean.'

She tries to picture herself many years in the future, doing ... doing what? Will she actually be able to get out of bed in the morning and not think of her child? She can't see it. It feels like she will be stuck here on this couch forever, simply waiting to die herself.

Her own mother is enjoying the attention, Anna is sure of it. When she's visiting them and people come over to the house, Vivian will greet them with a hug and dissolve into tears, whether she knows them or not. 'You barely knew her,' Anna wants to say to her. 'You found her too much and you hardly saw her.'

Anna knows that all of them, her mother, Keith's mother and Keith, are looking at her and finding her wanting.

'It's okay to cry,' Estelle had said to her a few days after the funeral. 'You're with family and you don't need to be brave. We're here to help.' Anna had wished, at the time, for the ability to fake tears, to satisfy her mother-in-law, but nothing would come. All she wanted was for everyone to go to their own homes and stay there, and give her some space to work out who she was now that she was no longer Maya's mother.

'You don't understand, Keith,' she had said, pulling her hand away hard so he would let go. She couldn't stand the feel of his skin against hers. 'The police don't just think this was my fault because I was a crap mother; they think I actually made it happen.'

'Why? That's unbelievable. She ran in front of a car. There was nothing you could have done once she started running.'

'I may have . . . maybe I . . .' Anna had said.

'Maybe what, Anna? What are you trying to say?'

Anna had looked at her husband and felt a cold, creeping exhaustion. She wasn't ready for this conversation. She would never be ready for it.

'Nothing, Keith, nothing . . . I'm just . . . so tired.'

'I'm sure you are. You don't have to go back tomorrow, you know. You can say you need some more time. This is them getting their paperwork in order. It can wait. I don't know what made you agree to do it in the first place.'

'No, I'll be fine. I want it done.'

'My mother says that . . .'

'You mother says what, Keith? Please tell me, because I really want to know.'

Keith shook his head. 'Nothing, Anna. I'll make dinner. Why don't you have a shower?'

'Good idea.'

Anna had stood under the pulsing heat, watching her fingers become like prunes. For the last two weeks, she has been able to stand under the shower as long as she wants. It is a strange sort of pleasure. Pleasurable and pleasure-less at the same time because, as her skin wrinkles, she looks at her hands and thinks about why she is able to stand there longer than fifteen minutes, longer than twenty minutes, longer than she has been able to for eleven years.

They had eaten their late dinner in silence. Anna had pushed her pasta around her plate, and then made her way through almost half a coconut cake that had been dropped off by one of her mother's friends. She ate quickly, compul-sively and quietly, standing up in the kitchen when Keith was watching the news.

She doesn't know what she will do when people decide to stop feeding them. She has never mastered the art of baking.

When Maya was alive, she tried to keep a minimal amount of sugar in the house. Maya was on a special diet that meant she couldn't have dairy, gluten or sugar. Some people in the autistic community swore by it. One family even claimed that it had cured their child. Keith and Anna had met them at their local autism awareness group. Keith had found the group online and suggested they attend one of their events, 'Just to see what it's like,' he said. Anna had, by then, already tried an autism group and wanted nothing more to do with them. 'I meet enough people at school,' she said.

'Well I'm going to go and I'm taking Maya. We hope you'll join us.'

'Maya doesn't hope anything,' Anna wanted to say but she went along to the picnic and it was there they met the Leigh family and their son, Aaron. Anna had stood on the fringes of the group, watching the children play and had seen Aaron but assumed he was the sibling of a child with autism. Even now she can still remember the giddy feeling of hope that suffused her body after being introduced to the family and told that Aaron was autistic. His mother, Sonya, had explained about the diet to the rapt audience of Anna and the other mothers. Anna had returned from the picnic and immediately emptied the fridge and pantry of the foodstuffs Sonya claimed were to blame for her son's autism diagnosis.

Aaron was in high school now, getting through life without spinning or rocking or staring at the wall when someone spoke to him. He still came along to fundraising events and Anna had watched him at the last picnic, had seen his eyes glaze over with boredom as he looked around him, and decided that he had nothing in common with the other children there.

'He may be on the very edge of the spectrum,' Dr Theo— the latest in a long line of doctors Maya had seen—had said when Anna told the story and asked about the possibility of a cure. By then Maya had been on the diet for two weeks but was not showing any signs of improving.

'I don't see any harm in the diet but don't expect a dramatic difference. Each child is different. What worked for this boy may not work for Maya,' Dr Theo said.

Whenever a doctor counselled acceptance and patience, Anna moved onto someone else, and Dr Theo was a paediatric specialist in autism who had trained all over the world. At only thirty years old, she was some kind of whiz-kid, and Anna had waited six months for an appointment with her. She thought Dr Theo would be the one who would finally manage to put together the right combination of diet and therapy to help Maya. But even the brilliant Dr Theo couldn't help Maya.

When Maya was five, there had been a spectacular year of progress. She'd been seeing a Dr Evans, who favoured a combination of routine and play therapy. Within weeks of starting on his program, Maya had acquired five words, and was using her iPad all the time to tell Anna and Keith what she wanted. If she asked for something to eat, she usually ate it. It felt like a small miracle and Anna started to believe that, one day, they would be able to do things that all other families did. She pictured Maya morphing into an ordinary child.

Anna wanted to take a walk in the local park on a sunny day and feed the ducks. In the early stages of her pregnancy with Maya, she and Keith had loved watching the children stand by the artificial lake and throw bread at the ducks. They had delighted in imagining their own giggling child celebrating a summer's day in the same way. It was such a small thing and yet it hadn't been possible. Maya was terrified of the ducks, and if someone shouted or laughed loudly, she freaked out and ran. She didn't understand the water, and twice, before Anna had simply given up taking her to the park, she had run straight into the lake before Anna could catch her.

She had watched Maya with her play therapist and projected forward to a future where she could say to her friends and family, 'Yes, she has come a long way, hasn't she? We didn't think it was possible but we're so grateful that she's making such great progress.' She had thought about the possibility of a mainstream school and seen a teenage Maya sitting with her in a coffee shop.

But just as suddenly as her improvement had begun, it had simply stopped. In fact, Maya had seemingly taken three steps back. And her tantrums had grown worse. Anything could set her off—a colour she didn't like, a food she didn't want to eat, Anna sitting in a chair she didn't want her to sit in, her DVD taking too long to load, the sun shining too brightly. Anna never knew what it would be. She spent all day, every day, moving slowly and trying to keep everything the way it had been the day before but she could never get it completely right. And when Maya threw a tantrum, she became violent. She would bite and kick and scratch and punch, and Anna had no choice but to hold her. If she let go, Maya would make for the front door, or she would kick and punch the walls, damaging her hands. So Anna held on and Maya used her as a punching bag. Afterwards, they would both feel exhausted, and peace would descend on their home for a couple of hours, but each time it happened, Anna felt a little more hope for a different future for her child drain away.

It seemed impossible to her, as she sat on her couch sipping tea, that she was going to be accused of murder in the morning. Would the police use her lie about Caro coming over to somehow make everything her fault?

It was almost laughable, but not funny at all. She had seen the way the two detectives had looked at each other— like they'd heard something, or seen something, and now they knew the answer.

She thinks about Walt's dark green eyes. Perhaps he is in bed next to Cynthia right now. Perhaps they are discussing her, discussing all the things she has said, and working out how to trap her into a confession. Perhaps Walt runs his hand slowly down Cynthia's body. Anna shivers in the heat, feeling Walt's hand touch her own skin. She shifts on the couch. A year ago, she had noticed that her period was late and experienced a brief moment of panic before she realised that she had not had sex for close to two years. Keith had given up approaching her; she couldn't make the leap from mother of an autistic child to lover. She had managed it every now and again when Maya was younger, but the older she got and the more violent she became, the less Anna could see herself as anything other than a parent of an autistic child, fighting to get through every day. There was no room for sex in that woman's life.

She could refuse to go back in the morning, she knew she could. Or she could tell Keith that she needed a lawyer and refuse to say anything else until they charged her with something. That was probably the wisest course of action but she had a feeling she would go back anyway. 'I have nothing to hide,' she says to the flickering television set.

But everyone has something to hide. Anna knew that Caro had sat in the interview room with different detectives and tried to hide the level of her drinking. She must have. She hid it from everyone else, or thought she did.

Over the years of their friendship, Anna had watched Caro's drinking get worse and worse, especially after her most recent pregnancy. She remembers the phone call from Geoff at seven in the morning. She was grateful, at the time, that Keith had still been home, and that he had told her he would sort out Maya and get her to school, so she could go and see Caro in the hospital.

'I held him as long as I could,' Caro had said, 'but they've taken him away now. He was so beautiful, Anna. You should have seen how beautiful he was.' Anna had never seen Caro so lost. With each miscarriage, she had seemed to shrink further and further into herself, questioning everything she had done. She wouldn't drink anything except herbal teas and only bought organic food. She turned getting and staying pregnant into her career, and Anna could see the strain on her face, on Geoff's face, and even on Lex's face, when their families occasionally saw each other.

In the same way that Anna searched for cures for autism, Caro became addicted to websites where women posted personal stories of their miscarriages. When she was past the three-month mark with Gideon, she relaxed a little, and then when she was past the five-month mark and knew she was having a boy, she threw herself into decorating the blue room for him. 'Everything happens for a reason,' she had said over and over again to Anna. 'If I hadn't lost those other babies, I wouldn't be having this little boy now. You just have to trust that everything happens for a reason.'

It had been difficult for Anna to be friends with Caro at that time. Her face radiated joy, and even when she walked she seemed lighter, despite her heavy belly. Anna found herself feeling slightly envious. She was still searching for her own reasons why things happened, and managed to dismiss Caro's years of heartbreak and simply think of her as 'lucky'.

When Gideon died, Caro was stunned. She believed she had reached a point in the pregnancy where, finally, the only outcome could be a healthy baby.

Anna had driven to the hospital and parked her car, and then waited a moment until she could find some words to say to Caro but all that she could think, and hate herself for thinking, was, 'Where's your reason now?'

'You're becoming a bitter woman, Anna,' her mother said to her every now and again.

'You and I both, Mum.'

'He had such tiny little hands, Anna,' said Caro, as she lay pale and still in the hospital bed. 'I forgot how tiny babies' hands are.' Her tears kept coming. 'I wish you could have seen him, Anna. He was so beautiful.'

'Oh, Caro,' Anna had said because there was nothing else to say.

She had seen the confusion on her friend's face and known that Caro was trying to find a way to reason through the tragedy, and failing. It had made Anna doubly ashamed of her own unkind thoughts.

She was unused to being the strong one in their relationship, unused to offering advice and comfort. She knew that sometimes she was so wrapped up in her daily struggle with Maya that she failed to see when her friends or family needed her, but she had tried with Caro. She had tried harder than ever on that day. She wanted to be a better person, a better friend.

In the weeks following Gideon's death, Anna called Caro almost every night and listened to her friend talk about her lost child. Finally, after two months, she asked, 'Will you try again?'

'No,' said Caro. Her voice was flat.

'But why? I know it's been really . . . really hard . . . but you're still young enough.'

'Geoff doesn't want to. At first, I didn't want to either. It felt like it was an impossible situation and I thought that maybe I'm not meant to have another child. But lately, I don't know, lately I am thinking about it. I mean, I pick up Lex from school, and there are all these other mothers with babies strapped to their chests and babies in prams, and I keep looking at them and thinking, "How come they've managed to get it right? How hard can it be?" You know?'

'Yeah, I know,' said Anna because she did know. She looked at other mothers all the time, wondering at their good fortune. She looked at harassed mothers in the grocery store, with four children all talking at once, and she thought, 'How come she gets to have four functioning children and I don't even get one?' But that thought wasn't one she shared with anyone, not even her therapists.

Anna spent a lot of time on the internet, looking at all the websites and reading all the blogs and the personal stories of parents of autistic children, and over and over again she read the word 'blessed'. It seemed to her that every other parent of an autistic child had managed to find the beauty in raising them, the hope and the joy and the humility that came with understanding and accepting their children for who they were. All of these parents talked about letting go of what they had imagined a child should be, of accepting the differences in their own children. Some talked of faith and most spoke of gratitude for the lessons they were learning. Anna envied their peace and happiness, and she kept searching for it in different places with different people.

She wanted her face to light up when she spoke about Maya, the same way Melanie's did when she spoke about her son, Jonah.

Anna had met Melanie at a local group for parents of autistic children that she attended a few times before she

decided it was not for her. They met once a month, to
discuss new therapies and treatments and any triumphs
they had experienced. Anna had been elated when she
found the group and she had hoped that there she would
find people she could speak to about how hard it was.
People who would understand that most days it was easier
not to leave the house when their child was home. People
who were scared that if they took their child somewhere,
he or she might attack another child, might hit or bite or
kick. She thought she would find another mother who
would sit with her in her lounge room, and the two of them
could watch their children spinning, or lining up blocks,
or simply staring at something only they could see, and she
wouldn't need to explain because the other mother would
understand. And, more than that—she would get how
Anna felt, her frustration, her anger and her worries.

She had Caro, but Caro sympathised and couldn't em-
pathise. Caro's child was fine.

At the first meeting she attended, Anna had listened
patiently while the parents described the different things
they were doing, and what was working and what wasn't,
waiting for someone to say something about just how hard
it was, about how angry they sometimes were because they
had to deal with a child with autism, but it never came.

Instead the catchword of the group seemed to be
'restraint,' as one parent after another told the group about
how they had managed to practice restraint in a difficult
situation and felt so much better for the achievement.

A woman named Deborah said, 'I walked into Benny's room and it was the most awful sight I'd ever seen. He'd smeared poo all over the walls—oh it was horrible and the smell, I don't need to tell you about the smell.' A few of the parents laughed but Anna closed her eyes. There was nothing funny about it. 'Anyway,' Deborah continued, 'I wanted to yell at him you know because he's nine now and we were way past that stage—he was even wiping himself in the bathroom—so believe me I was angry. But then I remembered about restraint and I thought, "well this is as good a time as any to practice that," so instead of yelling I went up to Benny really quietly and I said, "I think it's hose time, Benny," because he loves the hose and I knew he wouldn't argue. I kind of guided him without touching his hands until we were in the garden and then I turned on the hose and rinsed off his hands and he stood there with a dreamy look on his face. When his hands were clean I gave him the hose and let him water the flowers and I went in and cleaned up and by the time I was done he was really calm and the whole day was just easy. I was so grateful that I had restrained myself instead of just reacting.'

The group had applauded the woman and Anna had clapped along with them as she recalled a similar incident with Maya, where Maya had done the same thing in her own bedroom. Anna hadn't been able to muster the patience Deborah had described. Instead she had locked the door to Maya's room thinking, 'if she wants to be surrounded by shit, let her stay there surrounded by shit.' Keith had arrived home twenty minutes later as she had known he would and unlocked the door to Maya's room. 'That was cruel,' he had said to Anna and she had not even had the energy to reply. She had cleaned Maya's walls while Keith put her in the bath. Anna had berated herself for days afterwards, wondering at her own lack of humanity.

More stories like Deborah's had followed, and with each one Anna had felt her body slide further down in her seat. She wanted to put her arms up over her head and disappear, but she couldn't leave until she had asked the question.

At the end, she had raised her hand, almost hoping they wouldn't realise she wanted to say something but they had all looked at her, and she had thought, 'Here goes . . .'

'Um, I just wondered if anyone sometimes felt . . . I don't know . . . a little, um, upset about having to deal with all of this every day.'

One or two members of the group had chuckled, and then there had been mostly murmurs of 'no' and 'no way', and Anna was sure she'd heard the word 'blessed'.

'We all know how hard it can be, Anna,' said a man named Roy, and Anna watched everyone else nod their heads, 'but at this group, we feel that we are best served by focusing on the positive aspects of raising our very special children. It does no one any good to complain. We're all in the same boat here.'

Anna had stared at her feet as the meeting broke up and people walked over to the table loaded with cake and cookies.

She had made for the door but a woman with grey hair falling over her shoulders and down her back stopped her. She was dressed in a long, multicoloured skirt and she wore bracelets up to the elbow on both arms. 'Anna, I'm Melanie,' she said, touching Anna gently on the shoulder. 'I wanted to tell you not to worry about what Roy said. I know how hard it can be and I'm happy to talk if you'd like.'

'Oh yes, I mean . . . I have to go now but maybe another time? I would love to speak to someone who feels like I do.'

'Well, we all have our moments. My son's name is Jonah.'

'My daughter's called Maya.'

'What a beautiful name. I think names matter. I was drawn to the name "Jonah" when I was pregnant, though I've never even read the Bible, but I think I was guided to it because my boy would need to fight harder than most. "We're in the belly of this whale together," I always tell him.' And that was when her face had lit up, her eyes shining and her cheeks glowing. Anna had taken her number but had never called. She wasn't in the fight with Maya. She was fighting Maya, each and every day.

And she felt guilty about that. She questioned her attachment to Maya and her abilities as a mother. She knew that the only thing she should feel for her child was unconditional love, but the older Maya got, the harder it was to feel that love, and the more the resentment and anger took over. And when Maya physically attacked her, it was worse. You could leave an abusive husband but what about an abusive child—especially one who didn't really understand that she was hurting you? These thoughts and feelings were anathema to Anna, who had always pictured herself as a better mother than her own. 'My child won't be scared of my moods,' she had vowed, stroking her belly when she was pregnant. 'I will always make sure you know how much I love you and that you are the most important thing in my life,' she had whispered to a newborn Maya. 'I don't like you,' she had whispered to Maya as she watched her sleep after an intense tantrum that had left Anna with a broken wrist, and then she had felt her face flame, and she had stood in the shower hating herself and the terrible human being she had become.

'I sometimes feel like I've been cursed,' Caro had said in that long-ago conversation about trying again for another child. 'But then I think I have to be grateful for all that I have. That's what Geoff always says and sometimes I think he's right. Lex is great and we're doing okay. I should be grateful.' Caro had stopped to take a sip of something.

'What are you drinking?' Anna had asked.

'A glass of wine. Geoff brought home this great bottle of red. I haven't had any for so long, I forgot how much I liked the taste.'

Anna's tea is finished but she is still not tired, and she thinks about how she had watched Caro's drinking increase over the years. She would have wine when they had lunch together, saying, 'Might as well now that I'm never getting pregnant again.' And she would sip wine while they spoke at the end of most days. 'Just to unwind,' she would say but

Anna knew that it was more than that. She knew but she didn't have the energy to help her friend, because she was dealing with Maya and Keith, and her own terrible secrets.

'Don't you think you should get some rest?' asks Keith, startling Anna.

'I thought you were asleep.'

'I was, but I woke up and you weren't there. I was worried. Maybe you should take a pill or something.'

'I don't want to sleep, Keith.'

'What do you want then, Anna?'

'I want to stay awake.'

'No, I don't mean now. I mean, what exactly do you want? There's no way to make what's happened any easier but I feel like things would be better if we could talk to each other; if we could sit together and remember her. If we could somehow be a couple again, have a real marriage again.'

Anna slows her breathing. He makes her so fucking angry. She cannot find any space, any peace—even in the middle of the night, he is there, needing her to join him in his wallowing. 'What would you like me to remember first, Keith?' she says, not even attempting to keep the brittle tone out of her voice. 'Shall I remember the time I was trying to get her into her bedroom and she pushed me down the stairs? Maybe I should remember the time I put her dinner plate in front of her and it had corn on it, because I wanted her to give corn another try, and she picked up the plate and threw it at me so it hit my head and cut me? I guess

I could remember how she used to spit at me when she got angry, just before she hit me. I could remember that.'

'Anna, that wasn't her. She couldn't help that behaviour. She loved you, Anna, she was just struggling to be in this world.'

'And now she isn't,' says Anna. She gets up and heads towards the kitchen, leaving Keith in front of the flickering television set.

In the kitchen, she fills the kettle again. She has said the wrong thing, she knows that. She is always saying the wrong thing these days.

Tomorrow, when she goes back to the police station, she will have to make sure that she says only the right things.

'What do you want, Anna?' asks Keith, and Anna turns to find him standing behind her. He is shirtless, wearing only pyjama bottoms, and she looks at him, his thin frame and small shoulders. His hair is receding, and he squints a little because he is not wearing his glasses.

She knows that other women find him attractive. He has beautiful blue eyes and long dark lashes, and a smile that could grace a dental catalogue, but as she looks at her husband, all she can think is, 'What did I ever see in him?' But, more importantly than that, she wonders, 'What did I ever feel for him?'

She cannot help but compare him to the man she sat opposite today, and a picture of Walt and Cynthia entwined appears before her.

'Anna?'

'I just want to be left alone, Keith. Surely you can understand that?'

'I do, Anna,' he says. 'I get it, but what I want to know is how long you want to be left alone for. A week? A month? The rest of our lives?'

'What are you talking about, Keith?'

'Anna, do you think I don't see how you can't stand to be near me, how you don't want me to touch you? I see it, you know. I've seen it for years.'

'Keith, please. I don't want to have this conversation now. I'm tired and I have to be at the police station again tomorrow.'

'Yeah, you're tired. I know. I'm tired too. I lost my child two weeks ago and I don't know if I'll ever be able to sleep again, but I think that if I had a wife I could talk to, a wife I could touch and hold, then it would be easier to see a way forward, and I don't feel like I have that.'

Anna watches the kettle, waiting for it to boil again.

'You know, Keith, sometimes when your mother's words come out of your mouth, it feels like she's standing right here in my kitchen, and I have to say that I would rather not have your mother here all the time.'

'When did you turn into this person, Anna? You're so bitter and angry, and filled with . . . it feels like you're filled with hate. It feels like you hate me and sometimes it felt like you hated Maya.'

Anna shakes her head. 'You really do pick your moments don't you, Keith? What would you know about how I felt about Maya? You didn't want to know about anything except rainbows and sunshine. You never have. Even your own family find your incessant need to be positive about everything annoying.'

'There's nothing wrong with wanting to see everything in the best possible way, Anna.'

'So, how are you seeing this in the best possible way, Keith? What is the wonderful result of our daughter having been hit by a car?'

'I'm not talking about that, Anna. I'm talking about our lives before this. I know what kind of a child she was but I loved her through it, and I've always loved you; no matter how angry you get, and how resentful you become, I will always love you.'

Anna walks over to Keith and puts her hands on his face, looking for something, for anything, that makes her feel the way she is supposed to feel but there is nothing. Something has left her since Maya's death and inside she is empty.

'I don't feel the same way, Keith,' she says and then stops touching him.

Keith's eyes fill with tears. He had confronted her but Anna knows that he wasn't looking for anything other than reassurance. He is shocked, horrified, at the answer she has given him. Bad marriages muddle along for years without anyone saying anything. Her own parents had been married for forty-five years until her father died, and now her mother rhapsodised about the trips they'd taken and the love they'd shared. In her father's absence, her mother had rewritten their marriage and edited out the arguments, the weeks she took to her bed, the resentments and the loathing that had eventually been obvious to Anna and Peter.

Anna hadn't known what she was going to say to Keith, but now that the words are out there, she knows it was the right thing to have said them. She cannot live with him anymore, cannot pretend as her parents pretended. She is done. She feels some pity for Keith but mostly she is just irritated that he has pushed her now, in the middle of the night when she has her visit to the police station looming. She knows that she could have been kind, could have simply told him that she loved him, but she's tired of trying to be someone she's not. She's obviously failed at being the mother of an autistic child, failed at being any kind of mother at all. There is no reason for her not to fail at being a good wife and she has no interest in pretending that she is one.

'Do you want ... do you want a divorce?' says Keith, and Anna hears the hesitancy in his voice. He's pulled out the big guns, hoping to shock her back into the role she is supposed to be playing. Some couples discuss divorce every week, but Anna and Keith have only ever talked about it when they really felt they couldn't go on, and have always resolved to try again. Anna knows that Keith wants to be a good husband and that he wanted to be a good father, that he always thought they would find a way to make things better, but she has never felt the same way.

Each time, over the years, that she has found herself locked in an emotionally draining conversation about the state of their marriage, Anna has steered things towards resolution. Not because she wanted to remain married to Keith, but because she had always been terrified of being left alone with Maya.

'Do you, Anna?' Keith says and this time his voice is stronger, as though he is sure she will reply in the negative.

Anna feels something wash over her. For a moment, she isn't sure what it is and then she recognises the feeling. It is relief. She is relieved.

'Yes, Keith,' she says, 'I want a divorce.'

'You can't . . . Anna, what are you saying?'

'I'm saying that I want a divorce, Keith. You asked, I answered. That's what I want.' Anna concentrates on dunking her teabag in and out of her mug of boiled water, so that she doesn't have to look at him. He stands in the kitchen for a moment longer and she can feel him trying to find something to say but, for once, Keith only has his own words to rely on and Anna knows they are failing him.

He turns away from her and she hears him heading back to their bedroom. The door closes.

She will not go back to bed tonight. She will sleep on the couch.

'It's over,' she thinks. 'It's all over,' and again she has the sweet feeling but it is followed by a weight so heavy that she sinks to the kitchen floor.

'It's over,' she thinks again. 'All over.'

Chapter Sixteen

Caro walks into the police station with her head held high. 'I got through the night,' she thinks, and then she imagines firecrackers and banners and confetti because she got through the night.

She has watched programs about addicts and always found their need to celebrate one hundred sober days a little premature, a little ridiculous, but she understands it now, because if she could, she would celebrate every passing minute, despite how awful she feels.

She has not had a drink for twenty-four hours and she feels like . . . shit. But she is where she is supposed to be and, with a little help from Geoff, she has managed to shower and dress. Despite the blazing morning sun, she is dressed in jeans and a jumper because she is chilled and weak. 'You should be in hospital,' Geoff had said this morning as he helped her on with her pants.

Yesterday, Caro knows, she had rejected this pair of jeans as too tight but today they are looser at the waist. There is nothing left for her to throw up.

'I can tell them you're sick,' he said.

'No, it has to be done. It needs to be finished today. You understand, don't you?'

'It can be done later, when you feel better, when you've recovered.'

'I don't think I can recover until it's done, Geoff. The two are connected. Can you help me? Can you just help me?'

'I'm frightened for you—for us.'

'I know you are, and I know I should be, but . . .'

'But?'

'But I haven't had a drink for twenty-four hours. If you'd asked me two days ago, I would have told you there was nothing more frightening than the thought of giving up drinking. Twenty-four hours ago, the thought of going a day without a drink was impossible and I still can't quite believe I've done it. I thought I would feel better, but even though I don't, I want to keep going. If I can do this, I don't have to be afraid of anything else. I'll get through today and whatever comes after that. *We'll* get through whatever comes after that.'

'I think you need a lawyer,' he said again as he dropped her off.

'I know I do. I know I will, but today I'm just going to tell them what happened and let them take it from there.'

'Is there any chance that the test will come back and you were under the limit?' Geoff said.

Caro had looked at her husband and wanted to nod but she was through with lying about it. 'I don't think so,' she had said, but as she said the words, she had realised that she does have some doubt about it . . . there's something about her drinking that afternoon that's nagging at her but she can't remember what it is.

'Okay,' said Geoff. 'We'll deal with whatever happens. Tell them the story, make them understand.'

'You believe me now, Geoff, don't you?'

Geoff had looked out of the car window and said nothing for a moment, and Caro had felt her heart sink. If he didn't believe her, then how would she convince anyone else she was telling the truth?

'I do believe you,' he finally said. 'I didn't want to because it's not something I'd ever have believed of Anna. I mean . . . it's Anna.'

'I know,' she said. 'It's Anna.'

'Do you remember the time she invited us to a picnic in her garden?' asked Geoff.

'That was so long ago . . . it feels like forever.'

'Yeah, but it was a good day . . . sort of. I know we had to have it at her house because she needed Maya to feel safe, but do you remember how she spent the whole day trying to get Maya to come outside? She kept putting those little carob buttons that Maya was allowed to eat closer and closer to the door. She talked to her so softly that I couldn't hear what she was saying but she was so calm, so patient.'

'She was . . . she was a good mother, even though . . . Do you remember that when Maya did finally come outside, Anna was so happy, she was almost ecstatic. She kept laughing and then Maya started laughing too, and then we were all laughing at nothing more than a kid coming outside.

'I remember looking at Keith and thinking, "Look at us, two family men." I don't know what to say to him now. I feel like I should call him but I don't think he'd want to hear from me. I want to tell him that I'm . . . I'm so fucking sorry.'

'He may want to hear from you. You weren't driving. This had nothing to do with you,' said Caro.

'Don't go back to thinking you're alone, Caro. You're not alone,' said Geoff. 'You never have been and this has every-thing to do with me because we're a family—you and me and Lex and we're in this together. I just don't know how we're ever going to get past this.'

'We will,' said Caro. 'I hope we will. I have to believe we will,' knowing as she spoke that she didn't really mean it. She had no idea how she was going to get to the end of the day.

'You think?'

'I do.'

'Okay then.'

Caro had understood that Geoff was choosing to believe her because he loved her, because he needed her home and not in jail, but she also knew that she didn't really deserve his belief in her. They had lost their way as a couple and, in doing so, had lost their faith in each other. Caro had not been able to believe in Geoff for years. She had not trusted him or talked to him or turned to him. They had basically become strangers to each other.

But as she got out of the car to go into the police station, Caro knew that they had begun to find their way back to each other. The night before, they had both made a choice to begin that journey.

Caro had chosen to tell Geoff about the interview, about the dreadful humiliation she felt after throwing up in front of the detectives, about her fear for her future, because she knew they didn't believe her, and about the drinking. She had not minimised it or lied about it—she had told him everything. The words had come faster and faster, and gone all the way back to her clinging to her stillborn son in the hospital.

And Geoff had chosen to listen. He had not looked at the mess of a human being Caro was at that moment and turned away. Instead, he had sat on the bed next to her and listened. More importantly, he had heard. And then he had joined her in that long-ago hospital room, and they had remembered Gideon's small, perfect hands and the curls on his head.

They had talked for hours, sitting next to each other while Caro's body had thrown everything it had at her. She had felt like she was on fire one moment and immersed in ice the next. She had thrown up whatever Geoff gave her to eat or drink.

'I'm sorry,' she had wailed as he helped her into the shower for a second time. 'I'm so sorry.'

Geoff had not left her side. In the moments she was able to breathe, they had also talked about her drinking, and when it had begun and why.

'I wasn't just heartbroken after he died,' Caro had said, 'I was soul broken. I felt like I had been punished for some unimaginable sin.'

'But you seemed . . . you seemed like you were holding it together,' said Geoff. 'Once we came home from the hospital, you seemed . . . not happy but okay. You cleared out his room in a week. I couldn't believe it.'

'I couldn't look at his things. I felt stupid for having gone ahead and bought anything at all. I thought I should have known that I was never going to be allowed to have another child, and I couldn't look at my hope any longer. I thought I'd feel better once it was done but I just felt worse. One day after I'd dropped Lex at school, I took a whole bottle of vodka into the room, and cried and drank until I passed out. I was so scared when I woke up that I'd missed the end of school. I thought Lex would be standing out on the street.'

'What did you do? You didn't go and get her, did you? You didn't drive drunk with her in the car?'

'No,' said Caro quickly, 'I called my mum. She got her. I've never driven drunk with her in the car, Geoff.

I promise.' This is the one truth that Caro has clung to over the years—that she has always waited until she knew she was sober, or has called her mother or her sister for help. She has never driven drunk with Lex in the car, but she has driven drunk. It's not a distinction she explained to Geoff.

Sitting next to him with her hands over her stomach, she had realised she had been calling on others for help more and more. She has always had an excuse ready but it was possible that the sighs she has heard over the phone from her mother and her sister, and the few friends she has asked for assistance, were because it had begun to happen regularly. Too regularly.

'Why didn't they say anything?' Caro had thought but then had to admit to herself that they had said things. She had just chosen not to hear them.

'I took one of the teddy bears from the trash,' Geoff had said quietly. 'It was the one we took to the hospital for him. I couldn't believe you'd thrown it away.'

'I hated myself for that, I wanted it back so much, but I thought I would be better off if I got rid of everything. If I could simply pretend that he'd never happened.'

'But you didn't say anything to me? Why didn't you say anything to me? I thought you'd found a way to put it all behind you. You got involved in Lex's school. You always seemed to have something on the go, and when I got home at night, you were even kind of cheerful. I thought you were okay.'

'Were you okay, Geoff? Can either of us ever really be okay?'

'No, no, we can't and . . . I didn't want to say anything, because you were being so strong, but I felt a little . . . I don't know . . . resentful that you were so okay. I used to sit at my desk for hours during the day and think about his face, and then I'd come home and you'd be printing flyers for the bake sale at school, and the television would be blasting some stupid program, and it'd feel like you'd found a way to move on. It took me months, years even, to stop thinking about him. The day I came home and his room was empty, I couldn't believe it. I wanted to grab you and shake you, and make you tell me why you'd done it. I wanted to be able to see his stuff when I came home. I felt like having his room there the way we'd arranged it gave me more time to think about him, even though he'd never even made it through the front door.'

'I should have asked you, we should have done it together,' said Caro. She had stood up from the bed and made her way to the bathroom to throw up again.

'Do you still have the teddy?' she had asked when she returned to the bed.

'I do,' he said. 'He sits on my desk at work.'

She had taken Geoff's hand in hers. 'We missed each other,' she said. 'I got involved in Lex's school because I knew I couldn't sit at home and think about him. I didn't talk to you when you came home because you seemed to be doing just fine. You'd made your mind up that there'd be no more kids and you were fine with it, but I was so far from fine, Geoff. The only reason I seemed happy when you came through the door at night was because I'd dulled the pain with a drink, or two or three. It made everything so easy to deal with. I was drinking at night, Geoff, every night, and I was drinking more and more. You saw it. Lex saw it.'

'I saw it but I kept thinking I was being over cautious. No . . . that's not true. I didn't want to deal with it. I mean, I tried, but you were always so aggressive.'

'What if I can't stop?' asked Caro.

'I don't know . . . there are places you can go . . . help you can get . . . but, look, it's nearly twenty hours now.'

'It feels like a lifetime,' said Caro, and she allowed herself to imagine the clink and crack of ice cubes in her vodka.

'You have to do this, Caro,' said Geoff. 'You have to do it for Lex.'

Caro had felt her stomach turn over. Lex would be twelve soon. She was turning into a young woman, and her most significant memory of childhood would be of her mother with a wineglass in her hand. 'I've really fucked things up,' she said.

'We both have,' said Geoff. 'I'm forty-two and I feel like a kid, like I have no control over anything. I should have pushed you to get help. I should have made you talk about it, made you go to therapy. We both should have gone. It was stupid to think that we could just get on with our lives.'

'I wasn't ready for therapy. I wanted to try again, and when you said that we couldn't, it all felt so hopeless, and I felt locked into this life and this pain, like there was no way out.'

'But you agreed that we wouldn't try again. You agreed that it was too hard, and if you really wanted to give it another chance, why didn't you push me?'

Caro had made for the bathroom once again. When she'd finished throwing up, she climbed back onto the bed, and Geoff handed her a glass filled with water and lemon juice.

'The sour taste used to help you when you had morning sickness with Lex,' he said, and Caro had smiled and dutifully taken a sip. It was five o clock in the morning.

'I haven't had a drink for twenty-one hours,' she said.

'That's a good start,' said Geoff.

'I think I'm going to try and sleep a little.'

'Can I stay?'

'You can.'

Caro had rolled over onto her side and Geoff had done the same. She was surprised that their bodies still fitted together, that it still felt right.

She tried to breathe slowly, matching her breathing to his. Geoff was right. She hadn't pushed him because she had been terrified of another failed pregnancy, terrified that somehow she was being punished for some sin she couldn't name, and that she would continue to be punished over and over. She had imagined that if Geoff said without prompting that they should try again, she would somehow be able to change the outcome. She had waited and waited for him to say something, and had occasionally tried to prod him in the right direction, but he had never said the words she wanted to hear. And every time he didn't say them, every time he failed to do what she needed him to do, a drink made the situation bearable, and then another drink made it fine, and then another and another and another made everything black.

Today there would be no escape and no way to dull the pain. The only thing Caro can do is endure and that's what she plans to do. She locks eyes with Detective Sappington who is standing behind the police station counter.

'Hi, Caro,' she says. 'Thanks for coming back in.'

'You have no idea how far I've come to get here,' Caro wants to say, but knows Detective Sappington has no real interest in her life or who she is. 'I didn't really have a choice, did I?' she says instead.

'No, not really.'

Detective Sappington is holding a thin folder in her hands.

'Are those my results, Detective?' asks Caro.

The detective doesn't say anything but looks down at the folder, 'Please call me Susan. I think we're past formalities now,' she says.

Caro laughs.

'Throwing up in front of people does dispense with all the formalities,' she says. 'Can you do me a favour?'

'Depends what it is.'

'I think I know what the results are going to be and I'm sure you've looked at them already, so can you just leave it for now and let me tell you exactly what happened, and then we can get to what's in that folder?'

Susan looks at Caro, and Caro pushes her shoulders back. Whatever is going to happen today, she's ready to face it. She thinks Susan looks tired and wonders if the detective had been up all night as well.

'You'll tell me exactly what happened?' says Susan. 'No bullshit?'

'No bullshit,' says Caro, and holds back a laugh at how serious Susan looks when she says the word 'bullshit'.

'I haven't had a drink for twenty-four hours,' says Caro and covers her mouth with her hand. She wanted to tell someone, anyone, but Susan is probably not the best choice.

'Good for you,' says Susan.

'Well, I feel like absolute hell but it's a start.'

'All right then,' says Susan, nodding. 'Brian is waiting for us.'

Chapter Seventeen

'Anna, I'm hoping we can just get through what happened on the day of the accident. We want this over as much as you do,' says Walt.

He is dressed for the new day in jeans, and a blue shirt in a light fabric. He is less patient, more formal, despite his clothes.

Cynthia has her hair pulled back in a loose ponytail. Both detectives look well rested. 'Unfair,' thinks Anna. She sees them together in bed, sees them touching and then reluctantly leaving each other to shower and dress for the day, so they can come in and work out exactly how to make her pay for Maya's death—like she wasn't doing that every hour of every day already.

Anna thinks carefully about her words. They haven't

accused her of anything yet. All they've done is imply that she was somehow at fault. This morning, she had gone through the previous day thoroughly and realised that the detectives didn't know anything at all. *Caro obviously hasn't said anything to the two detectives interviewing her and, anyway, what would she say?* Caro had been drunk, Anna was sure of it. She'd heard her voice on the phone that day, heard the way Caro spoke slowly and clearly, as if she were trying to speak over the top of some noise only she could hear. Anna had known Caro long enough to know that meant she'd been drinking, and it was Saturday afternoon. Caro always drank on Saturday afternoon. And if she had said anything, it would be easy enough to discredit. She was an alcoholic. Her word meant nothing. Anna feels how cruel her words are as she thinks them, but there is no going back now. Someone has to pay for Maya's death, someone has to be blamed, and in a choice between herself and her best friend, Anna choses Caro.

'She'll be fine,' thinks Anna.

As she watches Walt check the camera before they begin, Anna thinks about Caro putting her arms around her the day they met. She sees Caro leaving Lex on a blanket in the park to chase with Anna after Maya as she ran to the water. She remembers Caro coming over one day with a gluten-free, sugar-free, dairy-free chocolate cake, saying, 'We can't have Maya missing out on the good stuff, can we?'

'God, this tastes awful,' Anna had said after they started on the cake.

'It does,' Caro had giggled, 'but look how much she's enjoying it.'

Maya had been sitting in front of the television, absorbed in her space video, while she ate her cake. Her eyes remained focused on the screen, but each time she'd taken another bite of cake, she'd smiled. 'You can't go past a good piece of cake,' said Caro.

Anna closes her eyes. She cannot think about Caro now.

'All you have to do,' she'd told herself in the mirror this morning, 'is repeat the same story.' Whatever Detective Anderson and Detective Moreno thought they knew meant nothing. Actual proof was the only thing that mattered and they would never have that. Caro wouldn't say anything, either because she couldn't remember anything or because she just wouldn't.

'Anna?' says Walt. 'Are you ready?'

She nods.

'How many times can you say the same thing different ways,' she thought as she'd dressed to return to the police station and the suffocating little interview room. She's not wearing a dress today: just her usual outfit of jeans and a T-shirt. She has brushed her hair back into a ponytail and made minimal effort with her make-up. 'Who cares, who cares, who cares?' she had thought to herself as she looked in the mirror.

She has not seen Keith this morning and assumes that he left without saying goodbye. She hopes that he simply doesn't come home. She would like to send him a text saying, *Please go and stay at your mother's house.* Since Maya was born, she hasn't had more than a few hours to herself during the school day. The idea of being in an apartment with only a silent cat for company had become one of her greatest fantasies.

'Walt, I've told you what happened. Maya had a bad day. She was sitting in front of the television when I thought it might be okay for me to get the post.

'I went outside and I left the door open, and then Maya came dashing out of the house. I tried to catch her but she was too strong for me. She kicked me, and I let go and she kept running, and as she got to the street, Caro was coming around the corner. Caro was driving quite fast and she was drunk, and she didn't see my child and she hit her, and that's exactly what happened.'

'You knew Caro would be coming around the corner.'

'I had known but I didn't remember. And even if I did, it makes no difference. She was drunk and she was speeding and she hit Maya.' As Anna says the words, she feels the sting of guilt. She doesn't want to talk about Caro this way. Caro, who dropped in on the bad days and the good days, and who could be counted on to bring milk and bread if Anna felt she couldn't leave the house, and who told Anna over and over again that she was a great mother, that she was doing her best with Maya—Caro should not be talked about this way.

'She wasn't speeding,' says Walt. 'We've checked and she was going less than the fifty kilometres she should have been going. In fact, she was basically coasting to a stop. If

Maya hadn't fallen and hit her head on the road, she'd be a little battered and bruised but she'd be fine.'

Anna looks at Walt, wondering at the cruelty of this statement. 'What is he trying to do?' she thinks.

'Well, that's not what happened, is it, Detective Anderson?' she says.

'How do they know all these things?' she thinks. 'How is it possible to measure all this, and to know exactly what Caro was doing and how fast she was going?' Caro's car is a four-wheel drive but a small one.

'Caro also says,' continues Walt, ploughing on without looking at Anna, 'and this is according to the detectives who were interviewing her yesterday, that you didn't try to stop Maya running out into the road. In fact, she says that you *pushed* her in front of the car.'

Walt says the words without emotion, as though he is reporting that Caro said it was a sunny day. He looks at Anna briefly, and then goes back to doodling on his pad, as though her reaction holds little interest for him. Cynthia, though, focuses her blue-eyed gaze on Anna.

Anna feels the words settle on her, feels the charge in the air. *Caro had said something.* In the same way that Anna was choosing herself over Caro, Caro was choosing herself over Anna.

'Stupid woman,' Anna thinks. 'Obviously she was going to do that.'

Now she regrets not taking any of Caro's calls but she'd been afraid. She knew that Caro wanted to comfort her, wanted to apologise to her, wanted to grieve with her; but she was also worried that Caro wanted to question her. If she had taken her calls, they could have discussed what had happened. Caro had been drinking and was probably confused about what she had seen. It would have been easy enough to convince her of that.

But now Caro has said the word 'pushed', and that word changes everything.

Anna chews on her lip. The silence grows.

'We think the reason she fell the way she did may have been because she was, indeed . . . pushed,' says Cynthia.

Anna looks from one detective to the other, and then glances quickly at the door and back again. *They know nothing. They think they know something but they know nothing. They're trying to push your buttons because they have no real idea.* Even though she repeats this to herself three times she can't convince herself of the truth of the statement.

'Anna, we're going to need you to say something here,' says Cynthia.

'She's lying,' says Anna. 'She's lying. You have to know that she's lying. She's a drunk and she's trying to prevent you from finding that out. She doesn't want anyone to know. It's her secret but I know all about it. Believe me . . .' she goes on, nodding her head as though she is vehemently agreeing with someone, 'I know. I know she drinks all day long. She drinks when Lex is at school and at night. She doesn't care about anything except alcohol. And she drives drunk all the time.

She's even driven drunk with Lex in the car. She should be in prison. She's not fit to be a mother. She shouldn't be allowed to drive a car. She's . . . she's a drunk.'

'Anna,' says Cynthia, 'you need to stay calm and listen to me. If Caro was drunk, it will show up in her blood tests. That's not really the issue now. What we'd like to discuss is why she'd say that you pushed Maya in front of the car. Is she right, Anna? Did you push Maya in front of the car?'

'She's such a bitch,' says Anna. 'All she knows how to do is lie and drink and feel sorry for herself. "Poor me . . . poor me . . . poor me." She has no idea what a hard life is. No idea at all.' Anna is looking down as she says this, talking to the tabletop.

'She was your best friend,' says Cynthia quietly.

Anna's head jerks up and she stares at Cynthia, causing her to sit back a little in her chair.

Walt folds his hands across his lap but doesn't say anything.

'She used to be my best friend,' says Anna. 'She killed my child, Cynthia. I think that would end most friendships pretty quickly—wouldn't you agree?'

'Anna,' says Cynthia, 'I'm a mother as well and my heart breaks for you, it really does. I can't imagine the pain you must be going through, but, as a mother, I have to confess that raising kids is not easy. It's never easy. I know all that crap on Facebook makes it look like a lot of mothers are living perfect lives but I know that's not the truth, and you know it too.'

'I don't think you have any idea about how hard it was,' says Anna. 'I'm sure your kids are fine, just average kids with average problems. You're just like Caroline ... just like all the other mothers out there who think they've got it tough because their kid throws a tantrum, or because they didn't get their eight hours of sleep last night, or because a teacher thinks their kid is badly behaved. You all think you know but really you have fuck-all idea.' As she says the words, Anna realises that she's angry at Caro. She's angry at her for hitting Maya with her car and for trying to blame it on her, but actually she's been angry with Caro for years. Yes, she'd had a hard time with the miscarriages and losing Gideon, but she still had Lex, who said her first word at ten months and at two years old would not shut up for a second. 'What colour is the sky in the dark, Mum? Why is that dog sitting down? Where is my dad? Can I have a lolly? I want Dora, Mum. I want my doggy. Why is it today?' Lex's endless commentary on everything she thought and saw was the background noise to every playdate she and Maya had until Lex stopped coming over forever, and all the while, as she listened to Lex talk and talk and talk, Anna would be saying to Maya, 'Say "Mum ... Mum ... Mum", Maya. Can you say "Mum"? *Unless your child couldn't talk to you, didn't look at you or smile at you, didn't even care whether you were there or not most of the time, you had no idea.*

'Maya was hard work,' says Cynthia.

'You have no fucking idea,' says Anna.

'Then tell me,' says Cynthia. 'Tell me how you managed to cope with a child who was so difficult, because I'm not sure I could have done it.'

'Tell me about your kids,' says Anna.

'Anna, Constable Moreno's children are really not something we want to discuss. You were talking about Maya; tell us what happened on the day of the accident. The moment you do that, you'll be allowed to go home.'

Anna looks down at her hands. 'Tell me about your children,' she says again. She needs to hear about Cynthia's life, needs to hear about her children. She doesn't know why.

Walt says, 'Anna . . .' and she detects a note of warning.

'It's okay, Walt,' says Cynthia. 'I don't mind talking about my boys. I have two boys, Anna,' she says, and Anna is forced to look up and at her as she talks.

'What are their names?'

'Joel, who's five; and Jarred, who's seven.'

'Joel and Jarred,' says Anna.

'Yes,' says Cynthia, and she sits forward in her chair a little, so she is closer to Anna.

'I didn't want to give them both J names but my ex-husband liked the idea.'

'How long have you been divorced?' Anna says and hears Walt sigh.

'Nearly three years now,' says Cynthia. 'The divorce was pretty hard on the boys but I think they'll be okay. I have to say that they can be as sweet as pie but there are moments . . . moments when I find them . . . awful.'

Cynthia nods as she says this.

'Kids can be awful,' says Anna.

'They can ... most days, I can calmly deal with Jarred throwing a tantrum because I made the wrong thing for dinner, or Joel saying, "I want to live with Dad," whenever I tell him it's bedtime, but sometimes it's just too much.'

'Yes,' says Anna quietly to Cynthia, 'sometimes it's just too much.'

Cynthia sits forward a little more, so she is even closer to Anna. Anna can smell her perfume, can even smell the mint of her mouthwash. 'Last week,' she says, 'Joel knocked on the bathroom door for five minutes straight because I wouldn't come out and give him an iceblock before dinner. It was just over an iceblock and it turned into a battle of wills, and when I came out, I wanted to grab him and shake him hard, just make him shut up.'

'What did you do?' asks Anna. Her voice is a whisper.

'Well, um, that's when I know I need to get out of the situation. I went back into the bathroom and locked the door, so I could get away from them both, because Jarred had already gone on at me about having more computer time. Joel wasn't having any of it and he kept banging on the door, driving me crazy. Eventually, I turned on the shower and just listened to the water until he went away. It was a bad day, an awful day, and when I came out of the bathroom, I was sorry I'd locked myself away, but it had given them both time to calm down and given me some space.'

'I never had any space,' says Anna. 'I couldn't leave Maya alone unless she was watching her DVD.'

'I imagine that would have made your life really difficult. Every mother I know sometimes needs a bit of time out from her kids—especially when they're being unreasonable,' says Cynthia, 'so tell me how you coped with never having that.'

'You don't get a choice,' says Anna. 'You don't get to choose if they look like you or your husband, or if they're good at sports, or clever or funny, and I didn't get a choice with Maya and autism. She could have been on the easy end of the spectrum but I didn't get to choose that either. I coped because I had no choice.'

Anna watches Cynthia sit back in her chair. Walt is sitting with his pen poised to write. The red record light on the camera draws her eye. She sits up straight and pushes a stray strand of hair behind her ear.

'I'm not saying I was happy,' she says, 'that would be stupid, but I didn't . . . push my child. That's a ridiculous thing to say, and so clearly from the mouth of a drunk that I'm surprised you've given it a single thought. I didn't push my child. I loved her. I sacrificed everything for her, everything. I even sacrificed another child for her, so why would I have tried to hurt her? She was it for me.'

Anna waits for the words to have the same effect they have on her when she only thinks them, but they don't.

'Sorry, did you say you sacrificed another child for Maya?' asks Walt slowly.

'Yes, Walt, that's what I said,' says Anna, and she holds his gaze, no longer interested in his beautiful green eyes. She wants to scratch at his face with the nails she is finally allowing to grow now that she doesn't have to avoid hurting Maya when she has to physically restrain her.

'You had a termination,' says Cynthia.

Anna starts to laugh. 'Oh, you're a clever one, Cynthia. Walt thought I had a body buried in my backyard.' She can hear an edge of hysteria in her words. She knows she is beginning to sound strange but doesn't seem able to rein herself in.

'I'm sorry, Anna,' says Walt.

'I'm not,' says Anna. 'It was my choice. I know that autism can run in families. I knew that there was a chance another child could be the same way and, no matter what Keith said, I couldn't seem to imagine any other outcome. I couldn't have dealt with two of them. I would rather have died.'

'What did Keith think?' asks Cynthia.

'What difference does that make? It has no bearing on what we're talking about today!'

Anna tries not to think about the night Keith found out about the termination. She had waited two days to tell him, until she felt physically strong enough to deal with his reaction. He had wanted her to keep the baby, had begged her to keep it. He had talked at her for days and days, trying to convince her that everything would be all right, promising to hire a full-time nanny if she needed one. 'With what money?' Anna had scoffed. 'Everything we have goes on therapy and doctors. How do you propose to pay for a nanny?'

'I'll go to my parents,' Keith had said. 'They'll understand. Everyone will help. Please, Anna, it'll be different this time. I know that this child will be fine and will make us a proper family. Please don't do anything until you've thought about it. I'll talk to my mother and see how much she can help. Everyone will want to help.'

He would not let it go and eventually Anna had agreed to wait, to give it some time before she made her decision, but she hadn't been able to. She had spent hours going over it again and again, trying to fit a new baby into the puzzle her family was, but no matter what image she tried to conjure up, no matter how hard she tried to envision the dream toddler she and Keith had once believed would be theirs, she couldn't see it. All she could see was a future of being shackled to two children who would need her for the rest of their lives.

She saw herself dragging them both by the hands through a shopping centre, with Maya screaming, and the new child spinning or flapping away from her. She saw the sleepless nights, and the dirty nappies that Maya had only stopped producing at five years old. She saw the endless hours trying to guess what was wrong with the new baby . . . 'Are you too hot? Too cold? Hungry? Tired? Hurt?' She saw the hours that she now had alone while Maya was at school disappear, swirling her back into a vortex of caring constantly for another living creature. There would be no rest or respite. She would be with a baby all day and all night, and when the baby was asleep, she would have to be with Maya. And how would Maya deal with a baby? In the middle of one of her tantrums, she had ripped the head off a teddy bear that was the size of a two-year-old child. Mid-tantrum, what would she do to a baby? And in the midst of all this worrying and caring and mothering, what would happen to Anna? There was little enough of her left as it was. How could there be enough for another human being who needed and wanted her constantly?

The thought made Anna throw up, even when the pregnancy hormones were not affecting her. After lying awake for a whole night, she had understood that she was not capable of sustaining even one positive thought about the child growing inside her, and it seemed kinder to her to let it go, rather than force it to deal with all her anger and fear.

She had booked the termination the next morning and was able to have it the same day. Caro had gone with her and Anna had arrived home before Maya's school was out. One, two, three, and it was done.

Two nights later, she had joined Keith on the couch after Maya had gone to bed.

'How are you feeling today?' he had asked gently.

'I'm fine, Keith.'

He had gone back to watching the television, but was clearly sensing something. Anna could always tell when Keith was avoiding a fight with her. He sat up straighter, did more cleaning up in the kitchen, or did what he did right then, which was switch the television channel from the news to a home-decorating show, because he knew she liked those.

'Don't you want to know why I'm fine?'

Keith had turned to look at her. 'Of course I want to know, Anna. I just hoped you were feeling okay today. I know you hate feeling nauseous.'

'I'm not nauseous.'

'That's great. I didn't realise it'd pass so soon. With Maya, you felt horrible for the whole time—remember?'

Afterwards, Anna had chastised herself for not taking a moment to phrase her words properly. As it was, even to her own ears, she sounded smug, and almost as if she were taking some sort of sadistic pleasure in her announcement. 'Keith, I'm not nauseous because I'm not pregnant anymore. I had a termination two days ago.'

'You . . . what?' said Keith without removing his eyes from the screen.

It made Anna nervous. She had expected yelling and the inevitable tears. She blundered on, 'I haven't been able to tell you because . . . because I know you wanted another child but I knew, Keith . . . please understand . . . that I knew that I couldn't do it.'

Keith hadn't said anything for about five minutes, and then he had finally switched off the television and stood up, moving across the room from her.

Anna wanted to get up and leave but could see he was breathing deeply, trying to make his anger dissipate.

'Say something, Keith, please! I'm really sorry but I know myself. I know what I can handle.'

'You evil bitch,' Keith had finally spat. He had rushed over to where she sat and loomed over her, raising his hand. 'How could you,' he sputtered. 'How could you do it without asking me? Without telling me? My child, you killed my child.'

Anna had never been afraid of Keith. He was short and slim, and could go for days without shaving. His curly blond hair and pudgy cheeks made him look younger than his years, and he was the least threatening person Anna knew, but that night she had been afraid he would actually hit her.

'Keith, what are you doing?' she had yelled.

'Be quiet,' he said. 'You'll wake Maya.'

Anna had stood up and pushed him out of her way. Even when he was so angry at his wife, he wanted to hurt her physically, he was still thinking about Maya, because if Maya woke up, the whole night descended into chaos. The whole *world* descended into chaos.

'I don't expect you to understand, Keith. I don't expect you to be happy about it, but you have to get that this was my body and my choice. I cannot have another child. I need to be here for Maya, and Maya only.'

'You're like a fucking robot, Anna. Don't you care? Aren't you heartbroken? What kind of a woman kills the baby she's carrying and doesn't feel a thing?'

When Anna thinks about that night now, she knows it was the end of her marriage. They had carried on together because Maya needed two parents, but she couldn't bear to have him touch her, and even though he had apologised, had apologised again and again, after a long talk with his mother, she had never been able to see him the same way.

'Keith thought . . . ,' says Anna to Cynthia, 'Keith thought that my decision to terminate made me an evil bitch.' Even now the words cause a pain in her chest. 'We don't have much of a marriage.' Anna has never said such a thing out loud before. She feels strangely freed. In fact, after last night, they didn't have a marriage at all, but Anna doesn't want to talk about that yet. She had slept on the couch with her mobile phone next to her, and had spent the night fighting the urge to call Caro and tell her what had happened. She knows that she should have removed Caro's number from her phone, or blocked her or something. In the days following Maya's death, Caro's calls to Anna's mobile had numbered in the hundreds. If she called the house, she got Keith, because Anna refused to answer the phone. It was bizarrely comforting to her to see evidence of Caro's attempts to contact her and to know that Caro was suffering as she was suffering. Her calls were proof of her guilt. They had to be.

'Would you say that you and Keith stayed together because of Maya?' asks Cynthia.

'Absolutely,' says Anna. 'How long did you stay with your husband because you didn't want to put your children through a divorce?'

'Too long,' says Cynthia. Walt clears his throat and Cynthia sits up straight.

'Would you say that on the day Maya died, you'd finally had enough?' asks Walt.

There is a moment of absolute silence in the room. Walt has asked the question without emotion and Anna can see him thinking that he's got her. She can see both detectives thinking that the good cop–bad cop routine has worked. Cynthia has engaged her, has connected with her as another mother, and then Walt has come in with the hard question. It's not the hardest question, because he hasn't asked, 'Did you kill your child, Anna?' But it's hard enough.

What neither of them understands is that Anna is watching herself, watching them and watching the camera. She is watching it recording all her words so that they may one day be used against her.

'No,' says Anna. 'I'd had enough every single day. Every time she hit me, or threw a tantrum, or broke something, or spat at me, I'd had enough. That day was no different to any other day. I loved my daughter, Detective. Despite everything, I loved her and I would never have done anything to hurt her.'

Anna shifts in her chair. 'What else have you got?' she thinks.

Chapter Eighteen

'You've got our attention, Caro. Tell us what you think we need to know,' says Susan.

'Okay, just give me a moment. This is really hard for me, you know.'

'We gave you all the time you needed yesterday and we didn't get very far.'

'I was sick.'

'You were in withdrawal,' says Brian.

'And I still am,' says Caro. 'I haven't had anything to drink since yesterday morning.'

'Well, good for you,' says Brian, and Caro smiles at him. 'The first few days are hard,' he says, 'but once your body recovers, it's going to be harder still. Now you can feel the effects that alcohol has had on your body but, afterwards, when you're feeling physically okay, it might be difficult to resist temptation.'

'This is not a therapy session, Detective Ng,' says Susan sharply. 'Caro, the accident. Let's just get to the accident.'

Caro holds up her hands to stave off Susan's aggression. She feels prickles of fear all over her skin. 'They're not going to believe me,' she thinks but knows there is nothing she can do but tell her story.

'Anna called me to come over to her house,' she says.

'Yes, you've said that already, and you also said that you'd only had a couple of glasses of wine,' says Susan.

'Well, I'm guessing that those blood-test results are going to say that's not the case,' says Caro, and stops talking.

'Well, actually—' says Brian, looking at the folder on the desk and then shaking his head, but Susan interrupts him: 'Why don't you just tell us the story, Caro?'

'Odd,' thinks Caro. She wonders how high the number actually is, wonders how she had thought she would be able to drive. She feels her stomach flip as the realisation of the course her life is now on hits her. She thinks about simply sitting back and refusing to speak. There is nothing she can say now to save herself, so why tell them what happened? Why drag Anna, who is already suffering, who already has suffered for years, into Caro's train crash of a life?

But then she remembers one afternoon when Maya was around seven. Anna and Keith had been invited to a wedding, and Caro had offered to babysit. It was the wedding of one of Keith's cousins, so none of their usual babysitters were available, and by then, Anna's mother refused to be alone with Maya.

'I can't ask you to do that,' Anna had said over the phone. 'You know how difficult it'll be.'

'I do, but I'm offering anyway. I'll come to your house, and leave Lex with Geoff, so I don't have to concentrate on anything else. She knows me, Anna, and it's one afternoon. I'll cope for one afternoon.'

Anna had hesitated for a few minutes, and in her silence, Caro had heard not only her friend's concern that Caro wouldn't be able to handle her child but her concern about the times when Anna had seen her a little the worse for wear.

'I'll be stone-cold sober, Anna,' she had said. Saying the words had hurt but she desperately wanted to give her friend one afternoon off. She had known Anna would never have said anything to her about her drinking. She would have supported Caro if she decided to give up, and turned a blind eye when she overdid things, but Anna would never judge her. 'Trust me,' Caro had said and finally Anna had agreed.

Caro had kept her promise. She had stayed away from alcohol the whole day she was going to babysit Maya, and arrived an hour early, so she could adjust to her being there.

'You look gorgeous,' she told Anna, who had looked quite startlingly beautiful. Not just well made-up and well dressed but lit up by the prospect of a free afternoon. 'You both look nice,' she had said when Keith walked into the room.

'Yes,' he had said, not even glancing at his wife, 'don't we.'

Anna had shrugged her shoulders and rolled her eyes at Caro, as if to say, 'Men!', but Caro knew that their marriage had never really recovered from Anna's termination the year before.

Their marriages, their failing marriages, were part of the ongoing stories of their lives. They felt they were both in the same situation, stuck with men they were no longer sure they wanted to be with but hampered by their children. Anna and Caro were closer than friends, closer than sisters. They texted each other all day and spoke every night. Caro had once pictured the two of them living side by side in a retirement home. She had never pictured them without each other. She had been able to imagine a time when her marriage to Geoff would be over, and when Lex would have a life completely separate from hers, but she had always seen Anna in her future.

'Thank you for doing this,' Anna had said before she left for the wedding. She had given Caro a quick, hard hug, and Caro had immediately regretted not making a similar offer sooner. Keith's family were fond of birthday dinners and picnic lunches and family holidays—none of which Anna and Keith ever got to attend.

'You'll be okay?' asked Anna.

'I'll be fine,' said Caro, 'just have a good time.'

Once Anna and Keith had left, Caro had sat on the couch, quietly watching Maya watching her space DVD. Anna had told her which snacks she could offer Maya and exactly when to offer them; in fact, she had left a run sheet specifying how the four hours with Maya were supposed to go.

Maya had watched the video five times while Caro sat there, every muscle tense, every sense alert. After the fifth time, she had stood up and looked around the room, and on seeing Caro, she had smiled. It was a genuine smile and in it Caro had read, *Don't be afraid. I'm going to help you get through this.* She had picked up her iPad and touched the icon meaning snack, and Caro had dutifully put seven— not six, not eight—rice crackers in a bowl, and half filled a red plastic cup with water and added exactly one tablespoon of apple juice. Maya had taken the bowl and the crackers, and sat at a small wooden table with matching chairs. She was too big for them, but Anna had told Caro that she was afraid to get rid of the furniture set. When she had finished eating, Maya had disappeared from the living room. Caro had been tempted to follow her, but she knew that the whole house was set up so as to let Maya wonder aimlessly from room to room. 'Sometimes she can do it for hours, for no apparent reason,' Anna had said.

Caro remained on the couch, fending off her desperation for a drink and refusing to look at the time. After a while, Maya had returned to the living room, holding a book, and then she had sat on the couch next to Caro and curled her legs under her, handing over the book. It was the classic story of the town mouse and the country mouse but with the language simplified to toddler level. Caro had read it to her, and then Maya had tapped the book, and she had read it again and again and again. She can't now recall how many times she read the book but, at some stage, Maya had let her head drop onto Caro's shoulder. She had never voluntarily touched her before. The trust she was displaying made Caro want to cry.

Caro had kept reading until she recognised the heavy sleep that all mothers learn to spot, and then had closed the book and sat quietly until Anna and Keith walked through the door. She hadn't wanted to move, being afraid to disturb Maya, afraid that the gentle look on the child's face would disappear as she opened her eyes. Caro had seen her then as a little girl, just like Lex was a little girl, and she had understood why it was always possible to love your child, regardless of everything else.

The next day, Anna had detailed a dreadful night with tantrums and no sleep. Caro had understood then that Maya really had tried to go easy on her—she had recognised that here was someone unused to dealing with her and had tried to help. When Caro had explained her theory to Anna, she had been unimpressed. 'She knows which environments are good for throwing fits.'

'Yes, but perhaps it means that you'll be able to get through to her eventually; that she's smart enough to know how to change her behaviour for me, so maybe—'

'So maybe nothing,' Anna had said. 'She has good days and bad days, good parts of the day and bad parts of the day. The day you babysat, she'd spent the whole morning writhing on the ground, screaming and kicking. She was probably just exhausted.'

Caro had left it because it was not her place to talk about someone else's child, especially a child with special needs. In the interview room, though, she can recall the feeling of Maya's head on her shoulder, and so, despite her friendship with Anna, she knows that she needs to tell the truth, whether she will be believed or not.

'When Anna called me that day, she sounded . . .' Caro thinks about what she is trying to say, 'She sounded different.'

'Different?'

'Yes, I don't know how to explain it. Usually, when she called me at the end, or in the middle, of a bad day, she'd be a little bit hysterical. No—not hysterical, just on edge, but laughing about it. She'd say something about what was going on, like "Maya threw one of her wooden blocks at me and it just missed my eye, so I'm going to look at that as a good thing," and then give a little laugh, and then she'd say something else and have another little laugh, and over the years, that became her—I think you call it a tell. I knew that if Anna was talking to me and the strange little laugh came out, usually followed by "Oh well, that's my life," that she needed a break and that it had been a difficult day with Maya. I always tried to talk to her for a while, or to go over there, so she could at least have some adult company. But when she called me on that day, her voice was kind of flat, like she'd taken drugs.'

Caro puts up her hand as Susan leans forward. She wanted to stop the detective from saying anything. 'Not that she was on drugs,' says Caro. 'Anna only drinks herbal tea and she won't take anything but over-the-counter pain medication. She just sounded like she'd taken something but I know she hadn't.

'She said, "I can't do this anymore," but nothing else. I asked her what had happened, and she told me that she'd been alone with Maya the whole day, and her voice still had this flat, dead kind of quality. I was worried about her, so I told her I'd come over and she said, "Yes, come over, Caro. Come over now," and then she put the phone down. I wanted her to tell me not to bother, like she sometimes did. I'd rather have talked to her for as long as she needed me to, but I called her back and it was engaged, and so I called her mobile but she didn't answer, so I felt like I had no choice but to go over there. I was worried.'

'Why didn't you just call her husband or get your husband to drive you, or wait until you had sobered up?' asks Brian.

'That would have been the right thing to do,' says Caro, irritated by his interruption, 'but, obviously, I didn't do that, so what's the point of asking the question? I was worried about her, really worried. In the ten years I'd known her, I had never heard Anna sound like that, so I got in my car and drove over there.

'Her house is in a cul-de-sac, and as I turned into it, I saw Anna and Maya out on the front lawn. They were physically fighting. They were kind of twisting around each other, like they were trying to make their way to the road one minute, and then back into the house the next. They are . . . shit . . . they *were* basically the same size, so they weren't getting very far.

'Maya was kicking out at Anna. I saw it and I sped up— just a little, to get there quicker—and then I slowed down in front of the house, but as I got there, they'd made their way right to the kerb, and for a split second, Anna looked at me and then she just pushed Maya, pushed her hard, right in front of my car. I wasn't going that fast—at least, I don't think I was. I did try to brake but Maya was already in front of the car and it . . . and I . . . hit her, and she bounced off the front of the bonnet and slammed down onto the road.'

Caro sits back and takes a deep breath. She realises that she's crying as she sees this and hears the sound of Maya's head hitting the road.

The image and the sound she had heard through her open window have played in her head on a continuous loop only alcohol could stop. Now that she doesn't have that option, she is overwhelmed by it anew and feels as though she might faint.

'Oh God,' she says, covering her mouth with her hand. 'I hit Maya. I hit her.'

'Yes,' says Susan. 'You hit her and she died.'

Caro winds her arms around herself and begins to rock back and forth. *I hit Maya, I hit Maya, I hit Maya*, plays in her head.

'I thought I was okay. I really thought I was okay to drive. I'd only had . . .' Caro stops rocking. She sits up. The afternoon before Anna's call comes back in full colour and she realises what's been niggling at her about her drinking.

'I'd only had one glass of wine,' she says.

'You must have had a lot of something else,' says Susan. She gives Brian a quick look and he looks again at the folder on the desk.

'No,' says Caro, as her memory of that afternoon now returns with the force of a punch. 'No, I hadn't. I had two shots of vodka—maybe three, because I poured myself a double the second time. I had one, and then I promised myself I wouldn't have another but I did, and then I opened the wine and poured myself a glass, and then I thought that I better have something to eat. There was some leftover pizza in the fridge, so I warmed that up—'

'Caro, I'm not sure where this is going,' says Susan.

'You need to listen,' says Caro and hears the forcefulness in her tone. 'I promised myself that I wouldn't drink the wine until the pizza was hot. I forced myself to clean the cutlery drawer so that I'd wait. When the pizza was warm, I took it out and turned around to put it on the bench, but I forgot the wine was there. I knocked over the wine bottle with the oven tray and that toppled the glass as well. I can't believe I didn't remember this. I spilled all the wine and broke the wineglass. I had to clean it up. I hadn't even had a sip yet.'

'Caro, this is not really the time to change your story,' says Brian.

'I'm not changing my story. I'm remembering what happened. I cleaned it up, and then sat down on the couch with my pizza and a new glass of wine. I'd only had a few sips when Anna called. Don't you get it? I wasn't drunk. I wasn't drunk at all. I don't care what those results say. I know I wasn't drunk.'

Caro sits forward and looks at Susan, willing the detective to believe her.

'Caro,' says Brian, 'you're digging yourself in deeper here. When the results do come back and show that you were over the limit, you will have lied to police officers. You're an alcoholic, Caro. It's pretty much a certainty that you were drunk at the time of the accident.'

Caro sits up and looks at Susan. 'What do you mean when they "do come back"? Don't you have the results right there?'

Susan hesitates, and then she shakes her head a little and Caro watches two small spots of colour appear on her cheeks. 'No,' she says.

'You bitch,' says Caro softly.

'Hey,' says Brian. 'Take it down a notch, Caro.'

'She made me think those were the results.'

'I never said they were,' says Susan. 'But you can bet when they do come back that they'll say you were way over the limit. All this other bullshit is just designed to throw us off and that's not going to happen. Your story about Anna pushing her own child into the road is too far-fetched even for Brian to believe; isn't that right, Brian?'

Before he can answer, Caro says, 'It's not a story. It's the truth. I know I hit Maya, I know I did, and I know I'm going to pay for that. I've relived that moment over and over again. I had to pull my best friend away from her daughter's body, so that the paramedics could get to her. If I'm standing in the kitchen, or the bathroom or the bedroom, and there's no other noise, I hear Anna screaming. I hear Maya hitting the road. The accident was my fault. I shouldn't have been driving because I had been drinking—even if I wasn't over the limit, I still shouldn't have been driving—but Anna pushed her in front of my car.'

'As you say, Caro,' says Susan, 'you'd been drinking. You were intoxicated. Probably more intoxicated than you're currently willing to admit but we'll have the truth in a few weeks. Maybe you think you saw Anna push Maya, but it's possible it's not the case.'

'I know what I saw,' says Caro. 'I will never forget it. I don't care if you believe me or not. I have nothing to gain from this, am I right?'

'We don't know,' says Brian.

'It will affect the case but will also mean that we have to focus on Anna. She is, or was, your best friend. Are you sure you want to do this?' asks Susan.

'I'm not sure of anything right now. I'm not even sure I want to wake up tomorrow,' says Caro. 'Not sure at all.'

Chapter Nineteen

'It must have been very difficult to always be patient with her,' says Cynthia.

Anna has relaxed in her chair. 'Aren't we done?' she asks.

'Not yet; I just want to get the final details.'

'Some days it was fine,' says Anna. 'On days when she'd been up a lot the night before, it was difficult. School days were easier, and days when Keith was home were fine.'

'Was she happy at school?' asks Cynthia.

Anna sits up again. 'She was . . .' her voice trails off.

'How much do they know?' she wonders. It's possible they have already been in touch with the school. It's possible that they know about the tantrums and about Maya hurting other children. For a moment, she doesn't know whether to be evasive or simply tell the truth. The longer she waits to speak, the more they will question her answer. In the end, she decides on truth. 'She was happy when she first started there. It's a great school, with a teacher-to-pupil ratio of one to three. It's almost impossible to get into.'

'So, she was happy at school?' asks Walt, and Anna understands that he's repeated the question because he thinks there is more to the answer.

'She was, but not lately. She's been getting aggressive with the other kids—you know, biting and kicking. I often had to pick her up early because of . . . an incident.'

'An incident?' says Walt. 'Can you give me an example of the kind of incident you're talking about?'

'It was usually to do with her hurting another child. A few days before she, she. . . died I had to pick her up because she bit another child,' says Anna. Walt seems to shrug his shoulders as if to say, 'so?' and Anna knows that he's filing this under normal childhood behaviour. 'It wasn't the first time she'd bitten another child but it was the first time she had drawn blood,' says Anna and she feels her mouth twist as she remembers the way that Mary had looked at Maya, as though despite being involved with autistic children her whole career she had never seen such a thing.

'And how was the school handling those . . . those incidents?' asks Walt while he writes.

'They were doing their best,' says Anna, 'they had strategies in place but a lot of the time they didn't work with Maya. They were doing everything they could, just like

I was doing everything I could. Some days she responded to the methods we were using, most days she didn't. I think the school was beginning to run out of options for dealing with her. I was supposed to meet with them the Monday after she died.'

'Do you think they were going to ask you to remove her from the school?' asks Cynthia gently.

Anna shrugs again. 'That school was costing us sixty thousand dollars a year. There's no way we would have been able to afford it without help from Keith's parents. They were used to dealing with kids like Maya. It's what we paid them to do. I'm sure they just wanted to try some different strategies or something,' says Anna, parroting Keith's words.

'That's a lot of money,' says Walt.

'Yes,' says Anna. 'A lot.' She and Keith had not taken a holiday since Maya was born. They rarely went out to eat, and when they did, Anna felt guilty because Keith's parents were helping them pay for the school and for Maya's extra therapy and then had to come over and babysit for them. Keith had missed out on promotions that would have meant travelling because he wanted to always be home for Maya, so his salary never increased to a point where they could afford to relax. Anna wonders what they will do with all the extra money and then remembers that she is no longer part of a 'we'. It's just her.

She doesn't think she has ever felt this tired in her life. Somewhere inside her, a voice is telling her to be careful, that Cynthia is being patient and kind for a reason, but she doesn't care anymore.

She has thought about taking her own life every day since Maya died. She feels a sense of peace in the middle of the night when she plans exactly how she is going to end it all. She even knows what clothes she is going to wear. She allows herself a dramatic funeral and imagines people shaking their heads at the sadness of her end. Her doctor has prescribed the strongest-available sleeping pills and she tells Keith she's taking them, but she's hoarding them. The growing pile and the thought of another prescription keep her functioning.

'You must allow yourself time to grieve,' her doctor had said. 'Here's a list of names. You need to talk to someone.'

'I don't think therapists are very effective,' said Anna. She is tired of listening to other people, tired of blocking out the voice in her head.

'You are doing the best you can,' each of her therapists told her. 'You're a great mother,' Caro told her, and Keith told her, and all the people who helped with Maya told her, but she knew that they weren't really believing it. What else could they say—'You're doing a crap job of loving this child'?

People say that you are never given more than you can handle, but Anna knows this isn't true. Caro was not equipped to handle the heartbreak of losing so many babies, of losing Gideon. And Anna has met many, many mothers with autistic children who handle it better than she did. They have more energy, greater reserves of strength and patience, and more love to give than she felt she had with Maya. Maya was too much for her to handle.

Whatever she did and however hard she tried, she never managed to deal with her child the way she knew she should have been able to.

'I don't think anyone can really conceive of the amount of money it takes to care for a special needs child until they have one,' says Anna. She twists her hands together, studying the prominent veins and dry skin as she remembers the pile of bills on the table by the front door that still have to be paid. Bills for occupational therapy and physical therapy and speech therapy—all of which were in addition to the school fees. 'I don't know how people manage if they don't have enough money or relatives to help them. Maya had every therapy that money could buy. Not that it ever made much of a difference.'

'Did you ... did you have any feelings of resentment towards Maya, Anna?' asks Cynthia softly. She sits forward and catches Anna's eye.

'Resentment?' says Anna, like she doesn't understand the question.

'Yes,' says Cynthia, 'did you perhaps resent her because she was so difficult and took up so much of your time? Because of the cost of the school, and because she used to lash out at you and hurt you?'

Anna smiles at Cynthia. 'I must say, I did feel a little resentful that my life was never going to be my own again—is that what you mean?'

She hears that her tone is flat. And her smile feels wrong, as though her lips haven't really moved.

'Yes,' Cynthia says. 'Something like that.'

Anna nods and starts talking again. 'I got angry and upset, especially when she attacked me and actually hurt me. All mothers have times when they wonder about the choice they made to have children, don't they? They take up so much time and energy. That's what used to drive my mother crazy when my brother and I were younger. I didn't understand it then, I thought she was mean and selfish, but I get it now. Kids demand everything and Maya demanded more than most. Of course I resented it, resented her. Don't tell me you've never had a bad thought about your kids, Cynthia, because then you'd be lying.' Anna smiles her strange smile again.

'I wouldn't say never,' says Cynthia. 'There's a reason they call it the hardest job there is.'

'Yeah, but most kids give something back. They smile at you when you smile at them, and then they learn to talk, and tell you what they see and hear and feel. They sit on your lap and let you read them stories. They wind their little arms around your neck and tell you that they love you, and then they get bigger and go into the world, and come home to tell you everything they've seen and heard. Your kids are going to grow up and get jobs and get married, and one day they'll bring you their children to play with, and you'll know that you've created this little group of human beings.'

'That feels like it's pretty far away, Anna.'

'Do you know what happens to an adult with autism?' asks Anna. 'I don't mean Asperger's, or someone at the lighter end of the spectrum; I mean someone severely affected by autism, like Maya was.' She is staring at the wall behind Walt's head. Her speech is slow and soft. She knows she is in a room with two detectives but also feels like she is alone, like her words don't really matter, because no one else can hear them.

She hasn't heard if Cynthia has answered her question, so she just continues speaking. 'They end up living in aged care facilities if their parents can't take care of them. I used to worry that I'd die and leave Maya alone in a world that still doesn't understand her disability. I used to see myself old and bent, pushing a walker, and still trying to get Maya to brush her teeth in the morning.

'She hated brushing her teeth. She didn't like the sound of the scrape of the toothbrush across her teeth and she didn't like the taste of any toothpaste I bought. It used to take ten minutes, twice a day, just for her to brush her teeth and that was if she was in a compliant mood. If not, there'd usually be a tantrum and teeth brushing would go out the door. They had to sedate her at the dentist's. I remember one visit where our dentist gave me a twenty-minute lecture on my responsibilities as a parent because Maya's teeth were in such a bad state. "You give her too much juice and too much junk food," he said.

'"I don't give her any of that," I said. "She's on a sugar-free, dairy-free, gluten-free diet."

"'You mothers with your ideas," he sneered. "Children need to eat proper food to grow. It is also your responsibility to make sure she brushes her teeth."

"'But—" I said.

"'But nothing. Gum disease in children is one hundred percent preventable."

'I just sat there listening to the idiot dentist, you know. What was I going to say?'

'It's getting late, Anna,' says Walt, looking at his watch. Anna looks at the detectives and, for a moment, forgets what she was saying. Then she nods like she understands. She knows what he wants her to talk about, she knows where he wants her to go, but she's not stupid. She'll draw this out for as long as she can because she can't explain what happened on her front lawn two weeks ago. She remembers what she was wearing, and she can feel the heat of the sun, smell the cut grass next door, but when she thinks about the last moments of Maya's life, the back of her head pricks with pins and needles. 'Was that me?' she thinks. 'Was that really me?'

Once Maya had stopped screaming, Anna had sat listening to the soft thumping sound for at least an hour. The whole house was silent, and even though Maya was locked in her room, far away from where Anna was sitting, the *thump, thump,* sound began to fill the house until it was the only thing Anna could hear. She felt it eating into her, taking her over. *Thump* ... pause ... *thump* ... pause ... *thump* ... pause ... *thump* ... pause ... *thump.*

She had tried turning on the television but hadn't found anything to watch that was distracting enough. She put her fingers in her ears but the thumping sound grew louder. It seemed to be taking over the whole house. She thought about calling Keith and telling him he needed to come home, but she didn't want him to know how badly she had fucked up.

'You can manage her yourself today, can't you, Anna?' he had asked when he was getting ready to leave that morning.

'I manage her myself every day, Keith.'

'Yes, but she goes to school and there's therapy after school, and I know that, sometimes, if you have to have her for a whole day, it can be difficult.'

Anna had taken a large sip of her coffee and refrained from answering. Keith went to work every day. Yes, he came home at six and, yes, he helped whenever he could, but he got to escape every single day. He got to have a cup of coffee without worrying about someone knocking it over. He got to go to the bathroom without having to make sure Maya was occupied and the door was locked. He got to just sit and think, without having to always have one eye on his child. Anna had heard other mothers complain about this, about how unequal it was, but the difference, the enormous difference, between her life and other mothers' lives was that by the time their children had reached the age of six or seven, the complaints slowed, and then they simply stopped and the children became 'Easy to deal with,' and 'Busy with their friends, and 'On their computers.'

Thump … pause … *thump* … pause … *thump* …
pause … *thump.*

'I can't, I can't, I can't,' Anna had muttered in time with
the thumping.

Thump … pause … *thump* … pause … *thump* …
pause … *thump.*

'She'll go to sleep soon,' she thought.

Thump … pause … *thump* … pause … *thump* …
pause … *thump.*

'Soon … soon.'

Thump … pause … *thump* … pause … *thump* …
pause … *thump.*

Thump … pause … *thump* … pause … *thump* …
pause … *thump.*

'This is never going to end,' she said aloud.

She had heard her voice on her mobile phone, asking
Caro to come over.

'I'll come over,' Caro had said, or something
like that.

'Yes, come over Caro,' Anna had said because this was
exactly what she wanted to hear. 'Come over now.' Then
she had switched off her mobile and taken the home phone
off the hook.

'Seven minutes,' Anna had thought.

Thump … pause … *thump* … pause … *thump.*

She had stood up and walked to Maya's room.

'It's going to be fine,' she had whispered, comforting
herself, soothing herself. Her voice sounded different. Her
body felt different.

She had leaned her head against the door, trying to breathe but feeling the air catch in her throat. She had watched her hands unlock Maya's bedroom door. Her hands, but not her hands, as her voice, but not her voice, whispered into the air: 'Fine, fine, it's going to be fine.'

She had not stayed to see if Maya was okay. She had simply turned and walked to the front door, unlocked it and, leaving it wide open, had stepped outside and breathed in the warm early evening air. Everything shimmered in the heat.

She had only been outside thirty seconds when she felt, rather than saw, Maya. She was standing in the doorway, looking out at the front garden and the road. Anna turned a little to watch her.

'Come on,' she muttered under her breath. 'Come on.'

And, in an instant, Maya was off. She bolted forward, but before she could get very far, Anna caught her and held her tightly by the shoulders.

'I knew you'd try to run,' she hissed at the child. She could smell her own curdled breath from all the coffee she'd had that day.

'Why do you have to be like this?' she asked, shaking her daughter, 'Why, why, tell me why?'

She started pulling Maya towards the road, yanking at her arms with all her strength as Maya pulled away from her.

'Say something, Maya,' she said, her breath coming in short bursts as they fought. 'Say, "Mum", Maya. Go on, fucking say the word for once in your life. Say, "Mum," or say anything, fucking anything at all . . . say, "I'm sorry, Mum." Why can't you say it, Maya, why can't you say it?'

Maya had tried to start screaming again but had already exhausted her voice, and a harsh squeak was all that came out.

'You hate me, don't you?' she said, looking into Maya's eyes and knowing it was true.

She pulled her towards the road, panting as her daughter fought being touched and held.

She heard a car turn into their road and knew it was Caro's. She pulled Maya again, and then felt everything drain away so that, inside her, everything was still and quiet and peaceful.

'Now go,' she whispered to Maya, 'Go.'

And she pushed Maya towards the road.

She pushed her hard.

Maya stumbled and turned, and fell right into the road as Caro approached.

Anna watched her.

She watched her stumble.

She watched her trip and then she felt herself start to move. She felt like she'd been slapped. The garden, the road, the car—everything—clicked sharply into focus.

'What have you done?' she screamed to herself. 'What have you done?'

'Maya, stop; Maya, no; stop, Maya!' she shouted but Maya was right there as Caro braked, and Anna heard the sound of metal hitting flesh and of the crack as Maya's head hit the road.

She watched the car hit her.

She watched Maya's head hit the road.

'Anna . . .' says Walt.

'Yes,' sighs Anna. 'I did resent her. I did, but that doesn't mean I didn't love her and it doesn't mean I killed her.'

She sits up and shakes her head. 'What are you thinking?' she says silently. 'Get a fucking grip.'

'Don't think I don't know what you're trying to do!' she says to Cynthia. 'You tell me about your bad days, and how you understand how hard it is to be a mother, and then maybe I'll tell you about my bad days—isn't that the way this is supposed to work?'

'Anna, I'm not—' says Cynthia.

'You're not trying to trap me? Of course you are. I didn't kill my child. My drunk ex-friend did and that's all there is to it. So, why don't the two of you just leave me the fuck alone?' Anna stands up and pushes her chair back. 'I'm done with this interview. I'm done with dealing with the two of you. Either charge me with something or let's declare this over.'

'You're free to go whenever you want, Anna,' says Walt.

'Good, then I'm going.' Anna pulls open the door of the interview room and stomps out into the corridor.

Anna hears Cynthia sigh and say, 'Fuck,' and she's pleased that she's pissed off the smug detective, with her average kids and good-looking boyfriend. 'Fuck her,' she thinks. *Fuck all of them.*

Chapter Twenty

'I'm going to ask you to repeat it one more time, Caro,' says Susan. 'Tell me what you saw.'

Caro has already repeated the story three, four, ten times. Her head is pounding, and her mouth is dry, despite the Diet Coke in front of her. She feels she could drink a river and still be thirsty.

'What I wouldn't give for a drink,' she thinks but resists saying anything. She can't stop now.

She takes another deep breath, 'I drove up to the house, and saw Maya and Anna fighting on the front lawn, right next to the street. It looked like Anna was trying to drag Maya up the front path to the road.'

'It looked like it?'

'It . . . no, it's what she was trying to do. I don't know why.'

Caro closes her eyes and sees the violence. She had never really seen Maya hurt Anna, only heard about it afterwards. She has seen cuts and bruises, and sprained wrists and scraped hands. 'She doesn't understand what she's doing,' said Anna when she was explaining what had happened when Maya shoved her head into the bathroom mirror. 'She didn't want to brush her teeth and I pushed too much. I should have known that she was restless, that she'd had a bad day at school, and I should have left it.'

'How will you cope when she's older?' Caro had asked. 'What will you do?'

They had been sitting in a coffee shop at the time. Anna had a large bandage across her forehead because of the cuts from the mirror's broken glass.

'I don't know,' she said. 'Keith says we'll think about it later.'

'And what do you say?' asked Caro.

'Sometimes I hope . . . sometimes I hope she kills me, so it doesn't have to be my problem,' Anna had said. Caro hadn't been able to think of a reply. Anna's tone was matter of fact and she was not trying to be funny.

'I started to slow down, but I was watching them and wasn't concentrating. I braked, I did, but I didn't brake fast enough.'

'Your reaction time was slowed,' says Susan.

Caro sighs. 'Yes, Detective,' she says, 'my reaction time was slowed, but it was shock that did it.'

Susan folds her arms across her chest and says nothing.

Caro hears herself and knows, really understands now, that what had happened came down to a matter of seconds, seconds she didn't have because she wasn't fully functioning. If she had registered the fighting and jammed on the brakes, she knows that she would never have seen the inside of this police station, but she hadn't. Instead, she had stared, in horror, at her friend and her friend's child wrestling on the front lawn and had kept driving until it was too late. Only when Maya's body had bounced off her car had she pushed down hard on the brakes. Only then.

'So, you drive up there, and you see Anna and Maya fighting, and then Anna pushes Maya into the road, and you brake but not hard enough, and you hit her?'

'Yes,' says Caro.

'Do you think Anna was trying to hurt her child? Do you think she planned to push her in front of the car? That she actually planned to do it, and if so, would you swear to this in a court of law?' asks Susan.

'In court? Why would I have to go to court?' A picture forms in Caro's head of herself and Anna facing each other in court. She has never been inside a courtroom. She can't imagine looking at her friend and telling a room full of people that Anna had killed her own daughter. It simply wasn't possible. That's not what was meant to happen, that's not what she wanted. She tries to breathe slowly to calm herself but everything is going too fast. She wasn't drunk, or was she? She saw Anna push Maya, or didn't she? Her stomach churns and her hands sweat. What was the right answer? What had she done? What was she doing?

Her plan had been to tell the police and have all of this go away. Have all of it go away somehow . . . It had really been no plan at all. She can't go to court and say Anna killed her own child. How can she do that?

'No, I couldn't do that,' she says. 'I couldn't testify against her. She was my friend and she's lost everything because of . . . No, I couldn't do that, I just wanted you to understand that it wasn't all my fault.'

Susan stands up and walks around the table to lean over Caro. 'Where exactly did you think this was leading, Caro? Have you simply been wasting our time? How did you think you were going to change anything if you're not willing to tell everyone, including a judge, what you saw, or thought you saw?' Susan shoves her hands into the pockets of her blue pants. She looks as though she would like to hit Caro.

'You don't believe me, do you?' asks Caro.

'No,' says Susan. 'I don't. We don't . . . right, Brian?'

'It is hard to understand, Caro,' he says. 'You were probably over the limit. I'm afraid I'm also finding all this a little hard to believe. Maybe you think it's what you saw, but chances are you weren't really able to judge the situation.'

'Fine,' says Caro, shrugging her shoulders. She has done her best. She's told her story and no one has believed her.

Even when she and Geoff had talked about it last night, he had expressed doubt that she had actually seen what she thinks she saw. She will be punished for Maya's death and rightly so. There is nothing more to say.

'What now?' she asks Susan.

'Now, I'm afraid, we need to charge you with dangerous driving occasioning death.'

'But what if I wasn't over the limit?' asks Caro in a small voice.

'You were driving the car that hit and killed a child,' says Susan.

'Can I call my husband before you do that? Can I call my lawyer?' Caro knows that Geoff will have to work quickly. They don't have a lawyer.

Susan and Brian look at each other. 'You can,' says Brian. 'It's your legal right.'

'I should have come in here with a lawyer, shouldn't I?'

'What's done is done,' says Susan, and Caro can see her shuffling this case to the back of her mind. 'This is my life,' she wants to say. 'Can't you see it imploding as I sit here? Have you no sympathy?' But as she opens her mouth to speak, she realises that she is not entitled to sympathy. She has killed someone, even if she didn't mean for it to happen. She cannot go back, and she will not be allowed to get away with this crime. Her only hope now is to keep moving forward, to take her punishment, and hope that when all of this is over, she still has some sort of a life to go back to.

She drops her head into her hands. 'What am I going to say to Lex?' she whispers. 'What am I going to say to my baby?'

But neither of the detectives has an answer for her.

Chapter Twenty-one

Anna marches towards the entrance to the police station, but as she does, the door of another interview room opens and Caro emerges with her own two detectives. She looks . . . broken.

Anna stops. She clenches her fists at her sides because her first instinct has been to put her arms around her friend.

'If you could just give us a moment, please, Mrs McAllen,' says the female detective, holding up a hand to indicate that Anna should stay away.

Caro lifts her head and looks at Anna.

Caro is not handcuffed, and the two detectives with her look relaxed, but there is something in the way she stands that makes Anna think of her as a prisoner. Caro's body language makes her look trapped, her eyes are blank.

Anna remembers Caro on the day they met. She remembers her putting her arms around a woman she didn't know and waiting for her to finish crying. She remembers her buying coffee and a ridiculously huge slice of chocolate cake for each of them, and letting Anna talk and talk and talk. Caro had thrown her a lifeline—one that she's been holding onto ever since. And, as she stands looking at the person she regards as her only true friend, Caro, once again, throws her a lifeline.

'I was over the limit, Anna; you don't have to worry anymore,' she says. 'I'm so . . . I'm so sorry, Anna. I shouldn't have come over.'

Anna gasps and feels as though she is cemented to the spot.

'Let's just move on,' says the male detective standing next to Caro, and even though she knows he's just trying to shift the group out of the corridor, Anna thinks, 'How can we ever move on?'

'You killed my child,' Anna whispers, trying the words out, feeling their rightness. She can feel the burn of anger feeding them, but underneath them, is another thread. She remembers the day Caro took her for the termination. She can see them sitting together in a cafe afterwards. Anna had sipped coffee and hadn't even tried to stop the tears.

Caro had sat with her hand on Anna's arm. 'You'll get through this,' she had said over and over again, and what Anna remembers the most is Caro's lack of judgement.

Only months before, she had stood at Caro's bedside and listened to her friend detail her baby's last moments. She had listened to her cry and drink, and cry some more, over the months that followed, and yet, when she had told her she needed to have a termination, Caro had only asked, 'Are you sure?', and when Anna had nodded emphatically, she had said, 'I'll come with you. I'll be there with you.'

Now, looking at Caro in the hallway, Anna is struck by just how much it would have taken for a woman grieving the death of her own baby to accompany another to a termination. She can't imagine what must have been going through Caro's mind.

The detectives begin moving away.

'Wait,' says Anna, and they stop and look at her.

'It wasn't her fault,' she says.

'Mrs McAllen, this is now a matter for the courts. Mrs Harman is going to be charged with dangerous driving occasioning death,' says the woman detective, and it seems to Anna that she is almost relishing the words.

Anna feels Cynthia behind her. She recognises her perfume. 'It wasn't her fault,' she says again. 'I called her. I knew she was coming and I let Maya out, and then I . . . I pushed her. I pushed her into the road.'

Anna feels her legs give way and she sinks to the floor. Caro moves away from the detectives and crouches down beside her, holding onto her.

'No, Anna,' says Caro. 'Don't say that. Take it back, please take it back.'

'I'm so sorry, Caro,' says Anna. Her words come out as a wail. 'I didn't mean it, I don't know what happened. I pushed her. I tried to pull her back, I did, but I pushed her first. I pushed her.

'I pushed her.

'I pushed her.

'I pushed her.'

Chapter Twenty-two

'Pick-up, pick-up, pick-up,' says Gabe.

'Not now, baby, Mummy's not feeling well. Go to Lexie.'

'Come here, Gaby, baby; Lexie will pick you up.'

Caro watches as Lex reaches down and picks up her little brother, and then smiles when Gabe snuggles into her shoulder, as he has done virtually since the day he was born.

'A fifteen-year-old sister, that's useful,' the nurse in the hospital had said. 'I bet you're going to help Mum out with this little one.'

'I am,' Lex had beamed. She'd been holding Gabe at the time, and Caro and Geoff had watched the two of them in wonder. 'He's the most beautiful thing I've ever seen,' Lex had said.

'Second only to you, my darling,' Caro had replied.

The blue room is no longer painted blue. Its walls are pale yellow and decorated with animal decals and it's always messy. This morning Caro had watched Gabe march his dinosaurs across the carpet to attack his train set. He doesn't like his teddies anymore, except for the small blue one he sleeps with at night. It's the teddy he has always slept with, ever since Geoff brought it home from work and placed it in his cot. 'Something that belonged to his brother,' he said. And Caro had closed her eyes and thought of Gideon for a moment.

'Mum, I'm hungry. I've been waiting and waiting and waiting,' says Gabe now.

'Told you, you should have packed a snack,' says Lex.

'I know,' Caro replies, 'but I thought we'd get here and the gate would open, and then we could all go for lunch. I didn't know we'd have to wait for so long. Let me check my purse . . . oh, great—here you go, Gabe—a muesli bar.'

'Don't wanna muesli bar.'

'Then you're not really hungry,' says Lex. 'Why don't you and I go for a walk to that park over there? Mum, call me when she's out.'

'Okay, love, thanks.'

Caro knows she should have left Lex and Gabe at home but she'd felt she needed her children with her today. Even though the presence of her children may cause some pain, even though they will be a reminder of what has been lost, she needed them with her. She turns to watch them walking hand in hand to the park, two beautiful copper-haired children. 'My babies,' she thinks, sending up a prayer of thanks, as she had done every day for the past three years since Gabe was born.

'What do you mean you're pregnant?' Geoff had said when she told him. 'Aren't you too old?'

'Women do have babies in their forties, Geoff. I didn't plan this but we have been . . . you know.'

Geoff had smiled and puffed out his chest a little.

'Men,' thought Caro.

Since she'd been released from prison, it had felt like she and Geoff were starting again. They couldn't seem to keep their hands off each other.

'Gross,' Lex said whenever she walked past them but Caro always caught a small smile on her daughter's face. Parents who held hands were better than parents separated by prison gates.

Caro had spent eighteen months in prison and was still on a good behaviour bond. She would never take another drink. Not ever. Her commitment to rehabilitation had meant she got out earlier than the three years she was sentenced to. The day she went into prison she had been clean and sober for six months. She had found herself tested every day during the long months of waiting for her trial to begin and then once that was over, waiting to be sentenced. When she looks back at those months now they have a surreal, dreamlike quality to them. They could have happened to someone else. Some days she knows that she attended two Alcoholics Anonymous meetings a day because the urge to drink was so strong that she felt like she couldn't breathe. She had felt as though she were under attack. The media chewed over the story, and new articles appeared on the internet every day. Caro and Geoff had to re-mortgage the house to pay for bail and a defence lawyer. And Lex had refused to speak to Caro as she dealt with taunts at school and having her whole life exposed. 'We'll get through this,' she can remember saying to Geoff over and over again but now she can remember little else about that time.

Her final reading was 0.06. It was considered at the low end of the range but she had still been over the limit. Caro had written the number down over and over again, in notebooks and on the back of shopping lists and on scrap pieces of paper that she'd placed in the freezer where her vodka used to be. Eventually she couldn't go anywhere in the house without seeing the number. 'Just stop it, stop it,' Lex had screamed at her one day when she found her compulsively scribbling the number on the pad of paper used for telephone messages. But Caro knew that she needed to see the number every day.

'You're torturing yourself,' said Geoff. 'Please stop.'

'I can't, Geoff, not yet,' she had replied. When she went into prison she'd stuck it up on the wall of her small cell. The number looked at her every day and she looked back, realising that the line between where she was and where she had been was as thin as .01.

Even though she had spilled the wine, even though she had remembered having only two shots, there had clearly been more or she wouldn't have been over the limit. Blood tests could not be disputed but memory could be.

She now has the number stuck to the fridge at home.

When her prison sentence finally began she was relieved. She wanted it over but she also knew that the temptation of alcohol would be kept at bay by the prison gates. She had not been able to meet anyone's eye for the first month of her sentence, believing that even in prison she was being judged for her terrible crime. She hated the routine of early mornings and all the sirens that chopped the days into pieces and head counts that made her feel like a child. But she was also grateful for it. Every morning she would wake up and counsel herself that all she needed to get through was breakfast before the siren sounded for work, and then all she needed to do was get through until lunch, and so on until the day was over. Then she could close her eyes and think about Geoff and Lex, worry about them and miss them. Once she was used to her surroundings she allowed herself to be drawn into conversations with the other women there and she found, not judgement, but understanding that there are mistakes people can make that change the course of their lives and the lives of others. Mistakes that had to be paid for but that could, eventually, be relegated to the past. She understood quickly that the only way she would survive her sentence was if she hung onto the possibility of a future where she could put her crime behind her.

Caro had made up her mind to use her time in prison constructively. It was a low-security prison, which focused on rehabilitation, and she had taken advantage of everything. She'd worked in the prison garden and learned basic first aid and she'd taken courses on business administration and marketing and computers. And she had written Geoff and Lex emails every day. She'd had to get used to them being scrutinised by the guards but after a while she hadn't cared. She just needed to stay in touch. First, she had apologised, then she had explained, and then she had simply kept writing. It had taken Lex six months to reply. Six months of Caro getting up every day with her heart in her mouth, wondering if today would be the day that her daughter chose to forgive her.

The first email had been brief: *Okay. I get it.* They had gotten longer over time, though. Some of Lex's emails were hard to read, like those where Lex told her how difficult it was at school because she was never allowed to forget that her mother was in prison. It made Caro's heart break for her child and sent her spiralling into intense self-recrimination; but in other emails Lex talked about books she was reading and movies she'd seen. Caro would write down the names of the books she mentioned and try to find them in the prison library so she and Lex could discuss them.

Geoff had never given up on her. He tried to write to her every day as well but was busy raising Lex alone and working. Caro tried not to let the guilt of being away from her family eat away at her, tried to see that her life was moving forward.

She also wrote to Anna, but never sent the emails. She was afraid of what her reaction would be, and also didn't know whether she would be allowed emails where she was.

One day in computer class, they had been learning about blogging as a way of journaling and Caro had decided, on a whim, to start her own blog. She called it *The Recovering Mummy*. She hadn't believed that anyone would ever read it and so had poured her heart out to the computer. She had talked about her appalling crime and about how she had let down her family, and about all the things that had led to her drinking.

One week after she started the blog, she had ten followers. The prison warden had been unsure of what to do. 'This may be seen as profiting from the proceeds of crime,' she said.

'But I'm not making any money. I'm just writing. I won't reply if you tell me I can't.'

'We have to be able to monitor every post, but we'll see how it goes,' she said.

Caro had been grateful for the chance and she had kept writing, hoping that her story might help even one person struggling to get through the day.

One week later, the number had jumped to a hundred, and by the time she was released from prison, she had thousands following her. Now she talked to people all over the world, and worked to get them help. Out in the suburbs, there were so many women suffering and hiding their addictions, and because Caro was one of them, they trusted her. She's had to learn about all forms of addiction and consult with doctors each time she writes about prescription medication or gambling or alcohol. Some posts are just about being a mother with two children, about getting through the laundry and the shopping and the cleaning but many are about the secret lives of those struggling to cope with the everyday world. Now, she was even making money from having advertising on her blog. Geoff liked to joke that he was on his way to being a 'kept man'. Caro was wary of the possibility of accusation that she was benefiting from her crime but her parole officer had assured her that she's in the clear on that. She funnelled a fair amount of money to halfway houses and charities that helped recovering addicts.

Sometimes at night, Caro lay in bed in the dark and cried at her good fortune.

The stigma of having gone to prison for drink driving and for killing a child would never leave her. At Lex's school she would always be the mother who had fucked up so spectacularly. But now she was also the mother who had changed her life for the better.

One week after her release, she had gone alone to pick up Lex from school. She could have simply stayed in the car, knowing that Lex would find her, but she had chosen to get out, chosen to go and stand right in the middle of the throng of mothers at the gate. She had stood on her own, and felt how the silence around her grew and grew and was then filled with whispers. She had lifted her chin and tensed her muscles. She repeated in her head, 'I can do this.' She imagined herself on top of a pile of wood and felt the whispers burning her. The muscles in her back tightened and a headache threatened but she didn't move until Lex emerged from school.

When Lex saw her, she stopped.

'I'll come out to the car,' she had said the night before and Caro had said she would wait for her, but she knew that this needed to be done.

For a moment, Lex had stared at her, and then Caro had seen her lift her chin the same way she had always done, and she had walked to her mother and kissed her on the cheek.

After that, Caro had gone every day to stand by the school gates and had felt her presence become less and less interesting, until one day one of her old acquaintances, Leeann, had broken off from her huddle and come over to her.

'You're looking really well,' Leeann had said.

'I'm feeling pretty good,' said Caro.

'I've read your blog . . . it's really good.'

'Thanks.'

'We're thinking of starting a book club, so we can read all the books our kids are reading. It's a bit silly but we want to be prepared. Did you maybe want to join us?'

'Yes, what a lovely idea,' Caro had said.

It was not forgiveness for what she had done, but rather acceptance of how far she had come. Caro was humbled by Leeann's choice to step forward and end her exclusion from the school community and she and Leeann had become, if not good friends, then at least close acquaintances. Sometimes Leeann would say something about her husband or about a bad day and it would make Caro realise again that few people were getting through the day without having to fight their own demons.

The desire for a drink was still there, would always be there. She attended meetings once a week at least, and when she felt more stressed than usual, went twice, or even three times, a week.

The day before her first scan when she was pregnant with Gabe, she had stood outside a bottle shop for an hour, fantasising about going in. Eventually, she had called Geoff at work. 'I can't move,' she said. 'Help me, I can't move.'

'I'm coming,' he had replied. 'Hold on.'

'Can you see there?' said the ultrasound technician, 'there's your baby's heartbeat. It's nice and strong, just what you want.'

'It won't last,' she had said to Geoff in the car on the way home.

'Maybe not, but maybe, just maybe it will. I know that you're prepared for the worst and I can't think any other way either but would it be so bad to include a few positive thoughts along with our worst case scenario thinking?'

'No,' Caro had agreed, 'not so bad.'

As her pregnancy with Gabe continued, she felt like she'd go mad. 'It would almost be a relief if it ended now,' she told Geoff one night when she was five months pregnant. 'I've done this before. I can handle it. I don't know how much longer I can handle holding onto hope.'

'You can handle it just like Lex and I are handling it, Caro; just like they tell you to do at your meetings. One day at a time.'

And she had.

Holding a healthy baby in her arms had seemed almost too miraculous to believe but Gabe was here to stay.

'Look, the doors are opening,' says Lex, she and Gabe having returned from the park without Caro realising.

Anna had agreed to be checked into a psychiatric facility for an indeterminate period. It was that or go to prison. Once she had admitted to pushing Maya in front of the car, she had not been able to stop.

'I pushed her, I pushed her, I pushed her,' she had wailed over and over again, and Caro recalled how nothing any-one at the police station said could induce her to stop or get up off the floor. Eventually, Walt had picked her up and put her on a couch. An ambulance had been called. Keith had been called. Anna had repeated her sin over and over, seemingly not even stopping to breathe until the paramed-ics gave her a shot of something that made her subside into silence.

Before she went to prison, Caro had reached out to Keith but he hadn't answered any of her emails or phone messages, and she didn't blame him.

Caro had read articles about Anna's story on the internet. 'Mothers in this situation often lack support from the medical community, or from their own communities,' was a quote that made Caro wince every time she thought about it. 'I tried,' she would say to herself. 'I tried.'

Caro holds her breath as she watches a woman emerge from the building.

It is Anna. She is as thin as Caro has ever seen her, but she walks with her shoulders back and, as she comes closer, Caro can see an uncertain smile on her face.

She had been shocked to receive the first letter from Anna six months ago. She had nearly thrown out the plain blue envelope with the junk mail until she looked at it more closely.

I've been following your blog. I'm not allowed to send emails but I am allowed on the computer under supervision. I googled you and found your blog. I wanted to see how you were and I wanted to apologise. I can almost see the shock on your face because 'sorry' seems like such an inadequate, simplistic word. It's taken me a long time to get to the place where I was ready to apologise. I read the words you write and I can hear your voice and I miss you. I can see why so many people follow you. You have a way of making everything seem . . . well, not fine but perhaps bearable? That's what you did for me even when your own life was so not bearable. I don't think you knew how much you meant to me, how much your words and your listening ear meant to me. I should have told you. I hope you know now. Every comment that says you are a 'lifesaver' is true. It's what you do, Caro. You see someone hurting and in pain and you step in to see how you can help.

I betrayed that in you. I betrayed your help and your kindness and your patience and your friendship.

I betrayed my daughter and my husband. I betrayed myself.

It's taken me years to admit these things, to admit what I did. I should have asked for help. I know that now. You did your best but you had your own child and Keith did his best but it was all too much for me. I should have shouted as loud as I could that I wasn't coping but I didn't know how to explain it. You're supposed to love your child no matter who they are or how much they hurt you. I still can't really explain what happened but all I can say is that not every woman is meant to be a mother and not every child can be loved. It sounds terrible but I have to admit the truth if I'm going to build a life for myself when I leave this place in a few months. I don't know if you heard but Keith filed for divorce as soon as I left home. I understand that. I don't blame him. Our marriage was over anyway. My mother told me that he has remarried and has a child. Apparently she is fine, so maybe the faulty gene lay with me. I wish him well, I really do. My mother has visited me every month while I've been here and she is waiting for me to get out so I can come and stay with her. We have a lot more to talk about now. We both failed at being mothers. I'm not saying that for sympathy. It's a fact. It's a fact that I needed to accept about myself and now that I have, I feel as though I can move on with my life. I know that people have said that all I needed was more support from those around me but I'm not sure about that. I don't know if there could ever have been enough support for me to be able to deal with Maya as she got bigger and older and stronger. There are some very special people in the world raising children with enormous difficulties but I wasn't meant to be one of them.

I hope you write back, Caro. I hope you can forgive me. I hope we can still have some kind of a friendship.

Caro had cried for days after that first letter. She had been angry and sad, and everything in between, but in the end, she had felt only sympathy for how lost Anna must have been feeling.

'*Dear Anna,*' she had begun in her head before deciding not to write back. '*Dear Anna,*' she had written on the first page of a pale pink writing pad and then torn off the sheet and crumpled it up. '*Dear Anna,*' she had finally started her letter to her friend.

I miss you. Sometimes I think about us laughing over cake and I feel an ache inside my body. We laughed a lot didn't we, even though our lives were falling apart? I know I've said "I'm sorry," countless times but I wanted to say it again. I'm sorry, Anna. I shouldn't have left my couch. I shouldn't have gotten into my car. I shouldn't have been there. But mostly I'm sorry that I failed to see you weren't just waving. I was wrapped up in my own life, consumed by my own pain and I didn't see you go under. I used to comfort myself with the idea that I was a good person and a good friend because I did try to help those around me. But now I know that you have no right to try and fix someone else if you, yourself, are broken.

Everything has changed in my life and I feel like I have the energy to be a better friend, to really help those who reach out to me.

It hasn't been an easy journey. Some nights in prison I used to want to scream into the silence at the unfairness of it all. I don't know why you and I had to travel such a hard road but I do know that if you walk it, every painful step, and if you keep walking it then there is something better at the end. I hope that you will let me take your hand and walk a little bit with you. I promise to be better this time because I am better. When you come home I'd love to be able to share a giant slab of chocolate mud cake with you and maybe a few more laughs.

Love, your friend, Caro

Anna's next letter had arrived after a week and then they arrived every week in response to Caro's replies.

It had taken Caro months to work up the courage to ask Anna the question that had been on her mind since the day her friend revealed the truth: *How did you know it was going to be my car that turned into the cul-de-sac? How could you be sure?*

When she finally wrote this down and sent it to Anna in a letter, she didn't hear from Anna for weeks. It was the first time in months that her letters had not arrived regularly.

'I'll never hear from her again,' she thought.

But finally, there was an answer. *It never occurred to me that it would be anyone else, Caro. You saved me. You always saved me.*

Caro had felt she should be angry, feel used, hate Anna for throwing her into the middle of a catastrophe, but in the end all she felt was desperate sorrow for someone who was so completely lost and who thought that she was utterly alone.

Anna's final letter had simply been a request: *Can you meet me when I leave the hospital? My mother has said she'll come but I think I would like it to be you. I am going to be living with my mother, but I would like to see you when I can and if you have the time. Can you meet me, Caro? Can you?*

'No way,' said Geoff when Caro told him.

But Caro had known what she would do. She had not argued, had not yelled or become tearful; she had simply stated what she would do.

'I'll come with you,' Geoff had said.

'No, I'll take the kids. It will make it less awkward.'

'Caro, don't be ridiculous. She's not sane. You can't expose our kids to her.'

'I know her, Geoff. We'll be fine.'

'Yeah,' said Lex, overhearing the conversation from the kitchen, where she was making Gabe her famous caramel salted popcorn. 'We'll be fine.'

'No use arguing with her,' said Caro.

'No,' agreed Geoff, 'not as she's going to be studying law, but I still don't think it's a good idea.'

'It may be the last time I see her, Geoff. I don't know what's going to happen. She may not want to see me again if she's trying to rebuild her life. I want her to see that I'm okay; that she doesn't have to worry about me.'

'Can't you just tell her in writing?'

'Give it a rest, Dad, I want to see her too,' said Lex coming into the room.'

'Why?' said Geoff.

Lex shrugged her shoulders and shovelled popcorn into her mouth. Geoff folded his arms and waited. 'I guess,' said Lex, swallowing, 'it's because she changed our lives.'

'That's my point,' said Geoff, 'she changed our lives. Your mother went to prison because of her.'

'I went to prison because of me, Geoff. You know that.'

'I know why you must hate her, Dad. I understand what she did to our family, but sometimes when I think about her I feel like the whole thing wasn't just black and white. I know that Mum would never have gone to prison without her but what if it had never happened and Mum had never stopped drinking . . .'

'You can't seriously be suggesting that what happened was a good thing, Lex?'

'No, Dad,' Lex had sighed and raised her eyebrow at her
father in a perfect imitation of his own gesture, 'but I think
that some lives need a giant catalyst to change their direction. I was never interested in law before I watched Mum
talk to the lawyer and read about the trial, and neither you
nor I know what life would have been like now if there had
never been a car accident. Personally, I don't think that you
and Mum would still be married and we certainly wouldn't
have Gabe.'

'Lex, I don't . . .'

'Dad, she was part of my childhood. Maya was part of
my childhood and I want to see Anna again. I want to see
that she's okay. I don't know why but I don't resent her for
what she did and I want to see her. I'm old enough to make
this decision myself . . . okay?'

'Okay,' Geoff had said shaking his head, 'but I still don't
like it.'

'I understand,' Caro had said, 'but you need to trust me
on this. Trust us.'

Caro watches Anna approach and feels the strong desire
for a drink wash over her. She tries to imagine what Anna
is thinking as she looks at her and her children. Caro has
not told Anna about Gabe. In their letters they have remi-
nisced about Maya and talked about Caro's work but Anna
has only asked once about Lex. Even though the question
was written down Caro had been able to sense how difficult it was for Anna to ask, how hard it would be for her to

avoid thinking about Maya at the age Lex was now. Discussing Gabe felt wrong because Caro sensed that Anna would rebuild her life without children and that for her to hear about Caro's good fortune would be too much for her to handle. She had felt herself unable to simply write that she had a son without having to rhapsodise about him. It had been easier to say nothing.

Anna's steps are small, hesitant as she gets closer.

'Maybe this was a bad idea,' thinks Caro and she feels she can almost taste the burn of vodka in the back of her throat and hear the clink of ice against the side of the glass. But then she feels Gabe's hand creep into hers and, at the same time, Lex leans down and rests her head on her shoulder.

'I can get through this,' she thinks.

Anna stops in front of Caro and her children. Her blonde hair is tied back, there are lines around her eyes and her skin is pale. She is holding a large duffle bag in front of her, as though to protect herself. She looks at Lex and her smile widens and then she studies Gabe.

'Oh, Caro,' she says, looking up so Caro can see the shine of tears in her eyes, 'I didn't know . . . he's . . . he's beautiful . . . they're both so . . . beautiful.'

'Hello, Anna,' Caro says and she can feels the tears slipping down her cheeks, 'Hello, old friend.'

Acknowledgements

Jane Palfreyman and the whole team at A&U.

Sarina Rowell for her copyediting skills.

Belinda Lee for always knowing the right thing to say.

Gaby Naher.

And as always, my mother, David, Mikhayla, Isabella and Jacob.